Under the Skylights

by
Henry Blake Fuller

Under the Skylights
by Henry Blake Fuller

Copyright © 2024

All Rights reserved.

No part of this publication may be reproduced, stored in a retrieval system, or transmitted in any form or by any means, electronic, mechanical, photocopying or Otherwise, without the written permission of the publisher.
The author/editor asserts the moral right to be identified as the author/editor of this work.

ISBN: 978-93-68097-87-7

Published by

DOUBLE 9 BOOKS

2/13-B, Ansari Road
Daryaganj, New Delhi – 110002
info@double9books.com
www.double9books.com
Tel. 011-40042856

This book is under public domain

ABOUT THE AUTHOR

Henry Blake Fuller was an American novelist and playwright born in 1857, in Chicago, Illinois. He is best known for his contributions to American literature in the late 19th and early 20th centuries, particularly for his realistic portrayals of urban life.

Fuller's most notable work, "Under the Skylights," explores the lives of diverse characters living in a boarding house in Chicago, reflecting the complexities of social class and individual aspirations. Other significant works include "The Cliff-Dwellers," "On the Stairs" and "With the Procession." His writing often delved into themes of identity, ambition, and the challenges of modern urban existence.

In addition to his novels, Fuller wrote plays and was involved in various literary and cultural organizations. He was recognized for his contributions by being inducted into the Chicago Literary Hall of Fame. Fuller passed away on 1929, but left a lasting impact on American literature through his insightful depictions of urban life.

CONTENTS

THE DOWNFALL OF ABNER JOYCE

I	9
II	11
III	14
IV	16
V	19
VI	21
VII	26
VIII	31
IX	34
X	40
XI	42
XII	44
XIII	47
XIV	50
XV	55
XVI	57
XVII	59
XVIII	63
XIX	66
XX	69
XXI	73
XXII	76
XXIII	79
XXIV	82

LITTLE O'GRADY vs. THE GRINDSTONE

I	86
II	90
III	94
IV	98
V	100
VI	104
VII	108
VIII	111
IX	114
X	118
XI	122
XII	125
XIII	131
XIV	135
XV	138
XVI	142
XVII	147
XVIII	150
XIX	155
XX	159
XXI	162
XXII	166
XXIII	169
XXIV	172
XXV	176
XXVI	182

DR. GOWDY AND THE SQUASH

I	184
II	186
III	188
IV	191
V	193
VI	196
VII	198
VIII	201
IX	203
X	205
XI	207
XII	210
XIII	213
XIV	216

THE DOWNFALL OF ABNER JOYCE

I

With the publication of his first book, *This Weary World*, Abner Joyce immediately took a place in literature. Or rather, he made it; the book was not like other books, and readers felt the field of fiction to be the richer by one very vital and authentic personality.

This Weary World was grim and it was rugged, but it was sincere and it was significant. Abner's intense earnestness had left but little room for the graces;—while he was bent upon being recognised as a "writer," yet to be a mere writer and nothing more would not have satisfied him at all. Here was the world with its many wrongs, with its numberless crying needs; and the thing for the strong young man to do was to help set matters right. This was a simple enough task, were it but approached with courage, zeal, determination. A few brief years, if lived strenuously and intensely, would suffice. "Man individually is all right enough," said Abner; "it is only collectively that he is wrong." What was at fault was the social scheme,— the general understanding, or lack of understanding. A short sharp hour's work before breakfast would count for a hundred times more than a feeble dawdling prolonged throughout the whole day. Abner rose betimes and did his hour's work; sweaty, panting, begrimed, hopeful, indignant, sincere, self-confident, he set his product full in the world's eye.

Abner's book comprised a dozen short stories—twelve clods of earth gathered, as it were, from the very fields across which he himself, a farmer's boy, had once guided the plough. The soil itself spoke, the intimate, humble ground; warmed by his own passionate sense of right, it steamed incense-like aloft and cried to the blue skies for justice. He pleaded for the farmer, the first, the oldest, the most necessary of all the world's workers; for the man who was the foundation of civilized society, yet who was yearly gravitating downward through new depths of slighting indifference, of careless contempt, of rank injustice and gross tyranny; for the man who sowed so plenteously, so laboriously, yet reaped so scantily and in such bitter and benumbing toil; for the man who lived indeed beneath the heavens, yet must forever fasten his solicitous eye upon the earth. All this revolted Abner; the indignation of a youth that had not yet made its compromise with the world burned on every page. Some of his stories seemed written not so much by the hand as by the fist, a fist quivering from the tension of muscles and sinews fully ready to act for truth and right; and there were paragraphs upon which the intent and blazing eye of the writer appeared to rest with no less fierceness, coldly printed as they were, than it had rested upon the manuscript itself.

"Men shall hear me—and heed me," Abner declared stoutly.

A few of those who read his book happened to meet him personally, and one or two of this number—clever but inconspicuous people—lucidly apprehended him for what he was: that rare phenomenon, the artist (such he was already calling himself)—the artist whose personality, whose opinions and whose work are in exact accord. The reading public—a body rather captious and blase, possibly—overlooked his rugged diction in favour of his novel point of view; and when word was passed around that the new author was actually in town a number of the *illuminati* expressed their gracious desire to meet him.

II

But Abner remained for some time ignorant of "society's" willingness to give him welcome. He was lodged in a remote and obscure quarter of the city and was already part of a little coterie from which earnestness had quite crowded out tact and in which the development of the energies left but scant room for the cultivation of the amenities. With this small group reform and oratory went hand in hand; its members talked to spare audiences on Sunday afternoons about the Readjusted Tax. Such a combination of matter and manner had pleased and attracted Abner from the start. The land question was *the* question, after all, and eloquence must help the contention of these ardent spirits toward a final issue in success. Abner thirstily imbibed the doctrine and added his tongue to the others. Nor was it a tongue altogether unschooled. For Abner had left the plough at sixteen to take a course in the Flatfield Academy, and after some three years there as a pupil he had remained as a teacher; he became the instructor in elocution. Here his allegiance was all to the old-time classic school, to the ideal that still survives, and inexpugnably, in the rustic breast and even in the national senate; the Roman Forum was never completely absent from his eye, and Daniel Webster remained the undimmed pattern of all that man—man mounted on his legs—should be.

Abner, then, went on speaking from the platform or distributing pamphlets, his own and others', at the door, and remained unconscious that Mrs. Palmer Pence was desirous of knowing him, that Leverett Whyland would have been interested in meeting him, and that Adrian Bond, whose work he knew without liking it, would have been glad to make him acquainted with their fellow authors. Nor did he enjoy any familiarity with Clytie Summers and her sociological studies, while Medora Giles, as yet, was not even a name.

Mrs. Palmer Pence remained, then, in the seclusion of her "gilded halls," as Abner phrased it, save for occasional excursions and alarums that vivified the columns devoted by the press to the doings of the polite world; and Adrian Bond kept between the covers of his two or three thin little books—a confinement richly deserved by a writer so futile, superficial and insincere; but Leverett Whyland was less easily evaded by anybody who "banged about town" and who happened to be interested in public matters.

Abner came against him at one of the sessions of the Tax Commission, a body that was hoping—almost against hope—to introduce some measure of reason and justice into the collection of the public funds.

"Huh! I shouldn't expect much from *him*!" commented Abner, as Whyland began to speak.

Whyland was a genial, gentlemanly fellow of thirty-eight or forty. He was in the world and of it, but was little the worse, thus far, for that. He had been singled out for favours, to a very exceptional degree, by that monster of inconsistency and injustice, the Unearned Increment, but his intentions toward society were still fairly good. If he may be capitalized (and surely he was rich enough to be), he might be described as hesitating whether to be a Plutocrat or a Good Citizen; perhaps he was hoping to be both.

Abner disliked and doubted him from the start. The fellow was almost foppish;—could anybody who wore such good clothes have also good motives and good principles? Abner disdained him too as a public speaker;—what could a man hope to accomplish by a few quiet colloquial remarks delivered in his ordinary voice? The man who expected to get attention should claim it by the strident shrillness of his tones, should be able to bend his two knees in eloquent unison, and send one clenched hand with a driving swoop into the palm of the other—and repeat as often as necessary. Abner questioned as well his mental powers, his quality of brain-fibre, his breadth of view. The feeble creature rested in no degree upon the great, broad, fundamental principles—principles whose adoption and enforcement would reshape and glorify human society as nothing else ever had done or ever could do. No, he fell back on mere expediency, mere practicability, weakly acquiescing in acknowledged and long-established evils, and trying for nothing more than fairness and justice on a foundation utterly unjust and vicious to begin with.

"Let me get out of this," said Abner.

But a few of his own intimates detained him at the door, and presently Whyland, who had ended his remarks and was on his way to other matters, overtook him. An officious bystander made the two acquainted, and Whyland, who identified Abner with the author of *This Weary World*, paused for a few smiling and good-humoured remarks.

"Glad to see you here," he said, with a kind of bright buoyancy. "It's a complicated question, but we shall straighten it out one way or another."

Abner stared at him sternly. The question was not complicated, but it *was* vital—too vital for smiles.

"There is only one way," he said: "our way."

"Our way?" asked Whyland, still smiling.

"The Readjusted Tax," pronounced Abner, with a gesture toward two or three of his supporters at his elbow.

"Ah, yes," said Whyland quickly, recognising the faces. "If the idea could only be applied!"

"It can be," said Abner severely. "It must be."

"Yes, it is a very complicated question," the other repeated. "I have read your stories," he went on immediately. "Two or three of them impressed me very much. I hope we shall become better acquainted."

"Thank you," said Abner stiffly. Whyland meant to be cordial, but Abner found him patronizing. He could not endure to be patronized by anybody, least of all by a person of mental calibre inferior to his own. He resented too the other's advantage in age (Whyland was ten or twelve years his senior), and his advantage in experience (for Whyland had lived in the city all his life, as Abner could not but feel).

"I should be glad if you could lunch with me at the club," said Whyland in the friendliest fashion possible. "I am on my way there now."

"Club"—fatal word; it chilled Abner in a second. He knew about clubs! Clubs were the places where the profligate children of Privilege drank improper drinks and told improper stories and kept improper hours. Abner, who was perfectly pure in word, thought and deed and always in bed betimes, shrank from a club as from a lazaret.

"Thank you," he responded bleakly; "but I am very busy."

"Another time, then," said Whyland, with unimpaired kindliness. "And we may be able to come to some agreement, after all," he added, in reference to the tax-levy.

"We are not likely to agree," said Abner gloomily.

Whyland went on, just a trifle dashed. Abner presently came to further knowledge of him—his wealth, position, influence, activity—and hardened his heart against him the more. He commented openly on the selfishness and greed of the Money Power in pungent phrases that did not all fall short of Whyland's ear. And when, later on, Leverett Whyland became less the "good citizen" and more the "plutocrat"—a course perhaps inevitable under certain circumstances—he would sometimes smile over those unsuccessful advances and would ask himself to what extent the discouraging unfaith of our Abner might be responsible for his choice and his fall.

III

Though Mrs. Palmer Pence kept looking forward, off and on, to the pleasure of making Abner's acquaintance, it was a full six months before the happy day finally came round. But when she read *The Rod of the Oppressor* that seemed to settle it; her salon would be incomplete without its author, and she must take steps to find him.

Abner's second book, in spirit and substance, was a good deal like his first: the man who has succeeded follows up his success, naturally, with something of the same sort. The new book was a novel, however,—the first of the long series that Abner was to put forth with the prodigal ease and carelessness of Nature herself; and it was as gloomy, strenuous and positive as its predecessor.

Abner, by this time, had enlarged his circle. Through the reformers he had become acquainted with a few journalists, and journalists had led on to versifiers and novelists, and these to a small clique of artists and musicians. Abner was now beginning to find his best account in a sort of decorous Bohemia and to feel that such, after all, was the atmosphere he had been really destined to breathe. The morals of his new associates were as correct as even he could have insisted upon, and their manners were kindly and not too ornate. They indulged in a number of little practices caught, he supposed, from "society," but after all their modes were pleasantly trustful and informal and presently quite ceased to irk and to intimidate him. Many members of his new circle were massed in one large building whose owner had attempted to name it the Warren Block; but the artists and the rest simply called it the Warren—sometimes the Burrow or the Rabbit-Hutch—and referred to themselves collectively as the Bunnies.

Abner found it hard to countenance such facetiousness in a world so full of pain; yet after all these dear people did much to cushion his discomfort, and before long hardly a Saturday afternoon came round without his dropping into one studio or another for a chat and a cup of tea. To tell the truth, Abner could hardly "chat" as yet, but he was beginning to learn, and he was becoming more reconciled as well to all the paraphernalia involved in the brewing of the draught. He was boarding rather roughly with a landlady who, like himself, was from "down state" and who had never cultivated fastidiousness in table-linen or in tableware, and he sniffed at the fanciful cups and spoons and pink candle-shades that helped to insure the attendance of the "desirable people," as the Burrow phrased it, and at the manifold methods of tea-making that were designed to turn the desirable people into profitable patrons. That is, he sniffed at the samovar and the lemons and so on; but when the rum came along he looked away sternly and in silence.

Well, the desirable people came in numbers—studios were the fad that year—and as soon as Mrs. Palmer Pence understood that Abner was to be met with somewhere in the Burrow she hastened to enroll herself among them.

Eudoxia Pence was a robust and vigorous woman in her prime—and by "prime" I mean about thirty-six. She was handsome and rich and intelligent and ambitious, and she was hesitating between a career as a Society Queen and a self-devotion to the Better Things: perhaps she was hoping to combine both. With her she brought her niece, Miss Clytie Summers, who had been in society but a month, yet who was enterprising enough to have joined already a class in sociological science, composed of girls that were quite the ones to know, and to have undertaken two or three little excursions into the slums. Clytie hardly felt sure just yet whether what she most wanted was to gain a Social Triumph or to lend a Helping Hand. It was Abner's lot to help influence her decision.

IV

The Bunnies could hardly believe their eyes when, one day, Mrs. Palmer Pence came rolling into the Burrow. She was well enough known indeed at the "rival shop"—by which the Bunnies meant a neighbouring edifice loftily denominated the Temple of Art, a vast structure full of theatres and recital-halls and studios and assembly-rooms and dramatic schools; but this was the first time she had favoured the humbler building, at least on the formal, official Saturday afternoon. Long had they looked for her coming, and now at last the most desirable of all the desirable people was here.

"Ah-h-h!" breathed Little O'Grady, who made reliefs in plastina.

It was for Mrs. Palmer Pence that the samovar steamed to-day in the dimly lighted studio of Stephen Giles, for her that the candles fluttered within their pink shades, for her that the white peppermints lay in orderly little rows upon the silver tray, for her that young Medora Giles, lately back to her brother from Paris, wore her freshest gown and drew tea with her prettiest smile. Mrs. Pence was building a new house and there was more than an even chance that Stephen Giles might decorate it. He held a middle ground between the "artist-architects" on the one hand and the painters on the other, and with this advantageous footing he was gradually drawing a strong cordon round "society" and was looking forward to a day not very distant when he might leave the Burrow for the Temple of Art itself.

Mrs. Pence sat liberally cushioned in her old carved pew and amiably sipped her tea beneath a jewelled censer and admired the dark beauty of the slender and graceful Medora. Presently she became so taken by the girl that (despite her own superabundant bulk) she must needs cross over and sit beside her and pat her hand at intervals. In certain extreme cases Eudoxia was willing to waive the matter of comparison with other women; but to find herself seated beside a man of lesser bulk than herself seriously inconvenienced her, while to realize herself standing beside a man of lesser stature embarrassed her most cruelly. As she was fond of mixed society, her liberal figure was on the move most of the time.

She was too enchanted with Medora Giles to be able to keep away from her, but the approach of Adrian Bond—he was a great studio dawdler—presently put her to rout. For Adrian was much too small. He was spare, he was meagre; he was sapless, like his books; and the part in his smoothly plastered black hair scarcely reached to her eyebrows. She felt herself swelling, distending, filling her place to repletion, to suffocation, and rose to flee. She was for seeking refuge in the brown beard of Stephen Giles, which was at least on a level with her own chin, when suddenly she perceived, in a dark corner of the place, a tower of strength more promising still—a man even taller, broader, bulkier than herself, a grand figure that might serve to reduce her to more desirable proportions.

"Who is he?" she asked Giles, as she seized him by the elbow. "Take me over there at once."

Giles laughed. "Why, that's Joyce," he said. "He's got so that he looks in on us now and then."

"Joyce? What Joyce?"

"Why, Joyce. The one, the only,—as we believe."

"Abner Joyce? *This Weary World? The Rod of the Oppressor?*"

"Exactly. Let me bring him over and present him."

"Whichever you like; arrange it between Mohammed and the Mountain just as you please." She looked over her shoulder; little Bond was following. "Waive all ceremony," she begged. "I will go to him."

Giles trundled her over toward the dusky canopy under which Abner stood chafing, conscious at once of his own powers and of his own social inexpertness. In particular had he looked out with bitterness upon the airy circulations of Adrian Bond—Adrian who smirked here and nodded there and chaffed a bit now and then with the blonde Clytie and openly philandered over the tea-urn with the brunette Medora. "That snip! That water-fly! That whipper-snapper! That— —"

Abner turned with a start. A worldly person, clad voluminously in furs, was extending a hand that sparkled with many rings and was composing a pair of smiling lips to say the pleasant thing. This attention was startlingly, embarrassingly sudden, but it was welcome and it was appropriate. Abner was little able to realize the quality of aggressive homage that resided in Mrs. Pence's resolute and unconventional advance, but it was natural enough that this showy woman should wish to manifest her appreciation of a gifted and rising author. He took her hand with a graceless gravity.

Mrs. Pence, upon a nearer view, found Abner all she had hoped. Confronted by his stalwart limbs and expansive shoulders, she was no longer a behemoth,—she felt almost like a sylph. She looked up frankly, and with a sense of growing comfort, into his broad face where a good strong growth of chestnut beard was bursting through his ruddy cheeks and swirling abundantly beneath his nose. She looked up higher, to his wide forehead, where a big shock of confident hair rolled and tumbled about with careless affluence. And with no great shyness she appraised his hands and his feet—those strong forceful hands that had dominated the lurching, self-willed plough, those sturdy feet that had resolutely tramped the miles of humpy furrow the ploughshare had turned up blackly to sun and air. She shrank. She dwindled. Her slender girlhood—that remote, incredible time—was on her once more.

"I shall never feel large again," she said.

How right she was! Nobody ever felt large for long when Abner Joyce happened to be about.

V

Abner regarded Mrs. Pence and her magnificence with a sombre intensity, far from ready to approve. He knew far more about her than she could know about him—thanks to the activities of a shamefully discriminating (or undiscriminating) press—and he was by no means prepared to give her his countenance. Face to face with her opulence and splendour he set the figure of his own mother—that sweet, patient, plaintive little presence, now docilely habituated, at the closing in of a long pinched life, to unremitting daily toil still unrewarded by ease and comfort or by any hope or promise or prospect of it. There was his father too—that good gray elder who had done so much faithful work, yet had so little to show for it, who had fished all day and had caught next to nothing, who had given four years out of his young life to the fight for freedom only to see the reward so shamefully fall elsewhere.... Abner evoked here a fanciful figure of Palmer Pence himself, whom he knew in a general way to be high up in some monstrous Trust. He saw a prosperous, domineering man who with a single turn of the hand had swept together a hundred little enterprises and at the same time had swept out a thousand of the lesser fry into the wide spaces of empty ruin, and who had insolently settled down beside his new machine to catch the rain of coins minted for him from the wrongs of an injured and insulted people....

Abner accepted in awkward silence Mrs. Pence's liberal and fluent praise of *The Rod of the Oppressor*,—aside from his deep-seated indignation he had not yet mastered any of those serviceable phrases by means of which such a volley may be returned; but he found words when she presently set foot in the roomy field of the betterment of local conditions. What she had in mind, it appeared, was a training-school—it might be called the Pence Institute if it went through—and she was ready to listen to any one who was likely to encourage her with hints or advice.

"So much energy, so much talent going to waste, so many young people tumbling up anyhow and presently tumbling over—all for lack of thorough and systematic training," she said, across her own broad bosom.

"I know of but one training that is needed," said Abner massively: "the training of the sense of social justice—such training of the public conscience as will insist upon seeing that each and every freeman gets an even chance."

"An even chance?" repeated Eudoxia, rather dashed. "What I think of offering is an even start. Doesn't it come to much the same thing?"

But Abner would none of it. Possessed of the fatalistic belief in the efficacy of mere legislation such as dominates the rural townships of the West, he grasped his companion firmly by the arm, set his sturdy legs in rapid motion, walked her from assembly hall to assembly hall through this State, that and the other, and finally fetched up with her under the dome of the national Capitol. Senators and representatives co-operated here, there and everywhere, the chosen spokesmen of the sovereign people; Abner seemed almost to have enrolled himself among them. Confronted with this august company, whose work it was to set things right, Eudoxia Pence felt smaller than ever. What were her imponderable emanations of goodwill and good intention when compared with the robust masculinity that was marching in firm phalanxes over solid ground toward the mastery of the great Problem? She drooped visibly. Little O'Grady, studying her pose and expression from afar, wrung his hands. "That fellow will drive her away. Ten to one we shall never see her profile here again!" Yes, Eudoxia was feeling, with a sudden faintness, that the Better Things might after all be beyond her reach. She looked about for herself without finding herself: she had dwindled away to nothingness.

VI

"Do you take her money—*such* money?" Abner asked of Giles with severity. Eudoxia had returned to Medora and the samovar.

"*Such* money?" returned Giles. "Is it different from other money? What do you mean?"

"Isn't her husband the head of some trust or other?"

"Why, yes, I believe so: the Feather-bed Trust, or the Air-and-Sunlight Trust—something of that sort; I've never looked into it closely."

"Yet you accept what it offers you."

"And give a good return for it. Yes, she had paid me already for my sketches—a prompt and business-like way of doing things that I should be glad to encounter oftener."

Abner shook his head sadly. "I thought we might come to be real friends."

"And I hope so yet. Anyway, it takes a little money to keep the tea-pot boiling."

Abner drifted back to the shelter of his canopy and darkly accused himself for his acceptance of such hospitality. He ought to go, to go at once, and never to come back. But before he found out how to go, Clytie Summers came along and hemmed him in.

Clytie was not at all afraid of big men; she had already found them easier to manage than little ones. Indeed she had pretty nearly come to the conclusion that a lively young girl with a trim figure and a bright, confident manner and a fetching mop of sunlit hair and a pair of wide, forthputting, blue eyes was predestined to have her own way with about everybody alike. But Clytie had never met an Abner Joyce.

And as soon as Clytie entered upon the particulars of her last slumming trip through the river wards she began to discover the difference. She chanced to mention incidentally certain low-grade places of amusement.

"What!" cried Abner; "you go to theatres—and *such* theatres?"

"Surely I do!" cried Clytie in turn, no less disconcerted than Abner himself. "Surely I go to theatres; don't you?"

"Never," replied Abner firmly. "I have other uses for my money." His rules of conduct marshalled themselves in a stiff row before him; forlorn Flatfield came into view. Neither his principles nor his practice of making monthly remittances to the farm permitted such excesses.

"Why, it doesn't *cost* anything," rejoined Clytie. "There's no admission charge. All you have to do is to buy a drink now and then."

"Buy a drink?"

"Beer—that will do. You can stay as long as you want to on a couple of glasses. Lots of our girls didn't take but one."

"Lots of——?"

"Yes, the whole class went. We found the place most interesting—and the audience. The men sit about with their hats on, you know, in a big hall full of round tables, drinking and smoking——"

"And you mixed up in such a——?"

"Well, no; not exactly. We had a box—as I suppose you would call it; three of them. Of course that *did* cost a little something. And then Mr. Whyland bought a few cigars——"

"Mr. Whyland——?"

"Yes, he was with us; he thought there ought to be at least one gentleman along. He couldn't smoke the cigars, but one of the girls happened to have some cigarettes——"

"Cigarettes?"

"Yes, and we found *their* smoke much more endurable. That was the worst about the place—the smoke; unless it was the performance——"

"Oh!" said Abner, with a groan of disgust.

"Well, it wasn't as bad as *that!*" returned Clytie. "It was only dull and stale and stupid; the same old sort of knockabouts and serio-comics you can see everywhere down town, only not a quarter so good—just cheap imitations. And all those poor fellows sat moping over their beer-mugs waiting, waiting, waiting for something new and entertaining to happen. I never felt so sorry for anybody in my life. We girls about made up our minds that we would get together a little fund and see if we couldn't do some missionary work in that neighbourhood—hire some real good artists"—Abner winced at this hideous perversion of the word—"hire some real good artists to go over there and let those poor creatures see what a first-class show was like; and Mr. Whyland promised to contribute——"

"Stop!" said Abner.

Clytie paused abruptly, astonished by his tone and by the expression on his face. The flush of innocent enthusiasm and high resolve left her cheek, her pretty little lips parted in amaze, and her wide blue eyes opened wider than ever. What a singular man! What a way of accepting her expression of interest in her kind, of receiving her plan for helping the other half to lead a happier life! Adrian Bond, a dozen, a hundred other men would have known how to give her credit for her kindly intentions toward the less fortunate, would have found a ready way to praise her, to compliment her....

Abner Joyce had a great respect for woman in general, but he entertained an utter detestation of anything like gallantry; in his chaste anxiety he leaned the other way. He was brusque; he often rode roughshod over feminine sensibilities. He was very slightly influenced by considerations of sex. He viewed everybody asexually, as a generalized human being. He dealt with women just as he dealt with men, and he treated young women just as he treated older ones. He treated Clytie just as he treated Eudoxia Pence, just as he would have treated Whyland himself—but with a little added severity, called forth by her peculiar presence and her specific offence. He brought her to book just as she deserved to be brought to book—a girl who went to low theatres and wore frizzled yellow hair and made eyes at strangers and took her share in the heartless amusements of plutocrats.

"Why, what is it?" asked Clytie. "Don't you think we ought to try to understand modern social conditions and do what we can to improve them? If you would only go through some of those streets in the river wards and into some of the houses—oh, dear me, dear me!"

But Abner would none of this. "Do you think your river wards, as you call them, are any worse than our barn-yard in the early days of March? Do you imagine your cheap vawdyville theatres are any more tiresome than our Main Street through the winter months?"

No, Abner's thoughts had been focused too long on the wrongs of the rural regions to be able to transfer themselves to the sufferings and injustices of the town. He saw the city collectively as the oppressor of the country, and Leverett Whyland, by reason of Clytie's innocent prattle, became the city incarnate in a single figure.

"I know your Mr. Whyland," he said. "I've met him; I know all about him. He lives on his rents. His property came to him by inheritance, and half its value to-day is due to the general rise brought about by the exertions of others. He is indebted for food, clothing and shelter to the unearned increment."

"Lives on his rents? Is there anything wrong in that? So do I, too—when they can be collected. And if you talk about the unearned increment, let me tell you there is such a thing as the unearned decrement."

"Nonsense. That's merely a backward swirl in a rushing stream."

"Not at all!" cried Clytie, now in the full heat of controversy. "If you were used to a big growing city, with all its sudden shifts and changes, you would understand. Even the new neighbourhoods get spoiled before they are half put together—builders treat one another so unfairly; while, as for the old ones—why, my poor dear father is coming to have row after row that he can't find tenants for at all, unless he were to let them to—to objectionable characters."

Clytie threw this out with all boldness. The matter was purely economic, sociological; they were talking quite as man to man. Abner brought every woman to this point sooner or later.

As for the troubles of landlords, he had no sympathy with them. And to him the most objectionable of all "objectionable characters" was the man who had a strong box stuffed with farm mortgages—town-dwellers, the great bulk of them. "Oh, the cities, the cities!" he groaned. Then, more cheerfully: "But never mind: they are passing."

"Passing? I like that! Do you know that eighteen and two-thirds per cent of the population of the United States lives in towns of one hundred thousand inhabitants and above, and that the number is increasing at the rate of——"

"They are disintegrating," pursued Abner stolidly. "By their own bulk—like a big snowball. And by their own badness. People are rolling back to the country—the country they came from. Improved transportation will do it." The troubles of the town were ephemeral—he waved them aside.

But his face was set in a frown—doubtless at the thought of the perdurable afflictions of the country.

"Don't worry over these passing difficulties that arise from a mere temporary congestion of population. They will take care of themselves. Meanwhile, don't sport with them; don't encourage your young friends to make them a vehicle of their own selfish pleasures; don't——"

Clytie caught her breath. So she was a mere frivolous, inconsequential butterfly, after all. Why try longer to lend the Helping Hand—why not cut things short and be satisfied with the Social Triumph and let it go at that? "I was meaning to ask you to dine with me some evening next week at a settlement I know, but now…."

"I never 'dine,'" said Abner.

VII

"I should be so glad to have you call." Mrs. Pence was peering about among the lanterns and tapestries and the stirring throng with the idea of picking up Clytie and taking leave. "My niece is staying with me just now, and I'm sure she would be glad to see you again too."

Abner looked about to help her find her charge. Clytie had gone over to the tea-table, where she was snapping vindictively at the half of a ginger-wafer somebody else had left and was gesticulating in the face of Medora Giles.

"I never met such a man in my life!" she was declaring. "I'll never speak to him again as long as I live! He's a bear; he's a brute!"

Little O'Grady, bringing forward another sliced lemon, shook in his shoes. "He'll have everybody scared away before long!" the poor fellow thought.

Medora smiled on Clytie. "Oh, not so bad as that, I hope," she said serenely. "Stephen, now, is beginning to have quite a liking for him. So earnest; so well-intentioned...."

"And you yourself?" asked Clytie.

"I haven't met him yet. I'm only on probation. He has looked me over—from afar, but has his doubts. I may get the benefit of them, or I may not."

"What doubts?"

"Why, I'm a renegade, a European. I'm effete, contaminate, taboo."

"Has he said so?"

"Said so? Do I need to have things 'said'?"

"Well, if you really are all this, you'll find it out soon enough."

"He's a touchstone, then?"

"Yes. And I'm a nonentity, lightly concerning myself about light nothings. He won't mince matters."

"Don't worry about me," said Medora confidently. "I shall know how to handle him."

Mrs. Pence kept on peering. Dusk was upon the place, and the few dim lights were more ineffectual than ever. "There she is," said Abner, with a bob of the head.

"Good-bye, then," said Eudoxia, grasping his hand effusively, as she took her first step toward Clytie. "Now, you *will* come and see us, won't you?"

"Thank you; but— —"

Abner paused for the evocation of an instantaneous vision of the household thus thrown open to him. Such opportunities for falsity, artificiality, downright humbuggery, for plutocratic upholstery and indecorous statues and light-minded paintings, for cynical and insolent servants, for the deployment of vast gains got by methods that at best were questionable! Could he accept such hospitality as this?

"Thank you. I might come, possibly, if I can find the time. But I warn you I am very busy."

"Make time," said Eudoxia good-humouredly, and passed along.

Abner made a good deal of time for the Burrow, but it was long before he brought himself to make any for Eudoxia Pence. He came to see a great deal of the Bunnies; in a month or two he quite had the run of the place. There were friendly fellows who heaved big lumps of clay upon huge nail-studded scantlings, and nice little girls who designed book-plates, and more mature ones who painted miniatures, and many earnest, earnest persons of both sexes who were hurrying, hurrying ahead on their wet canvases so that the next exhibition might not be incomplete by reason of lacking a "Smith," a "Jones," a "Robinson." Abner gave each and every one of these pleasant people his company and imparted to them his views on the great principles that underlie all the arts in common.

"So that's what you call it—a marquise," Abner observed on a certain occasion to one of the miniature painters. "This creature with a fluffy white wig and a low-necked dress is a marquise, is she? Do you like that sort of thing?"

"Why, yes,—rather," said the artist.

"Well, *I* don't," declared Abner, returning the trifle to the girl's hands.

"I'll paint my next sitter as a milkmaid—if she'll let me."

"*As* a milkmaid? No; paint the milkmaid herself. Deal with the verities. Like them before you paint them. Paint them *because* you like them."

"I don't know whether I should like milkmaids or not. I've never seen one."

"They don't exist," chimed in Adrian Bond, who was dawdling in the background. "The milkmaids are all men. And as for the dairy-farms themselves——!" He sank back among his cushions. "I visited one in the suburbs last month—the same time when I was going round among the markets. I have been of half a mind, lately," he said, more directly to Abner, "to do a large, serious thing based on local actualities; *The City's Maw*—something like that. My things so far, I know (none better) *are* slight, flimsy, exotic, factitious. The first-hand study of actuality, thought I——But no, no, no! It was a place fit only for a reporter in search of a—of a—I don't know what. I shall never drink coffee again; while as for milk punch——"

"And what is the artist," asked Abner, "but the reporter sublimated? Why must the artist go afield to dabble in far-fetched artificialities that have nothing to do with his own proper time and place? Our people go abroad for study, instead of staying at home and guarding their native quality. They return affected, lackadaisical, self-conscious—they bring the hothouse with them. Why, I have seen such a simple matter as the pouring of a cup of tea turned into——"

"You can't mean Medora Giles," said the miniaturist quickly, pausing amidst the laces of her bodice. "Don't make any mistake about Medora. When she goes in for all that sort of thing, she's merely 'creating atmosphere,' as we say,—she's simply after the 'envelopment,' in fact."

"She is just getting into tone," Bond re-enforced, "with the candle-shades and the peppermints."

"Medora," declared the painter, "is as sensible and capable a girl as I know. Why, the very dress she wore that afternoon——You noticed it?"

"I—I——" began Abner.

"No, you didn't—of course you didn't. Well, she made every stitch of it with her own hands." "And those tea-cakes, that afternoon," supplemented Bond. "She made every stitch of *them* with her own hands. She told me so herself, when I stayed afterward, to help wash things up."

"I may have done her an injustice," Abner acknowledged. "Perhaps I might like to know her, after all."

"You might be proud to," said Bond.

"And the favour would be the other way round," declared the painter stoutly.

Abner passed over any such possibility as this. "How long was she abroad?" he asked Bond.

"Let's see. She studied music in Leipsic two years; she plays the violin like an angel—up to a certain point. Then she was in Paris for another year. She paints a little—not enough to hurt."

"Leipsic? Two years?" pondered Abner. It seemed more staid, less vicious, after all, than if the whole time had been spent in Paris. The violin; painting. Both required technique; each art demanded long, close application. "Well, I dare say she is excusable." But here, he thought, was just where the other arts were at a disadvantage compared with literature: you might stay at home wherever you were, if a writer, and get your own technique.

"And you have done it," said Bond. "I admire some of
your things so much.
Your instinct for realities, your sturdy central grasp—"

"What man has done, man may do," rejoined Abner. "Yet what is technique, after all? There remains, as ever, the problem, the great Social Problem, to be solved."

"You think so?" queried Bond.

"Think that there is a social problem?"

"Think that it can be solved. I have my own idea there. It is a secret. I am willing to tell it to one person, but not to more,—I couldn't answer for the consequences. If Miss Wilbur will just stop her ears——"

The miniaturist laughed and laid her palms against her cheeks.

"You are sure you can't hear?" asked Bond, with his eye on her spreading fingers. "Well, then"—to Abner—"there *is* the great Human Problem, but it is not to be solved, nor was it designed that it should be. The world is only a big coral for us to cut our teeth upon, a proving-ground, a hotbed from which we shall presently be transplanted according to our several deserts. No power can solve the puzzle save the power that cut it up into pieces to start with. Try as we may, the blanket will always be just a little too small for the bedstead. Meanwhile, the thing for us to do is to go right along figuring, figuring, figuring on our little slates,—but rather for the sake of keeping busy than from any hope of reaching the 'answer' set down in the Great Book above."

"But——" began Abner; his orthodox sensibilities were
somewhat offended.

Miss Wilbur, who had heard every word, laughed outright.

"I beg," Bond hurried on, "that you won't communicate this to a living soul. I am the only one who suspects the real truth. If it came to be generally known all human motives would be lacking, all human activities would be paralyzed—the whole world would come to a standstill. Mum's the word. For if the problem is insoluble and meant to be, just as sure is it that we were not intended to suspect the truth."

Abner gasped—dredging the air for a word. "Of course," Bond went ahead, less fantastically, "I know I ought to shut my eyes to all this and start in to accomplish something more vital, more indigenous—less of the marquise and more of the milkmaid, in fact——"

"Write about the things you know and like," said Abner curtly.

His tone acknowledged his inability to keep pace with such whimsicalities or to sympathize with them.

"If to know and to like were one with me, as they appear to be with you! A boyhood in the country—what a grand beginning! But the things I know are the things I don't like, and the things I like are not always the things I know—oftener the things I feel." Bond was speaking with a greater sincerity than he usually permitted himself. The right touch just then might have determined his future: he was quite as willing to become a Veritist as to remain a mere Dilettante.

Abner tossed his head with a suppressed snort; he felt but little inclined to give encouragement to this manikin, this tidier-up after studio teas, this futile spinner of sophistications. No, the curse of a city boyhood was upon the fellow. Why look for anything great or vital from one born and bred in the vitiated air of the town?

"Oh, well," he said, half-contemptuously, and not half trying to hide his contempt, "you are doing very well as it is. Some of your work is not without traces of style; and I suppose style is what you are after. But meat for *me!*"

Bond lapsed back into his cushions, feeling a little hurt and very feeble and unimportant. Clearly the big thing, the sincere thing, the significant thing was beyond his reach. *The City's Maw* must remain unwritten.

VIII

Abner tramped down the corridor and walked in on Giles. He found the decorator busy over two or three large sketches for panels.

"For another Trust man?" he asked.

"No," replied Giles; "these are for a blameless old gentleman that has passed a life of honest toil in the wholesale hardware business. Don't you think he's entitled to a few flowers by this time?"

"What kind of flowers are they?"

"Passion-flowers and camellias."

"Humph! Do they grow round here?"

"Hardly. My old gentleman hasn't given himself a vacation for twenty-five years, and he wants to get as far away from 'here' as possible."

Abner gave another "Humph!" Wigs and brocades; passion-flowers and camellias. All this in a town that had just seen the completion of the eighteenth chapter of *Regeneration*. Well, regeneration was coming none too soon.

"What's the matter with Bond?" he asked suddenly.

"I do' know. Is anything?"

"I've just been talking with him, and he seemed sort of skittish and dissatisfied and paradoxical."

"He's often like that. We never notice."

"He seemed to shilly-shally considerable too. Has he got any convictions, any principles?"

"I can't say I've ever thought much about that. He never mentions such things himself, but I suppose he must have them about him somewhere. He generally behaves himself and treats other people kindly. Everybody trusts him and seems to believe in him. I presume he's got *something* inside that holds him up—moral framework, so to speak."

Abner shook his head. If the framework was there it ought to show through. Every articulation should tell; every rib should count.

"If a man has got principles and beliefs, why not come out flat-footedly with them *like* a man?"

"I do' know. Dare say Bond doesn't want to wear his heart on his sleeve. Hates to live in the show-window, you understand."

"He was fussing most about writing some new thing or other in a new way. I seem to have kind of started him up."

"He has been talking like that for quite a little while. He's tenderly interested—that's the real reason for it. He wants more reputation—something to lay at the dear one's feet, you know. And he wants bigger returns—though he *has* got something in the way of an independent income, I believe."

"Who is she?"

"That little Miss Summers."

"He may have her," said Abner quickly. "She may 'dine' *him* at her settlement." Then, more slowly: "Why, they hardly spoke to each other, that day—except once or twice to joke. They barely noticed each other."

"What should they have done? Sit side by side, holding hands?"

"Oh, the city, the city!" murmured Abner, overcome by the artificiality of urban society and the mockery in Giles's tone.

"You should have seen them in the country last summer."

"Them! In the country!"

"Why, yes; why not? We had them both out on the farm."

"Farm? Whose?"

"My father's. We try to do a little livening up for the old people every July and August. They got acquainted there; they took to it like ducks to water. That's where Bond got his idea for his cow masterpiece,—he may have spoken to you about it."

"Humph!" said Abner. Why heed such insignificant poachings as these on his own preserves?

"We're going out home week after next for the holidays," continued Giles. "Better go with us."

"So you're a farmer's boy?" pondered Abner. He looked again at the camellias, then at Giles's loose Parisian tie, and lastly at his finger-nails,—all too exquisite by half.

"Certainly. Brought up on burdock and smart-weed. That's why I'm so fond of this,"—with a wave toward one of his panels.

"Well, what do you say? Will you go? We should like first-rate to have you."

Abner considered. The invitation was as hearty and informal as he could have wished, and it would take him within thirty miles of Flatfield itself.

"Is your sister going along?"

"Surely. She will run the whole thing."

"Well," said Abner slowly, "I don't know but that I might find it interesting." This, Giles understood, was his rustic manner of accepting.

IX

Abner spent Christmas at the Giles farm, as Stephen had understood him to promise; and Medora, as her brother had engaged, "went along" too, and "ran the whole thing" from start to finish. Abner, with a secret interest compounded half of attraction, half of repulsion, promised himself a careful study of this "new type"—a type so bizarre, so artificial, and in all probability so thoroughly reprehensible.

Medora made up the rest of the party to suit herself. She had heard of Adrian Bond's struggles toward the indigenous, the simplified, and she was willing enough to give him a chance to see the cows in their winter quarters. Clytie Summers had begged very prettily for her glimpse too of the country at this time of year. "It's rather soon, I know, for that spring barn-yard; but I should so enjoy the ennui of some village Main Street in the early winter."

"Come along, then," said Medora. "We'll do part of our Christmas shopping there."

Giles accepted these two new recruits gladly. "Good thing for both of them," he declared to Joyce. "They'll make more progress on our farm in a week than they could in six months of studio teas."

This remark admitted of but one interpretation.

"Why!" said Abner; "do you want her to marry *him*?"—him, a fellow so slight, frivolous, invertebrate!

"Oh, he's a very decent little chap," returned Giles. "He'll be kind to her—he'll see she's taken good care of."

"But do you want him to marry *her*?"—her, so bold, so improper, so prone to seek entertainment in the woes of others!

"Oh, well, she's a very fair little chick," replied Giles patiently. "She'll get past her notions pretty soon and be just as good a wife as anybody could ask."

One of those quiescent, featureless Decembers was on the land—a November prolonged. The brown country-side, swept and garnished, was still awaiting the touch of winter's hand. The air was crisp yet passive, and abundant sunshine flooded alike the heights and hollows of the rolling uplands that spread through various shades of subdued umber and meditative blue toward the confines of a wavering, indeterminate horizon. The Giles homestead stood high on a bluff; and above the last of the islands that cluttered the river beneath it the spires of the village appeared, a mile or two down-stream.

"Now for the barn-yard!" cried Clytie, after the first roundabout view from the front of the bluff. "Adrian mustn't lose any time with his cows."

Giles led the way to a trim inclosure.

"Why, it's as dry as a bone!" she declared.

"Would you want us water-logged the whole year through?" asked Abner pungently.

"And as for ennui," she pursued, "I'm sure it isn't going to be found here—no more in winter than in summer. However"—with a wave of the hand toward the spires—"there is always the town."

No, the parents of Giles had taken strong measures to keep boredom at bay. They had their books and magazines; they had a pair of good trotters and a capacious carryall, with other like aids to locomotion in reserve; they had a telephone; they had a pianola, with a change of rolls once a month; they had neighbours of their own sort and were indomitable in keeping up neighbourly relations.

"I think you'll be able to stand it for a week," said Medora serenely.

"We've done it once before," said Bond.

"Don't be anxious about *us*!" added Clytie.

Medora Giles took Abner in her own special care. She knew pretty nearly what he thought of her, and she was inclined to amuse herself—though at the same time making no considerable concession—by placing herself before him in a more favourable light. In her dress, her manner, her bearing there was a certain half-alien delicacy, finesse, aloofness. She would not lay this altogether aside, even at home, even in the informal country; but she would provide a homely medium, suited to Abner's rustic vision, through which her exotic airs and graces might be more tolerantly perceived.

The illness of one of the servants came just here to assist her. She descended upon the kitchen, taking full charge and carrying Abner with her. She initiated him at the chopping-block, she conferred the second degree at the pump-handle, and by the time he was beating up eggs in a big yellow bowl beside the kitchen stove his eyes had come to be focused on her in quite a different fashion. Surely no one could be more deft, light-handed, practical. Was this the same young woman who had sat in the midst of that absurd outfit and had juggled rather affectedly and self-consciously with tea-urn and sugar-tongs and had palavered in empty nothings with a troop of overdressed and overmannered feather-heads? She was still graceful, still fluent, still endowed with that baffling little air of distinction; but she knew where things were—down to the last strainer or nutmeg-grater—and she knew how to use them. She was completely at home. And so—by this time—was he.

To deepen the impression, Medora asked Abner to help her lay the table. There were no studio gimcracks, mercifully, to put into place; but the tableware was as far removed, on the other hand, from the ugly, heavy, time-scarred things at Flatfield and from the careless crudities of his own boarding-house. Abner had had a tolerance, even a liking, for his landlady's indifference toward finicky table-furnishings; but now there came a sudden vision of her dining-room, and the spots on the table-cloth, the nicks in the crockery, the shabbiness of the lambrequin drooping from the mantel-piece, and the slovenliness of the sole handmaiden had never been so vivid.

"Shall I be able to go back there?" he asked himself.

Finally, to seal the matter completely, Medora led Abner to the place of honour and bade him eat the meal she had prepared. Abner ate and was hers. Even a good boarding-house, he now felt, was a mistake; the best, but a makeshift.

> During the day the telephone had made common property of the news of Abner's arrival, and the next morning, an hour or so after breakfast, the front yard resounded with the loud cry of, "What ho, neighbours!" and Leverett Whyland was revealed in a trig cart drawn by a handsome cob.

"Why, what's that man doing here?" Abner asked Giles, as they stood by the living-room window.

"He has a place three or four miles down the river," replied Giles, casting about for his hat. Clytie, meanwhile, had drubbed a glad welcome upon the adjoining window and then rushed out bareheaded to give greeting.

"He always comes out here with his family for Christmas," said Stephen.

"His family? Is he married? Has he a wife and children?"

"Yes."

"Yet he goes slam-banging around with a lot of young girls into all sorts of doubtful places?"

"Oh, I've heard something about that," said Giles. "Well, you wouldn't have them in charge of a bachelor, would you?"

"What's he farming for?" asked Abner, left behind with Medora.

"Sentiment," she replied. "He was born down there, and has never wanted to let the old place go. Do you think any the worse of him for that?"

Whyland had come to fetch the men and to show them his model farm. They spent the forenoon in going over this expensive place. Bond gave vent to all the "oh's" and "ah's" that indicate the perfect visitor. Abner took their host's various amateurish doings in glum silence. It was all very well to indulge in these costly contraptions as a pastime, but if the man had to get his actual living from the soil where would he be? Almost anybody could stand on two legs. How many on one?

"Do you make it pay?" Abner asked bluntly.

"Pay? I'm a by-word all over the county. Half the town lives on my lack of 'gumption.'"

"H'm," said Abner darkly. He was as far as ever from hitting it off with this smiling, dapper product of artificial city conditions.

"I came across some of your Readjusters the other day," observed Whyland, at the door of his hen-house—a prodigal place with a dozen wired-in "runs" for a dozen different varieties of poultry: "Leghorns, Plymouth Rocks, Jerseys, Angoras, Hambletonians and what not," as Bond irresponsibly remarked. "They say they haven't been seeing much of you lately."

Abner frowned. Whyland, he felt, was trying to put him at a disadvantage. But, in truth, it could not be denied that he had practically left one circle for another,—was showing himself much more disposed to favour the skylights of the studios than the footlights of the rostrum.

"I am still for the cause," he said. "But it can be helped from one side as well as from another. My next book——"

"I didn't dispute your idea; only its application. I should be glad if you *could* make it go. Anything would be better than the present horrible mess.

We have 'equality,' and to spare, in the Declaration and the Constitution, but whether or not we shall ever get it in our taxing——"

"I am glad to hear you speaking a word for the country people——" began Abner.

"The country people?" interrupted Whyland quickly, with a stare. Never more than when among his cattle and poultry was he moved to draw contrasts between the security of his possessions in the country and the insecurity of his possessions in town. "What I am thinking of is the city tax-payer. Urban democracy, working on a large scale, has declared itself finally, and what we have is the organization of the careless, the ignorant, the envious, brought about by the criminal and the semi-criminal, for the spoliation of the well-to-do."

Abner began to be ruffled by these cross-references to the city—they were out of place in the uncontaminated country. "I believe in the people," he declared, with his thoughts on the rustic portion of the population.

"So do I—within a certain range, and up to a certain point. But I do not believe in the populace," declared Whyland, with his thoughts on the urban portion.

"All the difference between potatoes and potato-parings," said Bond, catching at a passing feather.

"Soon it will be simply dog eat dog," said Whyland. "No course will be left, even for the best-disposed of us, but to fight the devil with fire. From the assessor and all his works——"

"Good Lord deliver us," intoned Bond, who fully shared Whyland's ideas.

Abner frowned. His religious sensibilities were affronted by this response.

"And from all his followers," added Whyland. "They threaten me in my own office—it comes to that. Well, what shall a man do? Shall he fight or shall he submit? Shall I go into court or shall I compromise with them?"

"It comes to one thing in the end," said Bond, "if you value your peace of mind. But even then you can put the best face on it."

Whyland sighed. "You mean that there is some choice between my bribing them and their blackmailing me? Well, I expect I may slip down several pegs this coming year—morally."

Abner drew away. He was absolutely without any intimacy with the intricacies of civic finances. He merely saw a man—his host—who seemed cynically to be avowing his own corruption and shame,—or at least his willingness to lean in that direction.

"Reform," he announced grandly, "will come only from the disinterested efforts of those who bring to the task pure motives and unimpeachable practices."

Whyland sighed again. He thought of his realty interests in town, as they lay exposed to spoliation, to confiscation. "I am afraid I shall not be a reformer," he said, in discouragement.

Abner shook a condemnatory head in full corroboration. And Whyland, who may have been looking for a prop to wavering principles, shook his own head too.

X

"Don't work so hard at it," said Medora, laying her violin on top of the pianola. "You shake the house. A minute more and you'll have that lamp toppling over. And you'll tire yourself out."

Abner wiped his damp brow and felt of his wilted collar. He never put less than his whole self into anything he attempted. "Tire myself? I'm strong enough, I guess."

"Well, use your strength to better advantage. Let me show you."

Medora slipped into his place, reset the roll, pulled a stop or two, and trod out a dozen ringing measures with no particular effort. "Like that."

"Very well," said Abner, resuming his seat docilely. The rest wondered; he seldom welcomed suggestions or accepted correction.

"Now let's try it once more," said Medora.

An evening devoted to literature was ending with a bit of music. Abner and Bond had both read unpublished manuscripts with the fierce joy that authors feel on such occasions, and the others had listened with patience if not with pleasure. Abner gave two or three of the newest chapters of *Regeneration*, and Bond read a few pages to show what progress an alien romanticist was making in homely fields nearer at hand. He had hoped for Abner's encouragement and approval in this new venture of his, but he got neither.

"The way to write about cows in a pasture," commented Abner, "is just to write about them—in a simple, straightforward style without any slant toward history or mythology, and without any cross-references to remote scenes of foreign travel. For instance, you speak of a Ranz——"

"Ranz des Vaches," said Medora: "a sort of thing the Alpine what's-his-name sings."

"It's for atmosphere," said Bond, on the defensive.

"Let the pasture furnish its own atmosphere. And you had something about a certain breed of cattle near Rome—Rome, was it?"

"Roman Campagna. Travel reminiscences."

"Travel is a mistake," declared Abner.

"So it is," broke in Clytie. "Squat on your own door-step, as Emerson says."

"Does he?—I think not," interposed Giles the elder. "What he does say is— —"

"We all know," interrupted Stephen, "and ignore the counsel."

Abner did not know, but he would not stoop to ask. "And there was a quotation from one of those old authors,—Theocritus?"

"Theocritus, yes. Historical perspective."

"Leave the past alone. Live in the present. The past,—bury it, forget it."

"So hard. Heir of the ages, you know. Good deal harder to forget than never to have learned at all. *That's* easy," jibed Bond, with a touch of temper.

"Oh, now!" cried Medora, fearful that another temper might respond.

"If you must bring in those old Greeks," Abner proceeded, "take their method and let the rest drop. All they knew, as I understand it, they learned from men and things close round them and from the nature in whose midst they lived. They didn't quote; they didn't range the world; they didn't go for sanction outside of themselves and their own environment."

"The Greeks didn't know so much," interjected Clytie.

"Oh, didn't they, though!" cried Adrian, sending a glance of thanks to counteract his contradiction. "They *finished* things. The temple wasn't complete till they had swept all the marble chips off the back stoop, and had kind of curry-combed down the front yard, and had— —"

"'Sh,'sh!" said Medora. Abner looked about, more puzzled than offended. "Let's have some music, before our breasts get too savage," said the girl, starting up.

> Bond followed with the rest. "I'll stick to my regular field," he said to Clytie, as he thrust his crumpled-up manuscript into his pocket. "Griffins, gorgons, hydras, chimeras dire,— but no more cows. I was never meant for a veritist."

"Samson is pulling down the temple," observed Clytie. "Crash goes the first pillar. Who will be next?"

"He'll be caught in the wreck," said Bond, in a shattered voice. "Just watch and see."

XI

Medora, long before Abner had learned to work the pedals of the pianola and to wrench any expression from its stops, had banished most of her "rolls" from sight. "Siegfried's Funeral March" was unintelligible to him; the tawdry, meretricious Italian overtures filled him with disgust. In the end the two confined themselves to patriotic airs and old-time domestic ditties. Medora accompanied on her second-best violin (which was kept at the farm) and Abner enjoyed a heart-warming sense of doing his full share in "Tenting Tonight" or "Lily Dale." The girl's parents had advanced far beyond this stage, but willingly relapsed into it now and then for Auld Lang Syne.

The final roll wound up with a quick snap.

"Well, you haven't told me what you thought of that last chapter," said Abner, putting the roll back in its box. He made no demand on Medora's interest to the exclusion of that of the others, however. His general glance around invited comment from any quarter. He had merely looked at her first.

"M—no," said Medora.

The girl, a few weeks before, had looked over *The Rod of the Oppressor*. *The Rod's* force had made itself felt most largely on economics; but in its blossoming it had put forth a few secondary sprigs, and one of these curled over in the direction of domestic life, of marital relation. Abner's chivalry—a chivalry totally guiltless of gallantry—had gone out to the suffering wife doomed to a lifelong yoking with a cruel, coarse-natured husband: must such a yoking *be* lifelong? he asked earnestly. Was it not right and just and reasonable that she should fly (with or without companion)—nor be too particular over the formalities of her departure? Medora had smiled and shaken her head; but now the question somehow seemed less remote than before. She paused over this bird-like irresponsibility and rather wondered that it should have the power to detain her.

The new chapters of *Regeneration* had taken up the same matter and had displayed it in a somewhat different light. Abner had got hold of the idea of limited partnership and had sought to apply it, in roundabout fashion, to the matrimonial relation. His treatment, far from suggesting an academic aloofness, was as concrete as characterization and conversation could make it; no one would have supposed, at first glance, that what chiefly moved him was a chaste abstract Platonic regard for the whole gentler sex. In short, people—such seemed to be his thesis—might very advantageously separate, and most informally too, as soon as they discovered they were incompatible.

"M—no," said Medora.

"Wouldn't that be rather upsetting?" asked her mother. Mrs. Giles was an easy-going old soul, from whom art, as personified by her own children, got slight consideration, and to whom literature, as embodied in a stranger, was little less than a joke. "Wouldn't it result in a good deal of a mix-up? What would have happened to you youngsters if your father and I had all at once taken it into our heads to— —"

"Mother!" said Medora.

"Oh, well," began Mrs. Giles, with the idea of making a gradual descent after her sudden aerial flight. "But, then," she resumed, "you must see that— —"

"Mother!" said Medora again. Abner, eager to defend his thesis, looked round in surprise.

"I agree with Mrs. Giles completely," spoke up Clytie, with much promptitude. "When I get married I want to get married for good. Most of the people I know are married in that way, and I believe it's the most satisfactory way in the long run— —"

"But— —" began Abner polemically.

Clytie shook her head. "No, it won't do. You've offered us the ballot, and we don't want it. And you've offered us—this, and we don't want that either. Consider it declined."

Abner stared at Clytie's brazen little face and disliked her more than ever.

"But don't *you* think— —" began Abner, turning to Bond.

Bond shook his head slowly and made no comment.

Abner looked round at Medora. She was ranging the music-roll boxes in an orderly row. Nobody could have been more intent upon her work.

"Well, it stands, all the same," said Abner defiantly.

XII

The clear, placid weather had been waiting several days for Sunday to come and possess it, and now Sunday was here. The young people stood bareheaded on the porch and looked down toward the village.

"Do I hear the church bells?" asked Abner. He was a punctilious observer of Sabbath ordinances and always reached a state of subdued inner bustle shortly after the finish of the Sunday breakfast.

"We sometimes make them out," replied Stephen Giles, "when the wind happens to blow right."

"We are all going down this morning, I suppose?" observed Abner, confidently taking the initiative.

"I expect so," replied Giles.

"Count me out," said Clytie.

"You do not go to church?" asked Abner.

"Not often."

"You have no religion?"

"Yes, I have," replied Clytie, with much pomp: "the religion of humanity."

"You run and get your things on," said Medora. "You'll find as much humanity at the First Church as you will anywhere else."

The party set out in two vehicles. Old Mr. Giles drove one and the "hired man" the other. Clytie, despite her best endeavours to go in company with Bond, found herself associated with Abner, and a spirit of unchristian perversity took complete possession of her.

She cast her eye about, viewing the prosperous country-side, the well-kept farms, the modest comfort symbolized in her host's equipage itself.

"You're a great sufferer, Mr. Giles," she said suddenly; "aren't you?"

The old gentleman let the lines fall slackly on the fat backs of his sleek horses. "How? What's that?"

"I say you're a great sufferer. You're a downtrodden slave."

"Why, am I? How do you make that out?"

"Well, if you don't know without having it explained to you! The world is against you—it's making a doormat of you."

Medora looked askant. What was the child up to now?

"Poor father," she said. "If he hasn't found it out yet, don't tell him."

"No wonder he hasn't found it out," returned Clytie, making a sudden veer. "Is he suffering for lack of fresh air and pure water? And does he have to pay an extra price for sunlight? And must he herd in a filthy slum full of awful plumbing and crowded by more awful neighbours? Does he have to put up with municipal neglect and corruption, and worry along on make-believe milk and doctored bread and adulterated medicines, and endure long hours in unsanitary places under a tyrannical foreman and in constant dread of fines——?"

Abner was beginning to shift uneasily upon his seat. "Clytie, please!" said Medora, laying her hand upon the other's.

"Well, they're realities!" declared Clytie stoutly.

"They're not *my* realities," growled Abner, without turning round.

"Can we pick and choose our realities?" asked Clytie sharply. "Well, if you are at liberty to pick yours, I am at liberty to pick mine. Yes, sir, I'll go to that settlement right after New-Year's, and I'll have a class in basket-making and hammock-weaving before I'm a month older."

"It will take more than basket-making to set the world right," said Abner.

"Basket-making is enough to teach boys the use of their hands and to keep them off the street at night," sputtered Clytie.

"Clytie, please!" said Medora once more.

Clytie fell into silence and nursed her wrath through a long service and through a hearty rustic sermon from the text, "Peace on earth, goodwill toward men." Abner, in exacerbated mood, watched her narrowly throughout, that he might tax her, if possible, with a humorous attitude toward the preacher or a quizzical treatment of his flock. He had not yet pardoned her "ways" along Main Street, on the occasion of one or two shopping excursions. She had not hesitated to banter the admiring young clerks that held their places behind those shop-fronts of galvanized iron in simulation of red brick and of cut limestone, and she had been startlingly free in her accosting of several time-honoured worthies encountered on the dislocated plank walks outside. "Now," said Abner, "if she sniggers at that old deacon's whiskers or says a single facetious word about the best bonnets of any of these worthy women round about us— —" But Clytie, outwardly, was propriety itself. Inwardly she was revolving burning plans to show Abner Joyce that none of his despising, disparaging, discouraging words could have the least power to move her from her purpose; and on the way back to the farm she declared herself—to Bond, in whose company, this time, she had contrived to be;—they sat on the back seat together.

"That's what I'll do," she stated, with great positiveness. "I'll go right over there as soon as I get back to town. I don't care if the streets *are* dirty, and the street-cars dirtier; and if I have to look after my own room, why, I will. I'll take along my biggest trunk and my full-length mirror and the very pick of my new clothes— —You know they like to have us dress; it interests them,—they take it as a great compliment— —"

"And all for Abner Joyce!" said Bond. "Another pillar of the temple tottering, eh? and trying to brace itself against the modern Samson."

"Not one bit! Not one speck!" cried Clytie. "Only— —"

"Well, there are others," said Bond. "I'm prostrate already, as you know. And Whyland, only a few mornings back, got a good jar that will help finish him, I'm thinking."

"Did he? And there's Aunt Eudoxia too. If you could have seen how discouraged she was after she came home from that first meeting with him, when he took the wind out of her training-school— —"

"But he isn't going to jar *you*? He isn't going to cause *you* to totter?"

"Not a jar! Not a tot! You'll see whether— —"

"Your object, then, is to show how much stronger you are than I am?"

Clytie suddenly paused in her impetuous rush. "Adrian," she breathed, with plaintive contrition, "I wish you wouldn't say such things—no, nor even think them."

Her fierce alertness fled. She leaned a little toward him, droopingly, a poor, feeble, timid child in need of some strong man to shield her from the rough world.

The other carriage reached home first. Medora alighted gaily on the horse-block. Abner helped her down with an earnest endeavour not to seem too attentive.

"Come," she said; "let's see how those pies have turned out—Cordelia is so absent-minded."

And Abner followed gladly.

XIII

Christmas-Day came with a slight flurry of snow. There was also a slight flurry in society: the Whylands drove over to the farmhouse for dinner.

Medora had suggested their presence to her mother, and Clytie had supported the suggestion: "the more the merrier," she declared. Whyland himself had jumped at the opportunity eagerly, and his wife, who had met Medora a number of times at the studio and in Paris and liked her, acquiesced after the due interposition of a few objections.

"About the children——" she began.

"They can take dinner with Murdock and his wife for once in their lives."

"I don't know whether I can be said to have called regularly on Mrs. Giles——"

"Is Christmas-day a time for such sophistications? And do you think that plain, simple people, like the Gileses——"

Mrs. Whyland allowed herself to be persuaded—as she had designed from the start.

She had no great fancy for a solitary Christmas dinner, such as her husband's rural tastes had so often condemned her to; besides, this new arrangement would give her an opportunity to take a look at Miss Clytie Summers, of whom she had heard things.

Medora received Edith Whyland with some empressement; she regarded her guest as the model of all that the young urban matron should be. Mrs. Whyland was rather languid, rather elegant, rather punctilious, rather evangelical, and Abner Joyce, before he realized what was happening to him, was launched upon a conversation with a woman who, as Clytie Summers intimated at the first opportunity, was really high in good society.

"One of the swells, I suppose you mean," said Abner.

"I mean nothing of the kind. Swell society is one thing and good society is another. If you don't quite manage to get good society, you do the next best thing and take swell society. *I'm* swell," said Clyde humbly. "But I'm going to be something better, pretty soon," she added hopefully.

Abner had his little talk with Edith Whyland, all unteased by consideration of the imperceptible nuances and infinitesimal gradations that characterize the social fabric. He thought her rather quiet and inexpressive; but he felt her to be a good woman, and was inclined to like her. She dwelt at some length on Dr. McElroy's Christmas sermon, and it presently transpired that, whether in town or country, she made it a point to attend services. Abner, who for some dim reason of his own had expected little from the wife of Leverett Whyland, put down as mere calumnies the reports that made her "fashionable." Through the dinner he talked to her confidently, almost confidentially; with half the bulk of Eudoxia Pence she made twice the impression; and by the time the feast had reached the raisins and hickory-nuts his tongue, working independently of his will, was promising to call upon her in town.

This outcome was highly gratifying to Medora—it was just the one, in fact, that she had hoped to bring about. City and country, oil and water were mixing, and she herself was acting as the third element that made the emulsion possible. From her place down the other side of the table she kept her eyes and ears open for all that was going on. She saw with joy that Abner was almost chatting. He had given over for the present the ponderous consideration of knotty abstractions; he totally forgot the unearned increment; and what he was offering to quiet and self-repressed Edith Whyland was being accepted—thanks to the training and temperament of his hearer—for "small talk." Yes, Abner had broken a large bill and was dealing out the change. He knew it; he was a little ashamed of it; yet at the same time he looked about with a kind of shy triumph to see whether any one were commenting upon his address.

To tell the truth, Abner felt his success to such a degree that presently he began to presume upon it. He had heard about the children, left behind for a lonely dinner with the farm superintendent, and he began to scent cruelty and injustice in their progenitors. The wrongs of the child—they too had their share in keeping our generous Abner in his perennial state of indignation. He became didactic, judicial, hortatory; Edith Whyland almost questioned her right to be a mother. But she understood the spirit that prompted this intense young man's admonitions and exhortations; his feelings did him credit. She made a brief and quiet defence of herself, and thought no worse of Abner for his championship, however mistaken, of distressed childhood. He understood and pardoned her; she understood and pardoned him. And the more she thought things over, the more—despite his heckling of her—she liked him.

"He's a fine, serious fellow, my dear," she said to Medora, "and I'm glad to have met him."

Medora flushed, wondering why Edith Whyland should have spoken just—just like that. And Edith, noting Medora's flush, considerately let the matter drop.

Mrs. Whyland also looked over Clytie Summers, and found no serious harm in her. "She is rather underbred—or 'modern,' I suppose I should call it, and she's more or less in a state of ferment; but I dare say she will come out all right in the end. However, my Evelyn shall never be taken through the slums: I think Leverett will be willing to draw the line there." And, "Remember!" she said to Abner, as she drove away.

Medora was delighted. She saw two steps into the future. Abner should call on Mrs. Whyland. And he should read from his own works at Mrs. Whyland's house. Why not? He read with much justness and expression; he was thoroughly accustomed to facing an audience. Indeed he had lately spoken of meditating a public tour, in order to familiarize the country with *This Weary World* and *The Rod of the Oppressor* and the newer work still unfinished. Well, then: the reading-tour, like one or two other things, should begin at home.

While these generous plans pulsed through the girl's heart and brain Abner, all unaware of the future now beginning to overshadow him, was out in the stable considering the case of a lame horse and inveighing against the general irksomeness of rural conditions. He threw back his abundant hair as he rose from the study of a dubious hoof,—a Samson unconscious of the shining shears that threatened him.

XIV

Abner, on his return to town, found its unpleasant precincts more crowded than ever with matters of doubtful expediency and propriety. Not that he felt the strain of any temptation; he knew that he was fully capable of keeping himself unspotted from the world — the world of urban society — if only people would leave him alone. Two dangers stood out before all others: his impending call upon Mrs. Whyland and the approaching annual fancy-dress ball of the Art Students' League. He had rashly committed himself to the one, and his officious friends of the studios were rapidly pushing him upon the other. He must indeed present himself beneath the roof of a man whom he could not regard as a "good citizen," and must thus seem to approve his host's improper composition, now imminent, with the powers that be; but he should bestir himself to withstand the pressure exerted by Giles, by Medora herself, by Bond, by mischievous Clytie Summers, by the whole idle horde of studio loungers to force him into such an atmosphere of frivolity, license and dissipation as could not but inwrap one of those wild student "dances."

"We should so like to have you present," said Medora. "It will be rather bright and lively, and you would be sure to meet any number of pleasant people. You would enjoy it, I know."

Abner shook his head. Fancy him, a serious man, with a reputation to nourish and to safeguard, caught up in any such fandango as that!

"I have never attended a dancing-party yet," he said. "I couldn't waltz if my life depended on it. And I wouldn't, either."

"You needn't," said Medora. "But you would be interested in the grand march. It's always very pictorial, and the girls are arranging to have it more so than ever this year."

Abner shook his head again. "I have never had any fancy togs on. I — I *couldn't* wear anything like that."

"You needn't. A great many of the gentlemen go in simple evening dress."

Abner shook his head a third time. "I thought you understood my principles on that point. Dress is a badge, an index. I could not openly brand myself as having surrendered to the — to the — —"

Medora sighed. "You are making a great many difficulties," she said. "But you will call on Mrs. Whyland?"

"I have promised, and I shall do so," he said, with all the good grace of a despairing bear caught in a trap.

"I think she suggested some—some afternoon?"

"Yes."

"You will go at about half-past four or five, possibly?"

"Yes."

Abner suddenly saw himself as he was six months before: little likelihood then of his devoting an afternoon—fruitful working hours of a crowded day—to the demands of mere social observances. Which of his Readjusters would have had the time or the inclination to do as he had bound himself to do? But now he was "running" less with reformers than with artists, and these ill-regulated spendthrift folk were prone to break up the day and send its fragments broadcast as they would, without forethought, scruple, compunction.

One day before long, then, Abner buttoned his handsome double-breasted frock-coat across his capacious chest and put on a neat white lawn tie and sallied forth to call on Edith Whyland. The day was sunny—almost deceptively so—and Abner, who knew the good points in his own figure and was glad to dispense with a heavy overcoat whenever possible, limited his panoply to a soft felt hat and a pair of good stout gloves. The wind came down the lake and sent the waves in small splashes over the gray sea-wall and teased the bare elms along the wide, winding roadway, and tousled Abner's abundant chestnut moustache and reddened his ruddy cheeks and nipped his vigorous nose—all as a reminder that January was here and ought not to be disregarded. But Abner was thinking less of meteorological conditions than of Mrs. Whyland's butler. He knew he could be brusquely haughty toward this menial, but could he be easy and indifferent? Yet was it right to seem coolly callous toward another human creature? But, on the other hand, might not a cheery, informal friendliness, he wondered, as his hand sought the bell-push, be misconstrued, be ridiculed, be resented, be taken advantage of....

The door was opened by a subdued young woman who wore a white cap and presented a small silver tray. Abner, who dispensed with calling cards on principle and who would have blushed to read his own name in script on a piece of white cardboard, asked in a stern voice if Mrs. Whyland was at home. The maid dropped the tray into the folds of her black dress; she seemed habituated enough to the sudden appearance of the cardless.

She looked up respectfully, admiringly—she had opened the door for a good many gentlemen, but seldom for so magnificent and masterful a creature as Abner—and said yes. But alas for the credit of her mistress and of her mistress' household: here was a lordly person who had arrived with the open expectation of meeting a "man" who should "announce" him!

Abner had come full of subject-matter; he knew just what he was going to say. And during the interval before Mrs. Whyland's appearance he should briefly run over his principal points. But he found Mrs. Whyland already on the ground. Nor was she alone. Two or three other ladies were chatting with her on minor topics, and before all of these had gone others arrived to take their places. Not a moment did he spend with her alone; briefly, it was her "day."

These ladies referred occasionally to matters musical and artistic—somebody had given a recital, somebody else was soon to exhibit certain pictures—but they had little to say about books and they made no recognition of Abner as an author. "More of this artificial social repression," he thought. "Why should they be afraid of 'boring' me, as they word it? They bore Bond—they are always buzzing Giles; I think I could endure a word or two." His eye roamed over the rich but subdued furnishings of the room. "No wonder that all spontaneity should be smothered here!" And when literary topics were finally broached he experienced less of comfort than of indignation. A sweet little woman moaned that she had attempted an authors' reading, but that her authors could not command a proper degree of attention from her guests. Her eyes flashed indignantly as she called to mind the ways of the people she had presumptuously ventured to entertain. "They were swells," she murmured bitterly. "Yes, swells;—it's a harsh word, but not undeserved. I never tried having so many people of that particular sort before, and they simply overrode me. They banded against me; being quite in the majority, they could keep one another in countenance. My poor authors were offended at the open way in which they were ignored. Poor dear Edward scarcely knew what to do with such a——"

The plaintive little creature lapsed into silence; great must have been her provocation thus to speak of her own guests. Abner's eyes blazed; his blood boiled with indignation. Such treatment constituted an affront to all art, to his own art—literature, to himself.

"I have heard of cases of that sort before," he blurted out. "Mr. Giles told me of one only yesterday. The victim in this case was a young gentlewoman"—Abner's lips caressed this taking word—"a young gentlewoman from the South. She had come to one of those houses"—everybody, with the help of Abner's tone, saw the insolent front of the place—"to tell some dialect stories and to sing a few little songs. The mob—it was nothing less—could hardly be reduced to order. All those people had seen one another the day before, and they were all going to see one another the day to follow, yet talk they would and must and did. Engagements, marriages, acceptances, excuses, compliments, tittle-tattle, personalities—a rolling flood of chatter and gossip. Mrs. Pence took her people for what they were, apparently, and kept up with the best of them herself. Now and then her husband would do a little feeble something to quiet the tempest, and then the poor girl, half crying with mortification, would attempt to resume her task. With her last word the flood would instantly rise and obliterate her once more— —"

Abner's voice vibrated with a hot anger over this indignity put upon a fellow "artist." His view of literature was sacramental, sacerdotal. All should reverence the altar; none should insult the humblest neophyte. Mrs. Whyland indulgently overlooked his reckless use of names and liked him none the less; and the little lady who had suffered on a similar occasion, though in a different role, gave him a glance of thanks.

"I know the type," said Mrs. Whyland. "It is commoner than it should be; others of us besides are much too thoughtless. You had too many at a time, my dear," she went on quietly. "A few scattered grains of gunpowder do no great harm, but a large number of them massed together will blow anything to ruin. Our motto should be, 'Few but fit,' eh? Or ought I to say, 'Fit though few'?"

Abner stayed on, and finally the last of the ladies rose to go. Abner was just about to throw open the stable door, preparatory to giving his hobbies an airing, when a latch-key was heard operating in the front door of the house itself. Then came a man's quick step, a tussle with a heavy winter overcoat, and Whyland himself appeared on the threshold.

He came in, tingling, exhilarated, cordial. His cordiality overflowed at once; he asked Abner to remain to dinner.

Abner had not looked for this; a mere call was as far as he had meant to go. He parried, he evaded, he shuffled toward the door.

"But where's your overcoat?" asked Whyland, looking about.

"I didn't wear one."

"On such a day as this!" exclaimed Edith.

"I am strong," said Abner.

"You'll find our winter stronger," said Whyland. "You are not out there in the country a hundred miles back from the lake. You must stay, of course."

Still Abner moved toward the door. *Could* any city man be as friendly as Whyland seemed? "It will be colder later on," he submitted.

"Our welcome will never be warmer." Whyland looked toward his wife—their rustic appeared to be exacting the observance of all the forms.

"You will stay, of course," said Edith Whyland; "I have hardly had a word with you. And when you do go, it must be in a cab."

Abner succumbed. He was snared, as he felt. Other rooms, still more handsomely, more lavishly appointed, seemed to yawn for him. And then came crystal and silver and porcelain and exquisite napery and the rare smack of new and nameless dishes to help bind him hard and fast. Abner was in a tremor; his first compromise with Mammon was at hand.

XV

Abner accepted his environment; after all, he might force the conversation to soar far above the mere materialities. His hobbies began to poke forth their noses, to whinny, to neigh; but some force stronger or more dexterous than himself seemed to be guiding the talk, and the name of Medora Giles began to mingle with the click of silver on china and to weave itself into the progress of the service.

"A very sweet girl," declared Edith Whyland. "Nothing pleased me more than her nice domestic ways at the farm. I had got the impression in Paris that, though she was quite the pride of their little coterie, she was not exactly looked upon as practical,—not considered particularly efficient, in a word."

Abner's thoughts instantly reverted to the farm-house kitchen. What were the paid services of menials, however deft and practised, compared with the intimate, personal exertions, the—the—yes, the ministrations of a woman like Medora Giles?

"She was probably just waiting for the chance," said Whyland heartily. "You don't often find talent and real practicality combined in one girl as they are in Miss Giles. Even little Clytie Summers——"

"We must not disparage little Clytie," said his wife gravely.

"Oh, Clytie!" returned Whyland, giving his head a careless, sidelong jerk. "Still, she's good fun." He laughed. "That child is always breaking out in some new place. The next place will probably be the students' ball. You'll be there to see?" he inquired of Abner.

"No wine, thank you," said Abner to the maid, placing his broad hand on the foot of a glass already turned down. "At the ball? I hardly think so. I never——"

"You might find it amusing," said Mrs. Whyland. "A good many of your friends will be there—ourselves among them."

"Yes," said Whyland, turning his eyes away from the uncontaminated glass, "my wife is a patroness, or whatever they call it. We go to help receive and to look on during the march and to see the dancing started."

"I should like to have a hand in helping Medora contrive a costume that would do her justice," said Mrs. Whyland. "She is really quite a beauty, and she has a great deal of distinction. Nothing could be better than her profile and those exquisite black eyebrows." Then, mindful of the presence of the children, she proceeded by means of graceful periphrase and carefully studied generalizations to a presentation of Medora's mental and spiritual attributes. She said many things, in the tone of kindly, half-veiled patronage; after all she was talking to a country man about a country maid. She even praised Abner himself by indirection—as one strand in the general rustic theme. The children, who caught every word and put this and that together with marvellous celerity and precision, were vastly impressed by the attributes of the invisible paragon. They looked at Abner's bigness with their own big eyes—though ignored by him, his interest being, despite his former championship of them, less in children than in "the child"—and envied him her acquaintance; and they began to ask that very evening how soon the admirable Medora might swim into their ken.

The first result from Abner's dinner with the Whylands was that Medora, thus formulated by the sympathetic and appreciative Edith, now became definitely crystallized in his mind; the second was that he changed his boarding-house. Mere crudity for its own sake no longer charmed. The curtains and bedspreads at the farm had served as the earliest prompters to this step, and the furnishings of the Whyland interior now decided him to take it. Mrs. Cole's stained and spotted lambrequin became more offensive than ever, and the industrious hands of Maggie, which did much more than merely to pass things at table, were now less easy to endure.

"I know I'm a fastidious, ungrateful wretch," he said to himself, as he saw his trunk started off to a better neighbourhood and prepared to follow it. "They've been very kind to me, and little Maggie would do almost anything for me"—little Maggie, whom he treated as a mere asexual biped and hectored in the most lordly way, and who yet entertained for him a puzzled, secret admiration;—"but I can't stand it any longer, that's all."

A few days later Bond called at Abner's old address and was referred by a grieved landlady to his new one. "I don't make out Mr. Joyce," said poor, hurt Mrs. Cole.

Bond went down the steps whistling, "They're after me, they're after me!" in a thoughtful undertone.

XVI

"Are you going to dress very much?" grimaced Giles, with a precious little intonation that caused Bond to laugh outright.

Abner, who was lounging under the Turkish canopy, pricked up his ears to catch the reply. Medora tossed aside one of her brother's sketches and turned her eyes on Abner.

"I don't know what *to* do," replied Bond. "We have had such a glut of Romeos and Mephistos and cowboys. It has occurred to me that I might go as a rough sketch—a *bozzetto*—of a gentleman."

"How would you get yourself up for that?" asked Giles.

"Just as you have often seen me. I should wear that old dress-suit with the shiny seams and the frayed facings, and a shirt-front seen more recently by the world than by the laundry, and a pair of shoes already quite familiar with tweeds and cheviots, and a little black bow—this last as a sort of sign that I am not fully in society, or if I am, only briefly at long, uncertain intervals. And a black Derby hat—or possibly a brown one."

Medora smiled, well pleased. This easy, jocular treatment of a serious and formal subject was just what she wanted. It would help show the listening Abner that the wearing of the social uniform was nothing very formidable after all, and did not necessarily doom one's moral and spiritual fibre to utter blight and ruin.

Abner set his lips. He might indeed go to their wretched "fandango" in the end—they had all been urging him, Stephen, Medora, everybody—but never as a cheap imitation of a swell so long as his own good, neat, well-made, every-day wardrobe existed as it was. He had turned down the wine-glass at Whyland's, and he would turn down the dress-coat here.

Medora, unconscious that her precious little seed had fallen, after all, on stony ground, turned toward Abner with a smile—an intent, observing one. "Did Mrs. Whyland speak to you about her 'evening'?"

"Her evening? What evening?"

"There, I knew she wouldn't dare. You frightened her almost to death."

"What do you mean?"

"Why, she had been thinking of having a few friends come in some night next week for a little reading and some music. But you were so violent in your comments on the behaviour of society that she didn't dare touch upon her plan. She was meaning to ask you to read two or three things from your *Weary World*, but——"

"Why——" began Abner.

"Read," put in Bond. "I'm going to."

"Why," began Abner once more, "I had no notion of offending her. But everything I said was the truth."

"She wasn't offended," said Giles, with a smile; "only 'skeered.' You must have been pretty tart."

"I can't help it. It makes me so hot to have such things happening——"

"I know," said Giles. "We're all made hot, now and then, in one way or another."

"You *will* read, won't you?" asked Medora, in accents of subdued pleading.

"Well, not *next* week," replied Abner, in the tone of one who held postponement to be as good as escape. "That tour of mine is coming off, after all. They have arranged a number of dates for me, and I shall go eastward for several readings and possibly a few lectures."

"How far eastward?" asked Medora eagerly. "As far as New York?"

"Maybe so," said Abner guardedly.

"How long shall you be gone?" she asked with great intentness.

"A fortnight or more," purred Abner complacently, under this show of interest. "I guess I can open the eyes of those Easterners to a thing or two."

Medora dropped her glance thoughtfully to the floor. An exchange of instruction seemed impending, and she could only hope that the East might prove a more considerate tutor to Abner than Abner threatened to be to the East.

XVII

The two long winding lines of gaily attired young people joined forces and the procession came marching down the hall by fours, by eights, by sixteens, and Abner sat against the wall next to Edith Whyland and watched the shifting spectacle with a sort of fearful joy. Eudoxia Pence, seated against the opposite wall, glanced across at him, when occasion once offered, and nodded and smiled, as if to say, "Isn't it lovely! Isn't it fascinating!" and Abner, in sudden alarm, recomposed his tell-tale face and frowningly responded with a grave bow.

Abner wore his double-breasted frock-coat and his white lawn tie; and Edith Whyland, who had come in a plain dark reception costume to stand in a row near the door with the wives of the professors at the Art Academy, now sat with him and brought him as far into drawing as might be with the abounding masculine figures in evening dress. Many of these appeared in the march itself, along with the sailors, the Indian chiefs and the young blades out of Perugino. Giles passed by as a Florentine noble of the late Quattrocento, in a black silk robe that muffled his slight indifference to a function familiar from many repetitions. Little O'Grady wore his plaster-flecked blue blouse over his shabby brown suit and hardily announced himself as Phidias. Medora walked with a languid grace as a Druid priestess, and Miss Wilbur, the miniaturist, showed forth as Madame Le Brun, without whose presence no fancy-dress ball could be regarded as complete.

High above the marching host rose dozens of the tall conical head-dresses of mediaeval France with their dependent veils. A great Parisian painter had just been exhibiting some mural decorations in the galleries of the Academy, and half the girls, from the life class down, wore candle-extinguishers on their heads and trailed full robes of startlingly figured chintz—a material that was expected to effect to the charitable eye and the friendly imagination the richness of brocade. Many of the younger men too had succumbed to the same influence and appeared in long skin-tight hose and bobby little doublets edged with fur.

"How can they? How can they?" wondered Abner.

The music abruptly changed its tempo and the march broke up into a waltz. Through the swirling dancers a single figure, clad in violet and green, zigzagged across to Eudoxia Pence and bowed over her for a word or two.

Eudoxia moved her lips and spread out her plump hands deprecatingly and shook her head with a smile.

"I should hope she *wouldn't*," thought Abner;—"not with a little squirt like that."

The figure immediately zigzagged back, with the same effect of eager, inquiring haste. It paused before Abner and Mrs. Whyland and suddenly sidled up. Abner recognised Adrian Bond.

"Clytie?" said Bond. "Has anybody seen or heard anything of Clytie Summers?"

"Well, well," said Mrs. Whyland, looking him over; "you are enrolled among the Boutet de Monvel boys too, are you?"

Bond ran his eye down his slim legs with fatuous complacency and fingered the fur fringe of his doublet and pushed his steep flat-topped cap over to a different angle. Abner looked at him with contemptuous amazement and would not even speak.

"Her aunt hasn't heard a word from her for a week," said Bond. "That settlement has claimed her, body and soul. All she does is to write home for more clothes. I expect she has completely forgotten all about our little affair to-night. I thought of course she was going to march with me, but— —"

And he darted away to resume his quest.

"She will come," said Mrs. Whyland. "And her cap will be higher and her veil longer and the pattern of her brocade bigger and more startling than anybody else can show."

Little O'Grady moved past with a Maid of Astolat, who wore white cloth-of-gold and carried a big lily above each ear and dropped a long full-flowered stalk over her partner's shoulder. Medora drifted by in company with a Mexican vaquero. Her white garments fluttered famously against the other's costume of yellow and black. She had let down her abundant dark hair and then carelessly caught it up again and woven into it a garland of mistletoe. She smiled on Abner with a plaintive, weary lifting of her eyebrows; she appeared to be "creating atmosphere" again, just as on the afternoon when he had first seen her pouring tea. She seemed a long way off. The occasion itself removed her one stage from him, and her costume another, and her bearing a third. Was this the same girl who had so dexterously snatched open the stove door in that farm-house kitchen and had been so active, as revealed by glimpses from the corridor, in beating up pillows and in casting sheets and coverlets to the morning air?

The waltz suddenly ended and the Mexican renounced Medora only a few steps beyond Abner. She came along and took a vacant chair next to Edith Whyland.

"Are you enjoying it?" she asked Abner.

"It is very instructive; it is most typical," he replied.

The orchestra presently began again, but Medora remained in her place.

"Aren't you dancing this time?" asked Mrs. Whyland.

"Yes," replied Medora deliberately; "I'm dancing with Mr. Joyce."

She handed Edith her card. Abner looked across to her with a startled, puzzled expression.

"So you are," said Mrs. Whyland. "J-o-y-c-e," she read, and handed the card back.

"I don't care for the redowa, anyway," Medora explained; "and I didn't want to dance with the man that was moving along in my direction to ask me. It was the only vacant line. What could I do? I looked about and saw you"—to Abner—"standing by the door——"

"I suppose I was tall enough to see," said Abner, feeling very huge and uncomfortable.

"A tower of strength, a city of refuge," suggested Mrs. Whyland.

"Precisely," said Medora. "So I snatched a pencil out of Adrian Bond's hand—he had just put himself down four times——"

"What impudence!" thought Abner savagely.

"—and scribbled this,"—dropping her eye on the card. "I hope you don't mind my having taken your name?" she concluded.

A sudden gust of gallantry swept over Abner. "Let me have the card," he said. "I have given my autograph a good many times"—looking at the faint pencilling—"but I don't recognise this." He drew out a lead-pencil and rewrote the name big and black above the other. "There," he said,—"a souvenir of the occasion." He handed the card back with the authentic autograph of a distinguished author. His name there wiped out not merely one scribble but all, even to the impertinent four traced by insignificant Bond. A man who could pen such a signature need have no regret for not being a carpet-knight besides.

Medora took back her card, highly gratified; her cavalier had made a long stride ahead. Abner himself rejoiced at his dexterity in asserting the man—almost the man of gallantry, at that—under the shield of the writer. Mrs. Whyland kindly refrained from entering upon an analysis to determine just what percentage of egotism was to be detected in Abner's act, and felt emboldened by such unlooked-for graciousness and by the sustaining presence of Medora to ask a favour for herself—that "evening" was still in her mind.

"You *will* read, won't you?" pleaded Medora.

"After my return from the East," acquiesced Abner.

The two women looked at each other, well pleased.

XVIII

Presently Leverett Whyland came along. The cares of the urban property-owner and of the gentleman farmer were alike cast aside; Abner had never known him to appear so natty, so buoyant, so juvenile. Another man accompanied him, a man older, larger, heavier, graver, with a close-clipped gray beard. This newcomer bowed to Mrs. Whyland with a repression that indicated but a distant acquaintance; and just as Medora was whisked away by a new partner—it was Bond, claiming the first of his four—Whyland introduced him to Abner: "Mr. Joyce, Mr. M'm——" Abner, occupied by Bond's appropriation of Medora, lost the name.

"And where is Clytie?" asked Whyland, looking about. "Has anybody seen or heard anything of little Clytie Summers?"

"No doubt she will appear presently," said his wife drily.

"And meanwhile——?" he suggested, motioning toward the floor.

"It might not look amiss," replied his wife, rising. They joined the dancers.

Abner was left alone with his new acquaintance, who, arriving at an instant apprehension of our young man's bulk, seriousness and essential alienation from the spirit of the affair, seized him as a spent and bewildered swimmer in strange waters lays hold upon some massive beam that happens to be drifting past. Abner clung in turn, glad to recognise a kindred spirit in the midst of this gaudy, frivolous throng. The two quickly found the common ground of serious interests. The circling, swinging dancers retired into the background; their place was quietly taken by the Balance of Trade, by the Condition of the Country, by Aggregations of Capital, by Land and Labour; and presently Abner was leading forth, all saddled and bridled, the Readjusted Tax.

"This is something like," he thought.

The other made observations and comments in a slow, grave, subdued tone. "Who is he?" wondered Abner. "What can he be connected with? Anyway, he's a fine, solid fellow—the kind Whyland might come to be with a little trying."

Stephen Giles passed by, guiding the billowy undulations of Eudoxia Pence. Eudoxia had a buoyancy that more than counteracted her bulk, and she wafted about, a substantial vision in lemon-coloured silk, for all to see. She looked at Abner's companion over Giles's shoulder.

"Enjoying yourself, dear?" she asked. Then she nodded to Abner and floated away.

Abner, instantly chilled, looked sidewise at his companion with a dawning censoriousness in his eyes. He had probably been talking, for a good ten minutes and in full view of the entire hall, to that arch-magnate of the trusts, Palmer Pence. He began to cast about for means to break up this calamitous situation. He welcomed the return of Leverett Whyland with his wife.

"Well, Pence," said Whyland, "how has the Amalgamated Association of Non-Dancers been doing?"

"Pence," Whyland had said. Yes, this was the Trust man, after all.

"First-rate," returned the other briefly, rising to go. "That's a fine, serious young fellow," he added, for Whyland's ear alone. "There's stuff in him."

"Been getting on with him, eh?" said Whyland ruefully. "Well, you're in luck."

Abner glowered gloomily across the thinning floor. Another dance had just ended and Whyland had skimmed away once again. Abner, forgetful of the presence of Edith Whyland, made indignant moan to himself over the perverse fate that had led him on toward friendliness with a man whose principles and whose public influence he could not approve.

There was a sudden stir about the distant doorway. Abner heard the clapping of hands and a few hearty, jubilant yaps frankly emitted by young barytone voices. "What now?" he wondered, with a sidelong glance at Edith Whyland.

Mrs. Whyland, herself half-risen, was looking toward the door, like everybody else. "Finally!" she said, with a pleased smile, and sank back into her place.

A tall, stalwart figure came through the crowd amidst a storm of hand-clapping and of cheers. The maids of mediaeval France fluttered their long veils, and their young male contemporaries waved their velvet caps.

It was a gentleman of sixty with a bunch of white whiskers on either jaw and a pair of flashing steel-gray eyes. He nodded brusquely here and there and looked about with a tight, fierce smile. "Hurrah! hurrah!" cried all the students, from the life class down to the cubes and cones.

"Who is he?" asked Abner.

"Why, that's Dr. Gowdy," replied his companion. "The ball would hardly *be* a ball without him here. He has led the grand march more than once——"

"A man of his age and dignity!" mumbled Abner.

"—but he is late to-night, for some reason. He is one of the Academy trustees," she added.

"Perhaps his patients kept him." Abner's tone implied that professional duties would set much more gracefully on such a figure than social diversions.

"His patients?"

"Yes. You said he was a doctor."

"But not a doctor of medicine. A doctor of theology."

"A minister?—a minister of the gospel?"

"He is, indeed. And I——"

"And you?"

"I am one of his parishioners. I sit under him every Sunday."

Abner was dumb. This professing Christian, this pattern of evangelicalism, could witness such things without pronouncing a single word of protest. "Is he going to dance?" he asked finally.

"I think not. He is coming over here presently to sit with me, just as you have been doing. You shall meet him."

Abner was dazed. Palmer Pence, doubtless, was here under protest; but this man, his superior in age, credit and renown, had apparently come of his own free will. He sat there staring at the smiling progress of the Rev. William S. Gowdy through the throng of jubilant students. He felt stunned, dislocated. It was all too much.

"Well, well," he heard Mrs. Whyland say. He looked about at her and then out upon the clearing floor.

"Well, well," said Mrs. Whyland once again. The wide, empty space before them was lending itself to a second grand entree, by a party of one. Clytie Summers had finally arrived.

XIX

Clytie came on with the brisk and confident walk that she had cultivated along the pavements of the shopping district, and she was dressed precisely as if about to enter upon one of her frequent excursions in that quarter on some crisp, late-autumn afternoon. She wore a very trig and jaunty tailor-made suit and a stunning little garnet-velvet toque. She tripped ahead in a solid but elegant pair of walking-shoes and was drawing on a tan glove with mannish stitchings over the back. The Boutet de Monvel girls, the contemporaries of Jeanne d'Arc, were immediately obliterated; Clytie became the most conspicuous figure in the whole big place.

She advanced tapping her heels, smoothing her gloves, and looking every shirt-front full in the face. Her forehead gathered in a soft little frown; he whom she sought was not in sight. She got a glimpse of Mrs. Pence and Medora Giles seated side by side in a far corner, and of Little O'Grady hovering near, with a covetous eye upon her aunt's profile; and she took the remaining space in a quick little walk that was almost a run.

"Adrian Bond?" she asked. "Tell me; has anybody seen or heard anything of Adrian Bond?"

"Well, Clytie child!" exclaimed her aunt, looking her over; "what's all this?"

Clytie passed her hand down the side of her thick fawn-coloured skirt and readjusted her toque. "These things were in that box you sent me day before yesterday."

"That box from London?"

"That box from London. I thought they were never coming. I wrote; I cabled; I implored friends to go to Regent Street every single day till they should be done. And here they are, finally—a month late; but I'm wearing them, all the same."

"Well, they're worth waiting for," said Medora. "I suppose they are just about the last word."

"Just about," replied Clytie complacently. "Meanwhile, where is Adrian Bond?"

"Here he comes now," said Medora.

Clytie turned. She beheld the mediaeval greens and violets. "Why, Adrian," she protested; "you told me you were coming disguised as a gentleman."

"I thought better of it," said Bond.

"But," she proceeded, "I—I— —" She spun round on one heel. "This is all for you. I thought that if you were coming disguised as a gentleman, it would be nice for me to come disguised as a lady. No use," she said regretfully. "Everybody knew me in a minute," she added.

Bond laughed. "I thought you weren't coming at all."

"But you got my note?"

"Not a word."

"Why, I wrote you how we were having a ball of our own, and how I couldn't come to this one till I had started off that one."

"What kind of a ball?" asked Mrs. Pence.

"One given by our Telephone Girls. I led the grand march with a lovely young bartender. I struck him all in a heap—can you wonder?—and he told me just what he thought of me. There wasn't much time to lead up to it. He was very direct; he took a short cut. Oh, I love the *people*! Why are the men in our set so shy— —!"

"What did he say?" asked Bond sharply.

"Oh, never mind! It was one of those cannon-ball compliments that leave you stunned and breathless, but willing to be stunned again. What do you think of my togs?" she asked, generally.

"Look at this jacket while it's a novelty," she went on without waiting for any response. "The girls were all tremendously taken by it; I noticed a dozen of them trying to see how it was made.—Oh, how do?" she said airily to Abner, who came up just then. Having perceived Medora in her remote corner, he had finally summoned enough resolution to make his first movement of the evening: leaving Edith Whyland in the company of Dr. Gowdy, he had succeeded in crossing the intervening leagues alone and unaided.

Abner frowned to find this pert little piece cutting in ahead of him in such a fashion. "How do you do?" he responded stiffly.

"They'll all be making ones like it," Clytie rattled on. "By next Sunday every street from Poplar Alley to Flat-iron Park will swarm with them, and not a milliner's window along the length of Green-gage Road but will have three or four of these toques on display. Yes, sir; I'm a power in the Ward already, let me tell you."

Bond placed his small hand on Abner's broad shoulder. "Isn't she a winner?" he murmured ecstatically. "If Medora, now, could only have done something as spirited and unconventional——"

"I have no fault to find with Miss Giles," retorted Abner in a stern undertone. "To me she is perfectly satisfactory. She will always do the right thing in the right way, and always be a lady."

Bond withdrew his hand. "Oh, come, I say," he began protestingly.

Abner ignored this. "How about the basket-weaving?" he asked Clytie.

"Well," Clytie responded hardily, "I found plenty teaching that already. I have chosen for my department instruction in tact, taste, dress and manners. Such instruction is badly needed, in more quarters than one."

Medora flushed. "Clytie Summers," she said, the first moment that the two were alone, "if ever you speak to Mr. Joyce like that again you need never come to our studio nor count me any longer among your acquaintances."

"Why, dear me——" began Clytie, with an affectation of puzzled innocence.

> "I mean it," said Medora, with an angry tear starting in her eye. "Mr. Joyce is too much of a man to be treated so by a child like you."

XX

Abner lingered on. He had meant to leave early, but it was as easy to stay as to go; besides, he felt the stirring of a curiosity to see what the closing hour of such an occasion might be like. Everything, thus far, had been most seemly, most decorous, full of a pleasant informality and a friendly, trustful goodwill; but the crucial point, he had read, always came about supper-time, after which the rout turned into an orgy.

Dr. Gowdy came across and launched himself upon Abner, just as he had done before, when Mrs. Whyland had first made them acquainted. He frankly admired the strength and the stature of the only man in the room who was taller and more robust than himself, as well as the intent sobriety of his glance and the laconic gravity of his speech.

"An admirable young fellow!" he had exclaimed to Edith Whyland, upon Abner's leaving them to cross over to Medora.

"Oh yes, yes!" she had returned with conviction.

"So serious."

"Oh yes,"—with less emphasis. She knew Abner was serious because he was puzzled.

"So grave."

"Yes,"—faintly. She knew Abner was grave because he was shocked.

"A painter?"

"A—an artist."

"He has personality. He will make a name for himself, I am sure."

The good Doctor, now alone with Abner, gave him a chance to celebrate himself, to make known what there was in him. But Abner remained inexpressive; and the Doctor, who himself was very ready of tongue and who, like all fluent people, was much impressed by reserve, presently went away with a higher opinion of Abner than ever.

Medora came up, extending her card. "I have secured another dance for you," she said. "Mr. Bond was kind enough to give it up. He will know what to do with the time. On this occasion, if you please, we might walk it out instead of sitting it out. At least we might walk to the supper-room."

Abner rose. He had never before offered his arm to a lady and was not sure that he had offered it now, yet Medora's fingers rested upon his coat-sleeve. For a few moments he felt himself, half proudly, half uncomfortably, a part of the spectacle, and then they entered the room where the spare refreshments were dispensed.

Medora found a place, and Abner, doing as he saw the other men do, went forward to traffic across a long table with a coloured waiter. He brought back to Medora what he saw the other men bringing—a spoonful of ice-cream with a thin slice of cake, and a cup of coffee of limited size. Truly the material for an orgy seemed rather scanty.

"I am glad you promised to read," said Medora. "It is a favour that Mrs. Whyland will appreciate very much."

Abner bowed. Surely it was a favour, and appreciation was no more than his due.

"I only wish you could have seen your way to being as nice to poor Mrs. Pence. I overheard her—didn't I?—asking you once more to call. Weren't you rather non-committal? Were you, strictly speaking, quite civil?"

"I was as civil as those silly, chattering people round her would let me be—that niece of hers and the rest. I'm sure I was careful to ask after her Training School."

"Oh, *that's* what made her look so dazed!"

"Why should it?" asked Abner, his spoon checked in mid-air.

"She could hardly have expected such an inquiry from *you*. Haven't I heard that you threw her down on this training-school idea, and threw her down pretty hard too, the very first time you met her? She wanted help, sympathy, encouragement, suggestions, and instead of that you gave her the—the marble heart, as they say. You made her feel so feeble and flimsy——"

"Did I?" asked Abner gropingly. Eudoxia loomed before him in all her largeness.

"You did. She was disposed to be a noble, useful worker, but now it seems as if she might drop to the level of a mere social leader. Do, please, treat Mrs. Whyland more considerately. She means to arrange quite a nice little programme, and it will be no disadvantage to you to take part in it. Mr. Bond will read one or two of his travel-sketches, and I may do a little something myself—a bit in the way of music, perhaps."

"H'm," said Abner. "Travel-sketches?" He ignored the promise of music.

"With folk-songs on the violin."

"I shall hope to offer something better worth while than travel-sketches," said Abner. "His things will hardly harmonize with mine, I'm afraid; but possibly they will serve as a sort of contrast."

"His things will be slight, of course, but the songs will help him out. Very simple arrangements; people don't care much for anything serious or heavy."

"I shall not show myself a mere frivolous entertainer—a simple filler-in of the leisure moments of the wealthy," said Abner.

Medora banished the violin—and herself. "What do you think of reading?" she asked.

"One or two pieces from my first book, I expect,—*Jim McKay's Defeat* and *Less Than the Beasts*, with possibly one of the later chapters in *Regeneration*."

"M—m," said Medora.

"You don't like *Regeneration*, I'm afraid; but there's going to be some good stuff in it, let me tell you. People will open their eyes and begin to think. This question of marriage——"

"You will read that part, then?"

"Why not? It's a vital question. It concerns everybody, at all times."

"Yes, it always has—for thousands of years."

"I don't know that I care for the thousands of years. I care for this year and next year."

"And a great deal of good thought has been put into it already."

"But not the best. The whole subject needs ventilating, shaking up."

"You would attack the fundamentals, then?"

"Why not? I'm a radical. I've always called myself such. I go to the root, without fear, without favour."

"Still, the present arrangement, resulting from the collective wisdom and experience of the race ..." said Medora, crumbling her last bit of cake.

"You make me think of Bond and his 'historical perspective.'"

"I meant to. It isn't enough to know at just what point in the road we are; we must know what steps we have taken, what course we have traversed, to reach it."

"I never look behind. The hopes and possibilities of the immediate future are the things that interest *me*. I shall read several chapters of *Regeneration*—not merely one—on my tour."

"On your tour, yes. But for Mrs. Whyland substitute something else. There was a story you wrote at the farm—the one about the girl and her step-mother—"

"H'm, yes," said Abner, with less enthusiasm than he usually showed for his own work. "*In Winter Weather*? H'm."

This was a short tale, of a somewhat grisly character, which Abner had composed during the holiday season. Bond had taxed him with using this work as a buffer to stave off other work of a practical nature such as was abundantly offered by Giles and his father about the farm; and, to tell the truth, Abner had limited his physical exertions to half-hour periods that most other men would have charged to the account of mere exercise.

"I *might* read that, I suppose," he said.

"And if there is any wild wind in it—why, I should be on hand with my violin, you know. I might be in white, as I am now, with snow-flakes in my hair;—they would show, I think, if this mistletoe does——"

"Not that it represents my best and most characteristic work," he went on, "or that it bears upon any of the great problems of the day...."

Medora dashed her spoon against her saucer. Was there no power equal to teaching this masterful, self-centred creature that a woman was a woman and not a cold abstraction composed merely of the generalized attributes of the race, male and female alike? She had been his guide to-night, when she might have left him to his own helpless flounderings: might he not try now to show some slight shade of interest in her as an individual, at least,—as a distinct personality?

"Shall we be moving?" she suggested. "It should not have taken so long to eat so little."

XXI

"Well, good luck on your trip," said Giles, accompanying Abner to the door of the studio.

"And let us hear from you once in a while," added Medora.

"Surely," said Abner. "Look for a clipping, now and then, to show you what they are saying of me."

"And for what you have to say of them we must wait until your return?" said Medora.

"Not necessarily," rejoined Abner. "I might"—with the emission of an obscure, self-conscious sound between a chortle and a gasp, instantly suppressed—"I might write."

"Do, by all means," said Stephen.

"We shall follow your course with the greatest interest," added Medora.

Almost forthwith began the receipt of newspapers—indifferently printed sheets from minor cities scattered across Indiana and Ohio. The first two or three of them came addressed to Giles, but all the subsequent ones were sent direct to Medora. These publications invariably praised Abner's presence—for he always towered magnificently on the lecture-platform, and his delivery—for he read resoundingly with a great deal of clearness and precision. But they frequently deplored the sombreness of his subject-matter, and as the tour came to extend farther east, these objections began to assume a jocular and satirical cast, until the seaboard itself was reached, when newspapers ceased altogether and letters began to take their place. These were addressed, with complete absence of subterfuge, to Medora, and they displayed an increasing tendency toward the drawing of comparisons between the East and the West, with the difference more and more in favour of the latter. Abner felt with growing keenness the formality and insincerity of an old society, its cynical note, its materialistic ideals, the intrenched injustice resulting from accumulated and inherited wealth, the conventions that hampered initiative and froze goodwill. "I shall be glad to get back West again," he wrote.

Medora smiled over these observations. "What would the poor dear fellow think of London or Paris, then, I wonder?" she said.

"I am glad to see that you will come back to us better satisfied with us," she wrote,—"if only by comparison. Meanwhile, remember that whether other audiences may be agreeable or the reverse, there is one audience waiting for you here with which you ought to feel at home and—by this time—in sympathy."

And indeed Abner faced Mrs. Whyland's little circle, when the time finally came round, with much less sense of irksomeness and repugnance than he had expected. Some twenty or thirty people assembled in the Whyland drawing-room on one mid-March evening, and he soon perceived, with a great relief, that they meant to respect both him and their hostess.

"There is every indication that they intend to behave," said Bond in a reassuring whisper. "Everything will go charmingly."

People arrived slowly and it was after nine before the slightest evidence that anything like a programme had been arranged came into view. Abner, by reason of this delay, would have had serious doubts of any real interest in his art if a number of ladies had not plied him in the interval with various little compliments and attentions. He found things to say in reply; he also engaged in converse with a number of gentlemen, who possibly had slight regard for literature but who could not help respecting his size and sincerity. He loomed up impressively in his frock-coat and steel-gray scarf, and nobody, as in the satiric East, was heard to comment on his lack of conformity with the customs of "society."

"Tkh!" said Whyland. "You have come again without your overcoat, they tell me."

The lake wind was fiercely hectoring the bare elm-trees before the house, and the electric globes registered their tortures on the wide reach of the curving roadway.

> Abner tossed his head carelessly, in proud boast of his own robustness. "What's three blocks?" he asked.

"Come into the dining-room and have something," said his host.

Abner shrank back. "You know I never take wine."

"Wine!" cried Whyland. "You want something different from wine. You want a good hot whisky——"

"No," said Abner. "No."

The male guests were mostly professional men and representatives of great corporate interests. They talked together in low undertones about familiar concerns during their half-hour or so of grace.

"I see you have begun stringing your wires," said one of them to Whyland. "We are meeting with them all over town."

"Yes, yes," replied Whyland, with the sprightly ingenuousness of a boy. "Whoever looks for a fair return on his money nowadays must keep a little in advance of legislation."

"Just what Pence was saying only yesterday."

"I snatched that great truth from my slight association with the Tax Commission," burbled Whyland. "Almost everything marked, spotted: property, real and personal; lands, lots, improvements; bonds, stocks, mortgages— —"

"Everything, in short, but franchises?"

"Franchises, yes. Nothing left but to turn one's attention to the public utilities— —"

"And to hope that legislation may lag as far behind and as long behind as possible."

"Precisely," said Whyland. "Meanwhile, we string our wires— —"

"Pence up one pole and you up the next—"

Whyland shrugged his shoulders and laughed. "And may it be long before they call us down!"

Abner listened to all this in silence, shaking his head sadly and conscious of a deep and growing depression. Here was Whyland, a clever, likeable fellow—and his host too—disintegrating before his very eyes.

Whyland looked askant at Abner. "Yes, yes, I know," he almost seemed to be saying. "But who can tell if a helping hand, extended at the critical moment, might not have...."

XXII

"Is that her? Is that her?" asked the children, the nursery door ajar.

"Yes, that is 'her,'" said their mother, as Medora, muffled in white and with her violin-case under her arm, slipped along through the hall.

"How soon is she going to play? And won't you please let us hear just one piece, mamma?"

"You may lean over the banister. But if you let anybody catch you at it— —"

"How soon is she going to begin?"

"Not for some time yet."

"Oh-h! Then won't you bring her in so that— —"

"'Sh! 'sh! And shut the door."

But the door opened again and the banister was called upon to shield, if it could, three little figures in white night-dresses as soon as Medora began to "illustrate" Adrian Bond. The children upstairs were delighted, and the grown-up children downstairs scarcely less so—for Medora knew the infirmities of the polite world and never tired its habitues by her suites and sonatas. She took her cue from Bond's crisp, brief sketches of amusing travel-types, and gave them a folk-song from the Bavarian highlands and one or two quaint bits that she had picked up in Brittany. Abner, who knew her abilities, was vastly disconcerted to find her thus minimizing herself; as for his own part of the performance, emphasis should not fail. No, these rich, comfortable, prosperous people should drink the cup to the dregs—the cup of mire, of slackness, of drudgery, of dull hopelessness that he alone could mix. To tell the truth, his auditors tasted of the cup with much docility and appeared to enjoy its novel flavour. They listened closely and applauded civilly—and waited for more of Bond and Medora.

Abner was piqued. The situation did not justify itself. There was no reason why Medora Giles should lend her talents to promote the success of Adrian Bond—Bond with his thin hair plastered so pitifully over his poor little skull and his insignificant face awry with a conventional society smirk. Yet how, pray, could she contribute to his own? What was there in any work of his for her to take hold upon? He himself could not claim charm for it, nor an alluring atmosphere, nor a soft poetical perspective, nor participation in the consecrated traditions so dear, apparently, to the sophisticated folk around him. Medora, in fact, had shaken herself loose from the farmyard, and if he were to follow her must he not do the same?

He meant to follow her—he had come to feel sure of that. He was not certain what it would lead to, he was not certain what he wanted it to lead to; but if he had not fully realized her to be most rare and desirable there were many round about him now to help open his eyes. Hers, after all, was the triumph; everybody was applauding her grace, her tact, her beauty, her dress, discreetly classical, her distinction; while she herself parried compliments with smiling good-humour in the very accents of society itself.

And he was to follow her with *Less Than the Beasts*. The farm-yard claimed him for its own once more. He must go in up to his knees, up to his middle, up to his chin. But as he progressed he forgot his surroundings, his auditory; all he felt was the fate of his poor heroine, the pitiful farm-drudge, sunk in hopeless wrong and misery. He read in his very best manner, with abundant feeling and full conviction, and for a moment his hearers felt with him. Then came a last elegiac paragraph, and here Abner's voice grew husky, his throat filled, he coughed, and as he laid aside his last sheet and turned to rise a quick pain darted through his chest; he coughed again and involuntarily raised his hand against his breast, and the acute and sudden pang was signalled clearly in his face.

Whyland advanced quickly. "*Now*," he said, in a low tone, "you must let me have *my* way—if it isn't too late. Come." He led Abner toward the dining-room.

"It is nothing," said Abner, on his return.

"It is something, I am sure," said Edith Whyland, with great solicitude.

"It is something serious, I feel certain," said Medora, pale as her dress.

"Nonsense!" exclaimed Abner. "I shall know just what to do as soon as I get home——" He clutched at his breast again.

"You will not go home to-night," said Whyland.

Abner did not go home that night, nor the next, nor the next. He was put to bed in an upper chamber and remained there. Outside was the gray welter of the lake. Its white-capped waves knocked viciously against the trembling sea-wall, and their spray, flying across the drenched bed of the Drive, stung on the window-panes as if to say, in every drop, "It is we, we who have brought you to this!"

Medora sent her brother next morning to make inquiries, and at noon she came herself.

"The nurse will be here in an hour or two," said Edith Whyland.

"I will stay till she arrives," said Medora.

For a fortnight Abner lay muffled in that big, luxurious bed and did as he was told.

"Men!" said Medora. "They don't know anything; they have no idea of looking after themselves. And the bigger they are, the more helpless."

Abner had his good days and his bad, and suffered the gentle tyranny of two or three solicitous women, and trusted that his sudden illness was making due public stir.

The Readjusters, who had lately been asking after him, first heard of his plight from the press. The same newspapers that brought them further details of the adventures of the new Pence-Whyland Franchise in the Common Council informed them that Abner Joyce—Abner, the one time foe of privilege—lay ill in Leverett Whyland's own house.

"He is no longer one of us," pronounced the Readjusters. "We disown him; we cast him off."

XXIII

On one of the earliest days in April, Abner, gaunt and tottering, went home to Flatfield. Leverett Whyland's own carriage took him to the station and Medora Giles's own hands arranged his cushions and coverlets.

"Spring is spring everywhere," said Whyland; "but it's just a little worse right here than anywhere else. If you're going to pick up now, home's the place to do it."

"It's only three hours," said Abner. "I can stand that."

He shook Whyland's hand gratefully at parting and held Medora's with a firm pressure as long as he dared and longer than he realized. It was a pressure that seemed to recognise her at last as an individual woman, and what his hand did not say his face said and said clearly. And as soon as he was a man again his tongue should say something too, and say it more clearly still.

Medora's image travelled along with him on the dingy window-pane and intercepted all the well-beloved phenomena of earliest-awakening spring. One slide followed another, like the pictures of a magic lantern. Now she was pouring tea, now she was baking bread; sometimes she was playing the violin, sometimes—and oftenest—she was measuring medicines or on guard against draughts. In any event the sum total was a matchless assemblage of grace, charm, talent, sympathy, efficiency. "I am not worthy of her," he said humbly. "But I must have her," he added, with resolution. He was not the author of this ruthless masculine paradox.

After another month of rest and of home nursing Abner undertook a second tour (in Iowa and Wisconsin, this time) to make sure of his re-established health and to build up again his shattered finances,—for sickness, even in the lap of luxury, is expensive.

He had refused as considerately as he could an offer from Whyland himself to do literary work. The Pence-Whyland syndicate had lately secured control of one of the daily newspapers, and Whyland had suggested semi-weekly articles at Abner's own figure. But Abner could not quite bring himself to print in a sheet that was the open and avowed champion of privilege and corruption.

"You think you won't, then?" asked Whyland, at the door of the Pullman.

"I don't believe I can," replied Abner mournfully.

"Oh, yes, you can too," returned Whyland. "In a week or two more you'll be as strong as ever."

"I—I think I'd rather not," said Abner, tendering an apologetic hand.

He wrote to Medora endless plaints about the discomforts of country hotels; and she, remembering how he had once luxuriated in these very crudities—he had called them authentic, characteristic, and other long words ending in *tic*—smiled broadly. It seemed as if that fortnight in the Whyland house had finally done for him.

"He will become quite like the rest of us in time," she said;—"and in no great time, either!"

In the early days of June Abner spoke. Medora listened and considered.

"I am like Clytie Summers——" she began slowly.

"You are not a bit like her!" interrupted Abner, with all haste.

"In one respect," Medora finished: "when I get married I want to get married for good. As Clytie says, it is the most satisfactory way in the long run, and the long run is what I have in mind."

Abner flushed. "I can promise you that, I think."

"You must."

"I do."

"We will dismiss the new theory."

"If you demand it."

The idea of limited matrimonial partnership therefore passed away. Then there loomed up the question of an engagement-ring.

"You agree with me, I hope," said Abner, "that all these symbolical follies might very well be done away with?"

"No," said Medora firmly; "folly—sheer, utter folly—claims me for a month at least. And as for symbols, they are the very bread of the race, and I am as much of the human tribe as anybody else is."

A few days later Medora was wearing her engagement-ring.

This step accomplished, Abner felt himself free to scale down to a minimum the customary attentions of a courtship.

Medora protested. "You are no more than a man, and I am no less than a woman. You must give all that a man is expected to give and I must have all that a woman is accustomed to receive."

The engagement lasted through the summer, and Medora was married at the farm in October. Abner's parents came the thirty miles across country to their son's wedding. His father disclosed a singularly buoyant and expansive nature; he lived in the blessings the day brought forth, and considered not too deeply—as the poet once counselled—the questions that had kept his son in the fume and heat of unquenchable discussion. Mrs. Joyce was quiet, demure, rock-rooted in her self-respecting gravity—a sweet, sympathetic, winning little woman. She advanced at once into the bustle of the household, and it was plain that nature had endowed her with a fondness for work for work's very sake, and that she was proud of her own activity and thoroughness. Abner, everybody saw, was immensely wrapped up in her. "A man who makes such a good son," said Giles to his wife, "will make a good husband."

"I expect him to," said Medora, overhearing. "And I intend to put on the last few finishing touches myself."

XXIV

One after another several carriages dismissed their occupants with slams that carried far and wide on the crisp air of the early December evening, and a variety of muffled figures toiled up the broad granite steps and disappeared in the maw of the cavernous round-arched entrance-porch. At both front and flank of the house a score of curtained windows permitted the escape of hints of hospitable intentions; and in point of fact Mr. and Mrs. Palmer Pence were giving a dinner for Mr. and Mrs. Adrian Bond.

Adrian and Clytie were but lately back from their wedding-trip. Adrian, after several years of unproductive traffic in exotic literature, had finally made a hit; he had been able not only to lay a telling piece of work at the dear one's feet, but also—by a slight discounting of future certainties—to put a good deal of money in his purse. He had at last found a way to turn his "European atmosphere" and his "historical perspective" to profitable account,—to write something that thousands were willing to read and to pay for. Thirty thousand was the number thus far; and that number, reached within six weeks, meant a hundred thousand before the "run" should be over. His method involved simply a familiar offhand treatment of royalty, backed up by an excess of beauty, bravery, sword-play, costume, and irresponsible and impossible incident. "The only wonder is," he said, "that I shouldn't have taken up with this before. Anybody can do it; almost everybody else has done it."

Clytie was delighted by this sudden showy stroke of fortune, and readily allowed Adrian's long string of hints and intimations—they had come rolling in thick and fast through the advancing summer—to solidify into a concrete proposal.

"With this and my little investments," he said fondly, "we might rub along very decently."

"I hope so," said Clytie.

"Let's try."

"Let's."

The Whylands were also of those who climbed the granite steps. Mrs. Whyland had required a little urging, as on some previous occasions.

"I hope you won't make difficulties," her husband had said. "Mrs. Pence is a nice enough woman, as women go; and since my new relations with her husband...."

"Well, if you think it necessary," she returned resignedly. At need she might find the means to avoid anything like a real intimacy; and, after all, there would be a certain satisfaction in finally seeing, with her own eyes, Clytie Summers as somebody's actual wife.

Last to arrive were the Joyces. Medora wore the wedding-gown that had astonished the country neighbours for ten miles around, and Abner was in the customary evening dress.

"A bachelor and a genius," Medora had declared, "may enjoy some latitude, but a married man must consider his wife."

Abner had dutifully considered. He who considers is like him who hesitates—lost.

"There will be wine," said Medora. "Drink it. There may be toasts. Be ready to respond."

Abner could think on his feet—speech would not fail. And his fortnight with the Whylands had reconciled him to more things than wine.

"Let me be proud of you," said Medora.

Abner shook to his centre. Had he married a Delilah and a Beatrice in one?

"And don't let's talk any more about our book than they talk of theirs," she counselled to end with.

Regeneration had appeared within a week of *My Lady's Honour* and was doing well enough among a certain class of hardy readers who did not shrink from problems. Some of the less grateful passages had been censored by Medora's own hand and the unfriendlier of the critics thus partially disarmed in advance. But *Regeneration* was no longer a burning matter; Medora's thoughts were on the great, new, different thing that Abner was now shaping. He had finally come to an apprehension of the city. In certain of its aspects it was as interestingly crass and crude as the country, and the deep roar of its wrongs and sufferings was becoming audible enough to his ears to exact some share of his attention. In *The Fumes of the Foundry* he was to show a bold advance into a new field. This book would depict the modern city in the making: the strenuous strugglings of traditionless millions; the rising of new powers, the intrusion of new factors; the hardy scorn of precedent, the decisive trampling upon conventions; the fight under new conditions for new objects and purposes, the plunging forward over a novel road toward some no less novel goal; the general clash of ill-defined, half-formulated forces. All this study would explain much that was obscure and justify much that appeared reprehensible. Such a book would find place and reason for Pences and for Whylands. Indulgence would come with understanding, and reconciliation to repellent ideals and to the men that embodied them might not unnaturally follow.

> Full of his own new idea, Abner felt a greater contempt than ever for Bond's late departure and for the facile success that had attended it.

"I know how you look upon me," said Bond cheerfully. "Yet who, more than you yourself, is responsible for my come-down?"

"I?"

"You. When the psychological moment was on me and I needed most of all your encouragement, you dashed me with cold water instead. Now see where I am!"

Abner presently disclosed himself as one of the major ornaments of the feast. He talked, with no lack of ease and dexterity, to three or four ladies he had never seen before in his life, and even showed his ability for give-and-take with their husbands, on the basis of mutual tolerance and consideration. The quiet dignity that was his natural though latent gift from one parent he had learned how to maintain with less of jealous and aggressive self-consciousness; and a kind of congenital geniality, his heritage from the other, had now made its belated appearance and begun to show forth its tardy glow. Everybody found Abner interesting; one or two even found him charming. Those who had never liked him before began to like him now; those who had liked him before now liked him more than ever. Medora looked across at him; her eyes shone with pleasure and pride.

Clytie sat between Pence and Whyland. Whyland's face had already begun to take on the peculiar hard-finish that follows upon success—success reached in a certain way. "How about the Settlement?" he asked.

Clytie shrugged her shoulders. "I have other interests now. Besides, I felt that my efforts on behalf of the Poor were more or less misunderstood and unappreciated." She glanced down the table toward Abner.

Whyland glanced in the same direction and shrugged his shoulders too. "I understand. I might have turned out to be an idealist myself if a certain hand had not pushed me down when it should have raised me up!"

"Ah!" sighed Clytie, who still saw the old Abner bigger than the new, "I am sure that both Adrian and I might have continued to be among the Earnest Ones, but for that ruthless creature!"

Abner sat on one side of Eudoxia Pence—Eudoxia gorgeous, affluent, worldly. Never had she disclosed herself at a further remove from all that was earnest, thoughtful, philanthropic, altruistic.

"No," she said, shaking her head with a pleasant pretence of melancholy, "I was presumptuous. I did not realize how little my poor hands could do toward untangling the tangled web of life." Eudoxia, talking to a literary man, was faithfully striving to take the literary tone. She had waited for a year now, but the tone was here and time had not impaired its quality. "There was a period when I felt the strongest impulse toward the Higher Things; but now—now my husband's growing success needs my attending step. I must walk beside him and try to find my satisfactions in the simple duties of a wife." She dropped her head in the proud humility of welcome defeat.

Yes, Abner had brought down, one after another, all the pillars of the temple. But he had dealt out his own fate along with the fate of the rest: crushed yet complacent, he lay among the ruins. The glamour of success and of association with the successful was dazzling him. The pomp and luxury of plutocracy inwrapped him, and he had a sudden sweet shuddering vision of himself dining with still others of the wealthy just because they *were* wealthy, and prominent, and successful. Yes, Abner had made his compromise with the world. He had conformed. He had reached an understanding with the children of Mammon. He—a great, original genius—had become just like other people. His downfall was complete.

LITTLE O'GRADY vs. THE GRINDSTONE

I

Mrs. Palmer Pence was a stock-holder in any number of banks—twenty shares here, fifty there, a hundred elsewhere; but she was a stock-holder and nothing more, while what she most desired was to be a director: to act on the board of one at least of these grandiose institutions would have given her a great deal of comfort. She was clever, she was forceful, she was ambitious,—but she was a woman; and however keen her desire, her fellow stockholders seemed bound by the ancient prejudice that barred woman from such a position of power and honour and left the whole flagrant monopoly with man.

"Such discrimination is miserably unjust," she would remonstrate.

Amongst her other holdings, Mrs. Pence had forty-five shares in the Grindstone National. This was her favourite bank. Her accounts with the great retail houses along Broad Street were always settled by checks on the Grindstone, as well as her obligations to the insatiable cormorants that trafficked in "robes and manteaux" farther up town. The bank was close to the shopping centre, and the paying-teller of the Grindstone was never happier than on those occasions when Eudoxia Pence would roll in voluminous and majestic and ask him to break a hundred-dollar bill.

This had last happened during the press of the Christmas shopping. As Eudoxia turned away from the window of the complaisant teller, a door opened for a moment in a near-by partition and gave her a glimpse of eight or ten elderly men seated round a long solid table whose top bore a litter of papers—among them, many big sheets of light brown. She saw what was going on,—a directors' meeting. Her unappeased longing rose and stirred once more within her, and a shadow crossed her broad handsome face—the face that Little O'Grady had resolutely pursued all over the hall the evening she had deigned to show it at the Art Students' dance, with his long fingers curved and straining as if ready to dig themselves instantly into the clay itself.

"I don't care so much about the other banks," she sighed; "but if I could only be one of the board here!"

The door closed immediately, but not before she had caught the essential mass and outline of the situation. This august though limited gathering was submitting to an harangue—it seemed nothing less—from a little fellow who stood before the fireplace and wagged a big head covered with frizzled sandy hair, and gave them glances of humorous determination from his narrow gray-green eyes, and waved a pair of long supple hands in their protesting faces. Yes, the faces were protesting all. "Who are you, to claim our attention in this summary fashion?" asked one. "What do you mean by thrusting yourself upon us quite unbidden?" asked another. "Why do you come here to complicate a question that is much too complicated for us already?" demanded a third.

Yes, the door closed immediately, yet Eudoxia Pence had a clairvoyant sense of what was going on behind that rather plebeian partition of black walnut and frosted glass. She knew how they must all be hesitating, fumbling, floundering—snared by a problem wholly new and unfamiliar, and readily falling victims to intimidation from the humblest source. The entire situation was as clear as sunlight in the gesture with which Jeremiah McNulty, blinking his ancient eyes, had laid down that sheet of yellow-brown paper and had scratched his gray old chin.

"They need *me*," said Eudoxia Pence. "Indeed, they might be glad to have me. I feel certain that, if left to themselves, they will end by doing something awful."

She was perfectly confident that she could be of service in the bank's affairs. Had she not always been successful with her own? So it pleased her to think—and indeed nothing had developed in connection with her private finances to bring her under the shadow of self-doubt. The elderly hand of her husband, which was deep in vaster concerns, seldom interfered in hers, and never obtrusively. Now and then he dropped for a moment his own interests—he was engaged in forming the trustful into trusts and in massing such combinations into combinations greater still—to steady or to direct his wife's; but in general Eudoxia was left to regard herself as the guiding force of her own fortunes, and to believe herself capable of almost anything in the field of general finance.

The Grindstone National Bank, after ten years of prosperity in rather shabby rented quarters, had determined to present a better face to the world by putting up a building of its own. The day was really past when an institution of such calibre could fittingly occupy a mere room or two in a big "block" given over to miscellaneous business purposes. It was little to the advantage of the Grindstone that it shared its entrance-way with a steamship company and a fire-insurance concern, and was roofed over by a dubious herd of lightweight loan brokers, and undermined by bootblacking parlours, and barnacled with peanut and banana stands. Such a situation called loudly for betterment.

"It's time to leave all that sort of thing behind," decreed Andrew P. Hill, waggling his short chin beard decisively and shutting his handsome porcelain teeth with a snap. "What we want is to make a show and advertise our business."

Hill was president of the Grindstone and its largest stock-holder. Mr. McNulty listened to his words, and so did Mr. Rosenberg, and so did Mr. Gibbons and Mr. Holbrook and the rest of the directors; and they had all finally agreed—all save Mr. Rosenberg—that the time was come for the Grindstone to put up its own building and to occupy that building entirely and exclusively. Mr. Rosenberg imaged a few suites for tenants, but he was voted down.

They had found a moderately old young man who knew his Paris and his Vienna and who could "render" elevations and perspectives with the best. This clever person gathered together Andrew P. Hill and Simon Rosenberg and Jeremiah McNulty and all the others of the hesitating little band and with infinite tact "shood" them gently, step by step, despite multiplied protests and backdrawings, up the rugged slopes of doubt toward the summit where stood and shone his own resplendent Ideal. Each of the flock took the trip as his particular training and temperament dictated. Andrew was a bit dazed, but none the less exhilarated; Jeremiah shook his head, yet kept his feet in motion; Simon grumbled that the whole business spelt little less than ruination. But Roscoe Orlando Gibbons, who had been about the world not a little and who drew sanction for the young architect's doings from more quarters of the Continent than one, instantly rose to the occasion and landed on the topmost pinnacle of the shining temple at a single swoop. Here he stood tiptoe and beckoned. This confident pose, this encouraging gesture, had its effect; the others toiled and scrambled up, each after his own fashion, but they all got there. Even old Oliver Dowd, who had once been a member of the state legislature and had won the title of watchdog of the treasury by opposing expenditures of any kind for any purpose whatever, finally fell into line. His name was the last to go down, but down it went after due delay; and presently the new building began to rise, only a street or two distant from the old.

The new Grindstone, of all the Temples of Finance within the town, was to be the most impressive, the most imposing, the most unmitigatedly monumental. The bold young architect had loftily renounced all economies of space, time, material, and had imagined a grandiose facade with a long colonnade of polished blue-granite pillars, a pompous attic story above, and a wide flight of marble steps below. The inside was to be quite as overbearingly classical as the outside. There was to be a sort of arched and columned court under a vast prismatic skylight; lunettes, spandrels, friezes and the like were to abound; and the opportunities for interior decoration were to be lavish, limitless.

Now these lunettes and spandrels were the things that were making all the trouble. The building itself was moving on well enough: the walls were all up; and half the columns—despite the groans of Simon Rosenberg—were in place. Here no hitch worth speaking of had occurred: merely a running short of material at the quarry, the bankruptcy of the first contractor, and a standstill of a month or two when all the bricklayers on the job had declined to work or to allow anybody else to work. Such trifles as these could be foreseen and allowed for; but not one of the Grindstone's devoted little band had ever grappled with a general decorative scheme for the embellishment of a great edifice raised to the greater glory of Six-per-cent, or had attempted to adjust the rival claims of a horde of painters, sculptors, modellers, and mosaickers all eager for a chance to distinguish themselves and to cut down the surplus and the undivided profits. No wonder that Jeremiah McNulty scratched his chin, and that Simon Rosenberg puckered up his yellow old face, and that Roscoe Orlando Gibbons ran his fingers through his florid side-whiskers as he tried to find some sanction and guidance in Berlin or in Rome, and that Andrew P. Hill frowned blackly upon all the rest for being as undecided as he was himself.

"This is awful!" he moaned. "We may have to calcimine the whole place in pale pink and let it go at that!"

The door opened and a deferential clerk announced the waiting presence of one of the Morrell Twins. Andrew, giving a sigh of relief, swept the drawings quickly aside and rose. Here, at last, his feet were back once more on solid ground.

II

While Richard Morrell charmed the ears of the Grindstone's directors with his tuneful periods, and dazzled their eyes by the slow waving to and fro of certain elegantly engraved certificates of stock, and made his determined chin and his big round shoulders say to the assembled body that there was no chance of his going away before he had carried his point, Eudoxia Pence was taking tea at the Temple of Art. The early twilight of mid-December had descended. "It's too late for any more shopping," said Eudoxia, "and I'm too tired." Though she was still on the right side of forty by a year or two, this advantage of youth was counterbalanced by the great effort of pushing her abundant bulk through the throng of Christmas strugglers that crowded shop and sidewalk alike. "Only to sit down for half an hour in some quiet place!" she panted. "I believe I'll just drop up and see Daffingdon for a bit. That will give me a chance at the same time to keep half an eye on Virgilia," she added soberly. "A hundred to one she'll be there; and if anybody's to blame *for* her being there, I'm that body."

The Temple of Art, after rooting itself in drama and oratory, after throwing out a sturdy limb of chaste traffic in bibelots here and instruments of music there and books and engravings elsewhere, and after putting forth much foliage in the shape of string-scraping and key-teasing and anguished vocalizing and determined paper-reading and indomitable lecture-hearing, blossomed forth at last in a number of skylights, and under one of these lofty covers Daffingdon Dill carried on his professional activities. Eudoxia sank down upon his big settle covered with Spanish leather, and took her tea and her biscuits, and declined the pink peppermints, and looked around to discover, by the dim help of the Japanese lantern and the battered old brass lamp from Damascus, just who might be present. Several people were scattered about in various dusky corners, and Virgilia Jeffreys was no doubt among them. "I don't know just how all this is going to end," sighed Eudoxia dubiously. "I presume I'm as responsible as anybody else," she added, in a reflective, judicial tone. "More so," she tacked on. "Altogether so," she added further, as she took a first sip.

Daffingdon Dill was a newcomer, but he had taken hold of things in a pretty confident, competent fashion and had made more of an impression in one year than many of his confreres had made in five or ten. To begin with, he had unhesitatingly quartered himself in the most desirable building the town could boast. Many of his colleagues, no less clever (save in this one respect), still lingered in the old Rabbit-Hutch, a building which had been good enough in its day but which belonged, like the building that Andrew P. Hill was preparing to leave, to a day now past. Fearful of the higher rents that more modern quarters exacted, they went on paying their monthly stipend to old Ezekiel Warren, with such regularity as circumstances would admit, and made no effort to escape the affectionate banter that grouped them under the common name of the Bunnies.

Dill kept his studio up to the general level of the Temple, and himself up to the general level of the studio. There was little trace of Bohemia about either. Society found his workroom a veritable *salon de reception*. He himself never permitted the painter to eclipse the gentleman. People who came late in the afternoon found his tall, slender figure inclosed in a coat of precisely the right length, shape, cut. People who came earlier found him in guise more professional but no less elegant. He took a great deal of pains with his handsome hands, which many visitors pressed with cautious, admiring respect, as something a little too good to be true, as something a little too fine for this workaday world, and with his well-grown beard, which hugged his cheeks closely to make a telling manifestation upon his chin, after the manner of Van Dyck. This beard cried, almost clamoured, for picturesque accessories, and when Daffingdon went to a costume ball he generally wore a ruff and carried a rapier. All these things had their effect, and when people said, "How much?" and Daffingdon with unblinking serenity said, "So much," they quailed sometimes, but they never tried to beat him down.

"Why, after all, you know," they would say to one another, as they reconsidered his effective presence and his expensive surroundings,—"why, after all, it isn't as if——" Then they would think of the Rabbit-Hutch and acknowledge that here was a great advance. The poor Bunnies would have blinked—and often had, you may be sure.

Daffingdon was a bachelor, and he was old enough or young enough for anything, being just thirty; and his sister Judith, who was some years his senior, sat behind his tea-urn on most occasions and made it possible for the young things of society to flutter in as freely as they willed. The young things came to little in themselves, but some of them had vainglorious mothers and ambitious, pomp-loving fathers, and who could tell in what richly promising crevice their light-minded chatter might lodge and sprout? So Daffingdon and his sister encouraged them to come, and the young things came gladly, willing enough to meet with a break in the social round that was already becoming monotonous; and among the others came Preciosa McNulty,—dear little Preciosa, pretty, warm-hearted, self-willed——But we will wait a bit for *her*, if you please.

Daffingdon had spent many years abroad and still kept *au courant* with European art matters in general; he knew what they were doing in Munich no less than in Paris, and letters with foreign postmarks were always dropping in on him to tempt his mind to little excursions backward across the sea. He kept himself more or less in touch too with the kindred arts, and readily passed in certain circles for a man of the most pronouncedly intellectual and cultivated type.

Thus, at least, Virgilia Jeffreys saw him. Virgilia herself was intellectual to excess and cultivated beyond the utmost bounds of reason; indeed, her people were beginning to wonder where in the world they were to find a husband for her. Not that Virgilia intimidated the men, but that the men disappointed Virgilia. They stayed where they always had stayed—close to the ground, whereas Virgilia, with each successive season, soared higher through the blue empyrean of general culture. She had not stopped with a mere going to college, nor even with a good deal of post-graduate work to supplement this, nor even with an extended range of travel to supplement that; she was still reading, writing, studying, debating as hard as ever, and paying dues to this improving institution and making copious observations at the other. She too had her foreign correspondents and knew just what was going on at Florence and what people were up to in Leipsic and Dresden. She possessed, so she considered, a wide outlook and the greatest possible breadth of interests, and she knew she was a dozen times too good for any man she had ever met.

There were scores of other girls like her—girls who were forging ahead while the men were standing still: a phenomenon with all the fine threatenings of a general calamity. Where should these girls go to find husbands? Virgilia herself had been very curt with a young real-estate dealer, who was that and nothing more; and she had been even more summary with a stock-broker's clerk who, flashing upon her all of a sudden, had pointed an unwavering forefinger toward a roseate, coruscating future, but who had finished his schooling at seventeen and had had neither time nor inclination since to make good his deficiencies. The first had just installed his bride in a house of significant breadth and pomposity, and the other, having detached himself from the parent office, was now executing a comet-like flight that set the entire town astare and agape.

"Well, that's nothing to me," said Virgilia disdainfully. "I couldn't have lived with either of them a month. I'm only twenty-six and I don't feel at all alarmed."

Then somebody or other had piloted her aunt Eudoxia toward the Temple of Art, and Eudoxia, after about so much of dawdling and of sipping and of nibbling and of gentle patronage and of dilettante comment and criticism through this studio and that, had opened up a like privilege to her niece. Together they had dawdled and sipped and suggested up one corridor and down another, and in due course they arrived at the studio of Daffingdon Dill, and presently they were as good as enrolled among the habitues of the place.

Eudoxia peered about among the tapestries and the sombre old furniture. "Yes, there she is over in the corner with Preciosa McNulty." Then she looked back toward Dill and sighed lightly. "I wonder how this thing is coming out? I wonder how I want it to come out? And I wonder how much responsibility I must really bear for the way it *does* come out?"

III

She handed back her cup to Dill. "What are those two girls giggling about?" she asked him.

Dill snatched a moment from his cares as host. Little had he expected to hear Virgilia Jeffreys taxed with giggling.

Yet giggling she was,—with some emphasis and spirit too. She seemed to have slipped back from sedate and dignified young womanhood to mere flippant girlishness and not to have gained appreciably by the transition. Preciosa McNulty, still a girl and giving no immediate promise of developing into anything more, shared with her the over-cushioned disorder of the Persian canopy and giggled too.

Preciosa could laugh and chatter easily, volubly, spontaneously—all this, as yet, was the natural utterance of her being. But Virgilia was keeping pace with her, was even surpassing her. Yet she showed evidences of effort, of self-consciousness, of serious intention; now and then the *arriere pensee* disclosed its puckered front.

This, and nothing but this, could excuse Virgilia to-day. For she was too old to giggle, far too learned, much too sober-minded. Dill himself felt this, and shook his head in reply to Eudoxia Pence's question, as he stepped away for a moment to accompany a pair of gracious amateurs to the door.

A little figure that was passing rapidly along the corridor stopped on seeing the door ajar and waved a long supple hand and wagged a frizzly flaxen poll and gave a humorous wink out of his gray-green eyes and called unabashedly, before he resumed his skurrying flight:

"I've got 'em on the run, Daff; I've got 'em on the run!"

"Oh, that little O'Grady!" sighed Dill genteelly; "he is impossible; he will end with disgracing us. What can the fellow be up to now?" he wondered, closing the door, and preparing to return to his study of Virgilia Jeffreys.

"Your poor grandfather!—can't I fancy him!" Virgilia was saying to Preciosa. She gave a light dab at the other's muff with her long slender hand. "Dear, puzzled old soul!"—and she crinkled up her narrow green eyes.

"Can't you?" Preciosa laughed back. "'I don't know anything about such things,' grandpa insisted. 'Go and see Mr. Hill, young man, or Mr.

Gibbons.' But the young man kept unrolling sheet after sheet. 'Grandpa,' I said, 'we shall miss the whole of the first act.' Then the young man *had* to go. He didn't want to, but he had to."

"The 'young man'!" laughed Virgilia, dandling a cushion. "Didn't he have any name?"

"Some queer one: Ig—Ig——I don't remember."

"Nor any address?"

"Some far-away street you never heard of."

"How ridiculous!" chirped Virgilia, throwing back her head. "Do let them give you another cup of tea or some more of those biscuits. Ask for what you want. Don't be backward, even if you are a newcomer."

"Dear me," said Preciosa; "don't tell me I'm bashful."

"Did his sketches amount to anything?" asked Virgilia, herself reaching for the biscuits.

"Well, there were plenty *of* them. By a quarter to eight they had covered all the tables and chairs and about two-thirds of the floor. There was every evidence of that young man's being after us—a regular siege. I have no doubt he was waiting outside all through dinner; he rang the bell the very minute poor unsuspecting grandpa turned up the gas in the front parlour. But that's nothing to the one just before him."

"What did *he* do?" asked Virgilia, with all her fine blonde intentness.

Preciosa threw back her mop of chestnut hair. "Followed grandpa all the way home and would hardly let him have his dinner. He had it this time, however. And then, as I say, he turned up the gas; and then——"

"And then the shower began?" suggested Virgilia, putting her delicate eyebrows through their paces.

"The downpour. I never knew anybody to talk faster, or give out more ideas, or wave his hands harder,—like this." Preciosa cast her muff away completely and abandoned her plump little fingers to unbridled pantomime. "The room was peopled—isn't that the way they say it, peopled?—in no time; a regular reception. There were ladies in Greek draperies seated on big cogged wheels with factory chimneys rising behind, and strong young fellows in leather aprons leaning against anvils and forges, and there were——"

"I know, I know," declared Virgilia, ducking her head into her cushion, with the effect of suppressing a shriek of laughter. "And more 'ladies' reading from scrolls to children standing at their knee. And all sorts of folks blowing trumpets and bestowing garlands; Commerce, Industry, Art, Manufacturing, Education, and the rest of them. Dear child! how good of you to call all these things 'ideas'! No wonder such novelties puzzled your poor dear grandfather!"

She clutched Preciosa's chubby little hand with her long white fingers, as if to squeeze from it an answering shriek.

But Preciosa contained herself. "And there was a lady engineer," she went on, after a short pause, "in a light blue himation—is that what they call it, himation?—and she was fluttering it out of the cab-window——"

"The Railway!" declared Virgilia, trying to laugh tears into her eyes.

"And one drawing showed a lot of Cupids nesting on top of a telegraph pole——"

"What did Jeremiah McNulty think of that?"

"—with their little pink heels dangling down just as cute——"

"In a bank!" cried Virgilia, in a perfect transport of merriment. Preciosa, with whom a growing admiration for these abundant decorative details seemed to be overlaying her sense of fun, stopped in her account and then complaisantly gave forth the laugh that Virgilia seemed to expect.

"Oh, these young men!" exclaimed Virgilia, with a gasp and a gurgle to indicate that the limit was nearly reached; "these young men whom you never heard of, whose names you can't pronounce, and who live you don't know where! They will be too much for your poor grandfather. Let him escape them while he can. He is too old and too busy for such annoyances. Let him find some other young man whose name is known and whose studio is in a civilized part of the town and who has done some rather good work for some rather nice people." Virgilia crinkled up her eyes in a little spasm of confidential merriment and then opened them on her surroundings—the rich sobriety of the furniture; the casual picturesque groupings of "nice people"; the shining tea-urn flanked by the candles in their fluted paper shades; the heavy gilded frames inclosing copies made by Dill in the galleries of Madrid and St. Petersburg; other canvases set against the base-boards face back so as at once to pique and to balk curiosity with regard to the host's own work; the graceful dignity of Dill himself, upon whom Virgilia's eyes rested last yet longest.

"I might mention Mr. Dill to grandpa," said Preciosa, with returning seriousness. This, her first intrusion into the strange, rich world of art, had rather impressed her, after all; such novel hospitality really required some acknowledgment.

"Do," said Virgilia, now in quite a gale. "Don't drink his tea for nothing! And if it's 'ideas' that are wanted," she went on, as she grasped Preciosa lightly by both shoulders and gave her a humorous shake, "this is the shop!"

Preciosa paused for a moment's consideration. She was not sure that Virgilia knew her well enough to shake her, nor had she supposed that Virgilia was giddy enough to shake anybody. Neither was she sure that what she most wanted was to ridicule the facile and voluminous sketches spread out so widely and so rapidly by that young man with the burning eyes and the quick, nervous hands and the big shock of wavy black hair. Still, it was as easy to laugh as not to laugh; besides, which of the two might better set the tone, and authoritatively? Virgilia, surely; by reason of her age—she was some six or eight years the senior, by reason of her stature—she was several inches the taller, and by reason of her standing as an habituee—surely she must know how to behave in a studio. So Preciosa tossed her pretty little head, and laughed, as she felt herself expected to.

"The shop, yes," she acquiesced gaily. "And if I come again——"

"If?" repeated Virgilia, raising her eyebrows archly.

"And when I come again," amended Preciosa, rising, "I might bring grandpa with me. I'm sure all this would be new to him."

"Do, by all means," cried Virgilia. "And don't be too long doing it. *We* won't keep him from his food and drink; *we* won't worry his poor tired brain, if we can help it; *we* won't give him ladies seated beneath factory chimneys; *we* won't——You are going? Goodbye, dear. So glad to have met you here. Aunt and I drop in quite frequently, and you should learn to do so too."

She gave Preciosa a parting smile, then composed her features to a look of grave intentness and turned about to impose this look upon Daffingdon Dill wherever found.

Her eyes found him on the opposite side of the room, in company with her aunt. Both of them were studying her with some seriousness and some surprise. Virgilia, having already resumed her customary facial expression, now took on her usual self-contained manner as well and crossed over to them.

IV

"Well, well, Virgilia," said her aunt, as the door closed on Preciosa, "you see more in that girl than I do."

"I see her grandfather," whispered Virgilia, with the obscure brevity of an oracle. She drew down her brows and looked at the wondering Dill,—or rather, through him, past him.

"Oh," replied her aunt softly. It was impossible that she should misunderstand; McNulty and Hill and the rest of them had just been in her own thoughts, on her own tongue. "I *shall* be responsible, after all," she said within herself. Then she gave Virgilia a slight frown of disapproval: it was not precisely a maidenly part that her niece had chosen to play; neither did it show the degree of deference due to an elder, a chaperon and—if you came right at it—to a stock-holder. "If this thing must be engineered," thought Eudoxia, "I think I should prefer to engineer it myself." Heaven pardon her, though, for ever having brought Virgilia Jeffreys to Daffingdon Dill's studio!

> She herself had come there full of Jeremiah McNulty and Andrew P. Hill and Roscoe Orlando Gibbons. "It's a big undertaking," she had told Dill. "They're struggling with it now, poor things. They need expert advice. If I were only one of the board of directors!"

Dill came up to the mark gingerly. "The air has been full of it for the last fortnight," he said, struggling between eagerness and professional dignity. "I know a number of fellows who have thought of going in for it."

"I suppose *you* haven't thought of going in?"

Dill drew himself up. "How can I?" He suggested the young physician who will starve but who will not infringe the Code by any practice that savours in the least of advertising, of soliciting. However, he was a thousand miles farther away from starvation than was Ignace Prochnow, for example; much better could he afford to await the arrival of an embassy.

Eudoxia Pence fumbled her boa. "Does Virgilia really want him? Does he want Virgilia? Do I want them to have each other? Shall I exert myself in his behalf?" Such were the questions she submitted to her own consideration as her eyes roved over the chatting, sipping throng. "Can he do for her all that a girl in her position would expect? Could such a fastidious, exacting young woman hope to find anybody she would like better—or as well?" Eudoxia had three or four swift successive visions of herself in a variety of circumstances and pleading or discouraging a variety of causes. Now, for example, she was saying to Virgilia, "Yes, he's a very nice fellow, I know; but he has only his wits and his brush, while you must always live as you always have lived—a rich girl to whom nothing has been denied." Again, she saw herself bent over the desk of Andrew P. Hill, with her forty-five shares clutched in her resolute hand, and saying, "I demand to be heard; I demand to have a voice in this momentous matter; I demand a fair and even chance for my nephew-in-law-to-be." Once more, she was wringing her hands and asking Virgilia in tones of piteous protest, "Why, oh why, didn't you take Richard Morrell when you could have got him?—a fine, promising, pushing fellow, with his million or more already, and barely thirty-five, just the right age for you!" Yet again, she was saying to that poor little vulgarian, Preciosa McNulty, "If Virgilia will, she will, and there's an end of it; therefore should you, dear child, promise me to use your influence with that loutish old peasant of a grandfather, you shall have the beatitude of actually pouring tea at one of my Thursday afternoons, and I'll even invite your mother to my next large reception——"

Eudoxia paused, struck suddenly by the earnest scrutiny of both Daffingdon and Virgilia. She saw that she had tied her boa into a double knot, and surmised that she had been doing the same with her features too.

V

By this time every "art circle" in the city knew from its centre to its circumference that the Grindstone National Bank was moving toward the elaborate decoration of its new building and that the board of directors was thinking of devoting some twenty thousand dollars or more to this purpose. The Temple of Art took on its reception smile; the Rabbit-Hutch began a nervous rummaging for ideas among cobwebs and dusty portfolios and forgotten canvases; decorators of drawing-rooms and libraries put on their thinking-caps and stood up their little lightning-rods; and one or two of the professors at the Art Academy began to overhaul their mythology and to sketch out broad but hazy schemes for a succession of thumping big masterpieces, and to wonder whether the directors would call on them or whether they should be summoned to meet the directors.

"Gee!" said Little O'Grady (whose *forte* was reliefs in plastina), as he hopped around Dill's studio on one leg; "but ain't it a godsend for us!"

Little O'Grady was celebrated for keeping the most untidy and harum-scarum quarters throughout the entire Rabbit-Hutch, and for being wholly beyond the reach of reproof or the range of intimidation. The stately sobriety of Dill's studio had no deterring effect upon him. Nothing could impress him; nobody could repress him. He said just what he thought to anybody and everybody, and acted just as he felt wherever he happened to be. Just now he felt like dancing a jig—and did so.

"But, dear me, where do *you* come in?" asked Dill, moving his easel a bit farther out of Little O'Grady's range.

"Where do I come in? Everywhere. I come in on the capitals of the columns round that court, which will all be modelled after special designs of me own——"

"I hadn't heard about them. I should suppose such things would follow established patterns."

> "So does the architect. But I shall convince him yet that he's mistaken." O'Grady gave a pirouette in recognition of his own powers of persuasion.

"And I come in on the mantel-piece in the president's private parlour," he continued. "It will be a low relief in bronze: 'The Genius of the West Lighting the Way to Further Progress,' or else, 'Commerce and Finance Uniting to Do Something or Other'—don't know what just yet, but shall hit on some notion or other in due time——"

"You've seen the plans, then? You've been striking up an acquaintance with the architect himself?" Dill frowned repugnance upon such a bit of indelicacy, such an indifference to professional etiquette.

"Well, perhaps I have. Why not? But if there's a president—I s'pose there is?"

"I suppose so."

"Then there'll sure be a parlour. And where there's a parlour there's a fireplace—see? A large official cavern with never any fire in it. And I come in on the drinking-fountains at each side of the main entrance: bronze dolphins twisted upside down and spouting water into marble basins."

"They're included too, are they?"

"Well, I suggested them. Don't those old coupon-clippers ever get thirsty? Sure they do. Well, can't I wet their whistles for them? I guess yes—and I told 'em so."

"Them? Whom?"

"The directors."

"You've seen them?"

"I attended a meeting of the board, as I suppose I might as well tell you," said Little O'Grady grandly.

"You did, eh?" returned Dill, balanced between reprobation of Little O'Grady's push and admiration for his nerve.

"Yep. I spoke a good word for myself. And one for the others—Gowan and Giles and you and Stalinski and——"

"Um," said Dill, none too well pleased. The last thing he desired was co-operation from the Rabbit-Hutch and association with the band of erratic, happy-go-lucky Bohemians that peopled it. "You're laying out a good deal of work for yourself," he remarked coldly, dismissing the Bunnies.

"Work? That's what I'm here for," declared O'Grady brightly. "And if I slip up on any of these little notions, why I'll just take a hand in the painting itself—didn't I help on a panorama once? Sure thing. There was a time when I could kind o' swing a brush, and I guess I could do it yet. Let's see: 'The Goddess of Finance,' in robes of saffron and purple, 'Declaring a Quarterly Dividend.' Gold background. Stock-holders summoned by the Genius of Thrift blowing fit to kill on a silver trumpet. Scene takes place in an autumnal grove of oranges and pomegranates—trees loaded down with golden eagles and half-eagles. Marble pavement strewn with fallen coupons. Couldn't I do a fairy-scene like that? I should say!" Little O'Grady threw out his leg again with sudden vehemence and toppled over among Dill's heaped-up cushions.

Dill laughed. "How are the other fellows over your way feeling about it?"

"Same as me—hopeful. We may have to sleep on excelsior for a while yet, but we shall soon stop eating it. And the first thing we do with the coin will be to give old Warren heart-disease by going down in a body and paying up all our back rent. I'm figuring on pulling out about two thousand for my share. Then if I want pie I can have it, without stopping to feel in my pocket first."

Little O'Grady babbled along as he delineated the mental state of the other Bunnies. They all felt the situation in the air—they all felt it in their bones. They all wanted a hand in things—a finger in the pie. There was Festus Gowan, who did little beyond landscapes, but who thought he could make some headway with faces and draperies if pushed to it. There was Mordreth, who did little but portraits—and "deaders" at that—but who fancied he might come out reasonably strong on landscape and on architectural accessories if somebody would only give him a chance. There was Felix Stalinski, who had lately left "spot-knocking" for general designing and who thought that if a man was able to turn out a good, effective poster he might consider himself equal to almost anything. And there was Stephen Giles, who had recently been decorating reception halls and dining-rooms for the high and mighty and who saw no reason why he shouldn't take a higher flight still and adorn the palaces where the money was made instead of those where it was spent. "No use in my talking to you about *him*, though," broke off Little O'Grady. "He ain't one of us any more. He's one of you, now."

"I hope you fellows don't feel that way——" began Dill.

"He's a renegade," declared Little O'Grady. "But never mind; we like him all the same. Some day he may be glad to leave the Temple and come back to us again at the Warren. That'll be all right. We'll welcome him; we'll share our last mouthful of excelsior with him." Little O'Grady gave another joyful kick into the air. "Well, his room didn't stay empty long; Gowan moved down right away, and a new man took Gowan's room only day before yesterday—so old Ezekiel won't lose more'n about fourteen dollars' rent, after all. Chap's got his name out already: Ignace Pr—Pr—— Well, anyway, it begins with a P. He makes rattling strong coffee, by the smell, and tinkles now and then on the thing-a-ma-jig. They say he's terrible smart—full of the real old stuff."

"Has Gowan been thinking up anything in particular?"

"Well, he's thinking he sees that money piled up in the bank vaults. We all do. And we want to get at it. Say, great thing to be working for a bank, eh? No flighty, shilly-shallying, notional women, but a lot of steady, sober business-men who'll make a good straight contract and keep it. No saying, 'Well, my daughter doesn't altogether fancy this,' or, 'I will take your sketches home to my husband and we will think about them,'—and then never telling us *what* they think. Sure pay, too. And prompt, as well. Quarter down, let us say, on submitting the general scheme of decoration; another quarter as soon as we begin actual work——Yes, sir, I almost feel as if I saw my way to meat once a day right through the week!"

VI

"Then I don't see but that he is about the man for us," said Roscoe Orlando Gibbons;—"at least he seems to provide a point for us to start from."

Jeremiah McNulty rescued some loose memoranda from the absent-minded pokings of his caller's plump forefinger and scratched his chin.

"You were pretty favourably impressed, weren't you?" asked Roscoe Orlando, leaning forward across the corner of the other's desk. "*I* was. I thought he had something in him, and something behind him. Seemed to me like a very dependable chap—for one in that line. These artists, you know,—erratic, notional, irresponsible. You never feel sure how you have them; you can't treat with them as you can with a downright, sensible, methodical business-man. I assure you I've heard the most astonishing tales about them. There's Whistley, for example—sort of sharp, perverse spoiled child, I should say. And the time my own brother-in-law had over the portrait painted by that man from Sweden! We've got to make up our minds to be patient with them, to humour them. But Dill, now——" Roscoe Orlando Gibbons ran his fingers through his graying whiskers and waited for Jeremiah's belated observation.

Jeremiah took his time in making it. He had accompanied his granddaughter to Daffingdon Dill's studio, but he was in no haste to formulate his impressions. His eyes were still blinking at the duskiness of the place, his nose was still sniffing the curious odour of burning pastilles, his ears were still full of the low-voiced chatter of a swarm of idle fashionables, and his feet (that humpy tiger-rug once passed) still had a lingering sense of the shining slipperiness of the brown polished floor. That floor!—poor Jeremiah had stood upon it as helpless as a cripple on a wide glare of ice, at a cruelly embarrassing disadvantage and wholly at the mercy of that original and anomalous person in the brown Van Dyck beard. Vainly had he cast about for something to lay hold of. None of the people there had he ever seen before; none of the topics bandied about so lightly and carelessly had he ever heard broached before. The sole prop upon which he had tried to repose his sinking spirit had looked indeed like an oak, but had turned out to be merely a broken reed. "That's the only man here," he had muttered, on looking across toward a stalwart, broad-shouldered figure standing half in the shadow of some frayed and discoloured drapery. "He's sort o' like one of those 'swells,' in that slick new coat and all, but I'll risk him." However, this robust young man had shown himself as prompt as any in his use of the teasing jargon of the place; he assumed on Jeremiah's part some interest and some knowledge and dogmatized as readily and energetically on the general concerns of culture as any of the others. Jeremiah, prostrate, soon moved away.

"Who is he—that tall young fellow over by that curtain?" he could not refrain from asking his granddaughter. How, he was thinking to himself,—how could such a big, vigorous young man betray such a range of trivial interests?

"Why, grandpa," Preciosa had returned reproachfully, "that's Mr. Joyce—Abner Joyce, the great writer. You've heard of him, surely?"

"H'm," said Jeremiah. He hadn't.

"And that lovely creature in the long, bottle-green coat," Preciosa went on, "is his wife. Isn't it stylish, though?—they're just back from London. Aren't they a splendid couple? And isn't she just the ideal type of the young matron——?"

Jeremiah touched bottom. It was all of a piece—everything was growing worse and worse. "Young matron," indeed!—where had his grandchild picked up that precious phrase? She was growing all too worldly-wise for his simple old mind. His abashed eyes turned away from her and began to blink at the twinkling candles on the tea-table; it stood there like an altar raised for the celebration of some strange, fearsome ritual—an incident in the dubious life toward which a heartless and ambitious daughter-in-law was pushing his poor little Preciosa. He almost felt like grasping her by the arm and bolting with her from the place.

But most uncertain of all these uncertainties had been the young painter himself. He could not be brought down to business. He dodged; he slipped away; he procrastinated. He wouldn't show his work; he wouldn't talk in figures; he wouldn't come within a mile of a contract. Instead, he slid about, asking people if they wouldn't have another biscuit, dropping a word to a lady here and there about Pater or Morelli (who were probably somewhere over there in the dark), confabulating determinedly with people who were pointed out as authors (more of them!), urging other people, who were musical, in the direction of the piano....

Some of these considerations Jeremiah haltingly placed before Roscoe Orlando.

"Oh, well," returned Roscoe, twiddling his fingers vaguely in the air, "you can't expect anything different on an 'afternoon.' There are occasions when a man must let down, must expand, must cultivate society a little. It was very much like that the first time I went there myself."

Roscoe Orlando's "first time" had been but a week before. Preciosa McNulty had communicated her novel impressions to his daughters, who, in turn, had commented on Preciosa's naivete in their father's hearing; then Roscoe Orlando, who had never hurt himself by overwork and who was developing a growing willingness to leave his maps and his plats and his subdivisions a little earlier in the afternoon, had determined to step round and patronize the new man.

"That we should never have met before!" said Roscoe Orlando to Daffingdon; "I can hardly credit it. Certainly it is no great thing in my own favour, for I really claim to know what is going on and to keep in touch with the better things. In my own defence I must say that I am an annual member of the Art Academy and that people who have etchings to sell invariably send me a copy of the catalogue. Your atelier is charming—most charming."

Roscoe Orlando was fat, florid and forty-eight, and as he began to expand he promised to take up a good deal of room. But Dill did not grudge the space when he learned that Roscoe Orlando was one of the directors of the Grindstone. Roscoe Orlando declared this with a broad, benevolent smile, accompanied by a confidential little gesture to indicate that a golden shower might soon descend and that it was by no means out of his power to help determine the favoured quarter.

"But this is no time to talk about that," declared Roscoe Orlando, casting an eye over the other visitors present. "I may drift in again before long and look at some of your things more seriously and have a little chat with you about our project."

Roscoe Orlando had somehow failed to drift in again, but he was now having the little chat—or trying to have it—with Jeremiah McNulty.

He looked across at the old man once more. "Yes, I rather think, after all, that if we were to try to arrange things with Dill we shouldn't be going much amiss."

Jeremiah scratched his chin slowly, and worked the tip of a square-toed boot against his waste-paper basket. "I dunno. It's a good deal of an undertaking," he declared.

"Surely," assented Roscoe Orlando. "Do we want it to be anything less? Don't we want to do something—a big thing, too—that will be a credit to ourselves and a real adornment to our city?"

Jeremiah puckered up his mouth and slowly blinked his little red eyes. "I've had one or two of those young painter fellows after me lately," he said in ruminative tone, as he picked at the green baize of his desk-top. He spoke with a slight querulousness, as if these wily and hardy adventurers had wilfully hit upon him as the weak spot in the defences, as the vulnerable point of the Grindstone. In particular he saw a pair of burning black eyes, a pair of eager, sinewy hands strewing drawings over the pink and gold brocades of his front parlour suite, and a shock of dark hair that swished about over a high square forehead as the work of hurried exposition raged along against a pitiless ticking of the marble-and-gilt clock and Preciosa's hasty adjustment of the green velvet toque.

"Haven't I had them after *me*!" cried Roscoe Orlando, jealous of his standing as an enlightened and sympathetic amateur. "But we ought to deal—really, we ought to—with painters of standing and responsibility, and no others. We must keep in mind such things as position, reputation, clientele. My partner, for example, once contracted—or tried to—for a large landscape of his stock-farm out beyond Glenwood Park; and the artist, sir——Well, you wouldn't believe the trouble we had before we got through. Our lawyer himself said that never in the whole course of his professional career had he——"

Jeremiah blinked and puckered a little more, and sighed as he abstractedly prodded among his pigeonholes. That slippery floor typified it all,—that dim room full of dusky corners! Ah, if he could only get that slim young man with the long coat and the pointed beard out on the black-and-white chequered pavement of the Grindstone, fair and square in the honest light of day! In such a situation a downright, straightforward old contractor could do himself something like justice. It would be playing a return match on his own ground.

"I dunno," said Jeremiah. "I'd 'most as soon not have anything to do with such matters and with that sort of people——"

He saw Dill as a dog might view a lizard, or a goat a swan; after all, there was no common ground for them—no way of coming together.

"But if it's got to be done," he concluded, "perhaps he would do as well to start with as anybody else."

"I think so," said Roscoe Orlando. "I'll speak about it in a day or so to Hill."

VII

Preciosa McNulty, after all, lost nothing of *The Princess Pattie* except half of the overture—a loss that, as operettas go, might indeed be counted a gain; but the succeeding activities of the prima donna, the ponderous basso and the brace of "comedians" were subject to a series of very sensible impediments and interruptions. Several times—and often at the most inopportune of moments—a swarthy, earnest young man walked across the stage, throwing out big sheets of brown paper right and left and looking at her and her alone. He wore one unvarying expression—a mingling of reproach and of admiration. His eyes said across the footlights: "You are a heartless, cruel little creature, but that green velvet hat looks amazingly well on your chestnut hair—so amazingly well that I almost forgive you. Yet an hour lost by you from the theatre is nothing, while an hour gained by me here in your home almost makes the difference between life and death." Yes, there the young man was, fifty feet away from her, yet she could plainly see the blood pulsing through his veined hands and could almost hear the ideas ticking in his brain. How they had ticked, to be sure, and clicked and clanked and jarred and rattled and rumbled—a perfect factory, a perfect foundry of ideas! Preciosa, who had never had a dozen ideas in her life, and had seldom encountered a human brain running full force and full time, was a good deal impressed. "I shouldn't wonder but what he *was* a pretty smart fellow, after all. It was rather sudden, the way I brought him up. Yes, I'm afraid I'm a real cruel girl," said Preciosa complacently, and reverted to the deplorable antics of the "comedians."

Within a day or two Preciosa began to notice the railway trains. Whenever she was detained at a "grade crossing" she caught herself looking at the locomotive to find a lady in a blue himation. Then the telegraph poles began to trouble her; she got into the habit of glancing aloft for nests of Cupids, and once or twice she thought she saw them. Then her father's letter-heads began to affect her. They sometimes lay carelessly about the house, and whenever she saw the tall chimney of his sash-and-blind factory looming above the blank date-line she always looked for a female in Greek drapery seated on a cogged wheel at the base of it.

"This won't do," she told herself. "Dear me, I don't even know his name. Why, for heaven's sake, didn't I pay better attention?"

Not knowing his name did not prevent her from thinking about him, nor even from talking about him. When Virgilia Jeffreys started her up, she went on because she couldn't stop and because she didn't want to, anyway. She would not deny herself *that* small comfort.

Preciosa was the pride and the hope of the McNultys—especially of her mother. This ambitious lady had lived long in obscurity—a prosperous, well-fed obscurity, but an obscurity all the same—and now she was tired of it and was rebelling against it and was meaning to emerge from it. Every inch of her tall, meagre figure was straining with the wish to attract attention; every feature of her thin, eager, big-eyed face showed forth the tense desire to shine. She realized that Preciosa was the only one of them who could raise the family to a higher level and bring it within range of the glamouring illumination of "society." The child's grandfather doted on her, true, but had never been quite able to leave behind him the lusty young peasant of the bogs. He had a regrettable taste in foot-gear, a teasingly uncertain fashion of lapsing back into his shirtsleeves at table, and a slight brogue that had stood a good deal of smothering without ever reaching the point of actually giving up the ghost. The girl's father lived and thought in terms of blinds and frames and panellings; he could never bring himself into sympathy with his wife's social yearnings or even realize the verity of their existence. Their boy was too young; besides, what can be done with a boy, anyway? As for herself, she had begun too late; she was a little too stiff, too diffident; society slightly intimidated her; she felt sure she could never hope to associate in easy, intimate fashion—even should the most abundant opportunity present—with the ladies whose names were so often printed in the papers. She might serve as a chaperon, a supernumerary, perhaps, but as a leading figure, no.

There remained only Preciosa. But Preciosa would suffice. So the child was bundled out at the earliest moment. She was made to fence at the Young Ladies' Athletic League, where the Gibbons girls went, and rather enjoyed it. She was made to study and discuss at the Philomathian Club, of which Virgilia Jeffreys was a shining light, and enjoyed it not at all. Then she began to go to musicales and dramatic matinees at the Temple of Art, finding a wide range of novel diversion at these little functions and making some acquaintances worth while. "And as soon as spring is fairly here," said her indefatigable mother, "she shall join a good golf club; and then things will really have begun to move."

But things had begun to move already. The fairest, topmost blossom on the family tree had set itself to swaying in the gentle breezes of sentiment, regardless of the dotings of the gnarled old root, of the indifference of the sturdy trunk, of the solicitous rustlings of the foliage. The blossom began to peer over and to look down, as if conscious of the honest, earthy odour of the dear lowly soil itself—though not, perhaps, the soil of the links. Preciosa was preparing to revert.

"No," she said again, "I don't even know his name."

VIII

When Ignace Prochnow found himself able to move into the Rabbit-Hutch, he congratulated himself on having made a marked advance in fortune.

"Oh, Lord!" thought Little O'Grady, upon Prochnow's venturing this disclosure, which he made in all sincerity and simplicity and with a complete absence of false shame; "how must he have lived before!"

The Rabbit-Hutch, the Warren, the Burrow—it went by all of these names—was a hapless property that was trying to pay taxes on itself between the ebbing of one tide of prosperity and the hoped-for flood of another. Centres were shifting, values were see-sawing, and old Ezekiel Warren was waiting for the nature of the neighbourhood to declare itself with something like distinctness. Meanwhile,—as regarded its upper floors, at least,—broken panes of glass were seldom mended, sagging doors seldom rehung, smoky ceilings seldom whitewashed, and the corridors rarely swept, save when the tenants formed themselves into a street-cleaning brigade, as Little O'Grady called it, and co-operated to make an immense but futile dust and stir.

"You're in a palace, sure," declared Little O'Grady, on the occasion of his first call upon the newcomer. This took place the third day of Prochnow's tenancy—he had scarcely got his poor belongings into shape and had barely affixed his name to the door. But Little O'Grady cared nothing for conventions; he was ready to overstep any boundary, to break through any barrier. "How did it occur to you to come among us?" he asked, sitting down on the bed. "What made you want to be a Bunny?"

"I found I must be where I could reach people, and where I could give them a chance to reach me."

Prochnow spoke with a slight accent—slight, but quaint and pungent. To have come among the Anglo-Saxons three or four years sooner would have been an advantage; to have deferred coming three or four years longer, a calamity.

"Yep, they 'reach' us good and hard," said O'Grady; "processions of millionairesses and peeresses marching through the halls with gold crowns on their heads and bags of double-eagles in both hands—nit. We *did* have a real swell, though—once. She called when Giles was here—it convulsed the premises. We all lost our sleep and appetite and thought of nothing else for a month. It was Mrs. Pence—expect you haven't heard of her. Money to burn—husband head of some tremendous trust or other—house as big as a hotel—handsomest profile in six states. 'Stevy,' says I to Giles, 'Stevy, for the love of heaven, introjooce me. Take a quart of me heart's blood, but only give me a chance to do her lovely head.' He wouldn't. She came when he had one of those good big rooms lower down—very fair, nothing like these of ours up here. He did wonders about fixing it up, too. But now we've lost him; he's gone, and taken my best chance with him." Little O'Grady rocked to and fro in melancholy mood and the cot creaked and swayed in unison.

"Show me something," he said suddenly, jerking himself back to his own bright humour. "I've smelt your coffee and I've heard your mandolin, and now I want to see your pictures."

"I've just sold one or two of my best ones," said Prochnow. "That's why I was able to come here."

"Sold a picture!" cried Little O'Grady, with staring eyes. "Sold a—— Have you spent the money?"

"Most of it."

"Well, let it pass. Only we generally look for a supper after the sale of a picture. We had one six months ago. We're getting hungry again. But let that pass too. Show me something."

Prochnow looked at Little O'Grady, openly and unaffectedly appraising him. Little O'Grady jovially blinked his gray-green eyes and tossed his fluffy, sandy hair. "Don't make any mistake about me; I can appreciate a good thing. What's that big roll of brown paper behind the washstand?"

Prochnow reached for it. "Just a scheme for decoration I got up two or three years ago. It didn't quite—how do you say?—come off."

"Such things seldom do," said the other. "That's the trouble. Let's look."

"It isn't much," said Prochnow, undoing the roll. "It isn't quite what I would do now. It's the sort of thing I show to ordinary people."

"It will do to begin on. H'm, I see; just a lot of ladies playing at Commerce and Education and Industry and so on. Still, those cherubs up in the air are well done." He glanced over behind the wood-box. "Bust open that portfolio."

Prochnow looked at his visitor again—longer, more studiously.

"Oh, come now," said Little O'Grady, "you'll have me red-headed in a minute. I'm no chump; I know a good thing when I see it."

Prochnow opened the portfolio and handed out several sketches one after another. "These are more recent," he said;—"all within the last few months."

Little O'Grady snatched them, devoured them, immediately took fire. Prochnow caught the flame and burned and blazed in return. "Whew! this is warm stuff!" cried Little O'Grady, who had not an envious bone in his body; "and you—you're a wonder!" Little O'Grady made a last sudden grab. "Oh, this, this!" He dropped the sheet and threw up both hands. Then, being still seated on the cot, he threw up both feet. Then he placed his feet upon the floor and rose on them and gave Ignace Prochnow a set oratorical appreciation of his qualities as a thinker and a draughtsman, and then, swept away by a sudden impulse to spread the news of this magnificent new "find" right under their own roof, he rushed downstairs to communicate his discovery to Festus Gowan.

"Will return in half an hour," said the card on Gowan's door; so Little O'Grady sped back upstairs and burst in on Mordreth.

Mordreth was sitting composedly before a half-finished portrait of an elderly man of rustic mien. About him were disposed a number of helps and accessories: a pair of old-fashioned gold spectacles, an envelope containing a lock of gray hair, two or three faded photographs, and a steel engraving extracted from the *Early Settlers of Illinois*. With these aids he was hoping to hit the taste and satisfy the memory of certain surviving grandchildren.

Little O'Grady ignored the presence of any third person and let himself out. "He's a genius, Mark; he's full of the real stuff. He can draw to beat the band, and he's got ideas to burn—throws them out as a volcano does hot stones. And I expect he can paint too, from what little I saw—says he's just sold off all his best things. Yes, sir, he's an out-and-out genius and we've got to treat him right; we must let him in on this bank scheme of ours—that's all there is about it!"

IX

"Well, it comes to this, then," said Virgilia. "We must give them something definite—a fully outlined—*projet*; and we must give it to them as soon as possible." She cleared away the ruck of evening papers from the library table, sent her younger sister off with arithmetic and geography to the dining-room, extracted a few sheets of monogrammed paper from the silver stationery-rack close by, and turned on two or three more lights in the electrolier overhead. "Now, then. We'll choke off that foolish notion of theirs; we'll smother it before it has a chance to mature."

She put a pen into Daffingdon's hand, with the open expectation of immediate results. She herself always thought better with a pen in her hand and a writing-pad under it; no doubt a painter would respond to the same stimulus.

Daffingdon bit at the end of the penholder and made a dog-ear on the topmost of the steel-gray sheets.

"Come," said Virgilia. "Whatever follies may have begun to churn in their poor weak noddles, we will *not* draw upon the early pages of the local annals, we will not attempt to reconstruct the odious architecture of the primitive prairie town. Come; there are twelve large lunettes, you say?"

"Yes."

"Well, now, just how shall we handle them?"

"I had thought of a general colour-scheme in umber and sienna; though Giles's idea of shading the six on the left into purple and olive and the six on the right into——"

"Dear me! Can we hope to impress Andrew P. Hill with any such idea as that? No; we must have our theme, our subject—our series of subjects."

"I don't want to be simply pictorial," said Daffingdon reluctantly; "and surely you can't expect me to let my work run into mere literature."

"They're business-men," returned Virgilia. "For our own credit—for our own salvation, indeed—we must be clear-cut and definite. Even if we are artists we mustn't give those hard-headed old fellows any chance to accuse us of wabbling, of shilly-shallying. We must try to be as business-like as they are. So let's get in our work—and get it in first."

Daffingdon's eyes roamed the rugs, the hangings, the furniture. "'The Genius of the City,'" he murmured vaguely, "'Encouraging—Encouraging'—"

"Yes, yes," spoke Virgilia, doing a little encouraging herself.

"Or, 'The—The Westward Star of Empire Illuminating the'— —" proceeded Daffingdon mistily, raising his eyes toward the electrolier.

"Yes, yes," responded Virgilia quickly, by way of further encouragement.

"Or—or—'The Triumphal March of Progress through Our'— —" Daffingdon confusedly dipped the wrong end of the penholder into the big sprawling inkstand.

Virgilia's teeth began to feel for her lips, and her eyebrows to draw themselves down in an impatient little frown of disappointment. Not through "Our Midst," she hoped. What was the matter with her idol? What had he done with all his fund of information? What had become of his ideas, his imagination? She felt that if she were to approach a bit closer to his pedestal and sound him with her knuckles he would be found hollow. What a calamity in such a discovery! She put her hand behind her back and kept her distance.

"'The Genius of the City,'" she mused; "'The Star of Empire.' Those might do for single subjects but not for a general scheme. 'The March of Progress '—that might be better as a broad working basis, although— —" She saw the "lady" seated on the cogged wheel beneath the factory chimney and stopped.

"'The Prairie-Schooner'—'The Bridging of the Mississippi'—'The Last of the Buffaloes'—' The Corner-Stones of New Capitols'— —" pursued Daffingdon brokenly.

"Would you care very much for that sort of thing?" asked Virgilia.

"No."

"Nor I. Come, let me tell you; I have it: 'The History of Banking in all Ages'! There, what do you think of that?" she asked, rising with an air of triumph.

Dill hesitated. "I don't believe I know so very much about the history of banking."

"Don't you? But *I* do—enough and more than enough for the present purpose. Come, tell me, isn't that a promising idea? What a series it would make!—so picturesque, so varied, so magnificent!"

Daffingdon looked up at his Egeria; her visible inspiration almost cowed him. "Isn't that a pretty large theme?" he questioned. "Wouldn't it require a good deal of thought and study— —?"

"Thought? Study? Surely it would. But *I* think and study all the time! Let me see; where shall we begin? With the Jews and Lombards in England, Think what you have!—contrast, costumes, situations, everything. Then take the 'Lombards' in Italy itself; the founding of the earliest banks in Venice, Lucca, Genoa, Florence; the glamour of it, the spectacularity of it, the dealings with popes and with foreign kings! And there were the Fuggers at Augsburg who trafficked with emperors: houses with those step-ladder gables, and people with puffed elbows and slashed sleeves and feathers of all colours in those wide hats. And then the way that kings and emperors treated the bankers: Edward the Second refusing to repay his Florentine loans and bringing the whole city to ruin; Charles the First sallying out to the Mint and boldly appropriating every penny stored there—plain, barefaced robbery. Then, later, the armies of Revolutionary France pillaging banks everywhere—grenadiers, musketeers and cuirassiers in full activity. Among others, the Bank of Amsterdam—the one that loaned all those millions of florins to the East India Company. And that brings in, you see, turbans, temples, jewels, palm-trees, and what not besides— —"

"So much trouble," breathed Daffingdon; "so much effort; such an expense for costumes."

"And if you want to enlarge the scheme," pursued Virgilia, waiving all considerations of trouble, effort and expense, "so as to include coining, money-changing and all that, why, think what you have then! The brokers at Corinth, the *mensarii* in the Roman Forum. And think of the ducats designed by Da Vinci and by Cellini! And all the Byzantine coins in Gibbon—the student's edition is full of them! Why, there are even the Assyrian tablets— you must have heard about the discovery of the records of that old Babylonian bank. Think of the costumes, the architecture, the square curled beards, the flat winged lions, and all. Why, dear me, I see the whole series of lunettes as good as arranged for, and work laid out for a dozen of you, or more!" cried Virgilia, as she pounced upon a sheet of paper and snatched the pen from Dill.

"A dozen?" he murmured. "A hundred!"

"Nonsense!" she returned. "Four or five of you could manage it very handily. You, and Giles, and——"

"The Academy would expect recognition," said Dill. "One of the professors for a third. And somebody or other from the Warren, I suppose, for a fourth."

"Three subjects apiece, then," said Virgilia. "Go in and win!—By the way, did I mention Phidion of Argos? He was one of the primitive coiners. And then there was Athelstane, who regulated minting among the early Saxons...."

X

Dill passed out into the cool starry night to recover his breath and to regain his composure. It was as if he had struggled through a whirlpool or had wrenched himself away from the downpour of a cataract. Virgilia's interest, her enthusiasm, her co-operation had reared itself above him and toppled over on him just like a high, ponderous wall; the bricks bruised him, the dust of scattered mortar filled his lungs and his eyes. "Such a mind!" he thought; "such readiness; such a fund of information!" Never before had anybody offered so panting, so militant a participation in his doings. He doubted too whether Virgilia could ever have felt so extreme an interest in the doings of any other man whomsoever. Certainly it was a fair surmise that Richard Morrell, during the formative period of the Pin-and-Needle Combine, had never so succeeded in enlisting her sympathy and support,—otherwise she would not have turned him off in the summary fashion that had kept society smiling and gossiping for a fortnight.

As Daffingdon walked thoughtfully down the quiet street a deep sense of gratitude stirred within him—he felt himself prompted to the most chivalrous of acknowledgments. He saw himself taking her hand—with such deliberation as to preclude any shock of surprise, and looking into her eyes as ardently and earnestly as good taste would permit; and heard himself saying, in a voice as tremulous with passion as the voice of a well-bred gentleman could be allowed to become, such things as should make quite unmistakable his appreciation of her qualities both as an amateur and a woman. Certainly if this great undertaking went through he should be able to say all that was in him and to maintain it to the last word. She had turned a deaf ear to others, but there was reason to think she might listen to him.

Then all at once the magnitude of the scheme rose before him; such a vast expenditure of time on books of plates in libraries—and weeks and months to be devoted to sketches, to compositions, to colour-schemes of this sort and that; such a tremendous outlay for models, for costumes, for multifarious accessories! But as Daffingdon gradually pulled himself together, a comforting little sense of flattery came to soothe his bruises and to clear his eyes. Yes, she believed in him. This brilliant and learned young woman had impetuously placed her boundless stores of erudition at his disposal; she had loaded the work of twenty men on his shoulders and was confidently expecting him to carry off the whole vast undertaking with jaunty ease. He must not fail. Fortunately, she was willing to admit the co-operation of a few of his brother artists.

Dill laid her plan—their plan—before two or three of his own guild, experimentally. They gaped at it as a plainsman would gape at the Himalayas. Nor was it, as has been said, the smallest of mouthfuls to himself. However, the distinguished assistance of a young woman of fashion, means and cultivation was not a matter to hide under a bushel; besides, some firm, concrete scheme must be put promptly before the Nine Old Men of the Bank before they should have glued their desires undetachably upon some crude, preposterous plan of their own.

"It would cost like smoke," said Giles, "but it's an idea."

"Let's try it on," said the Academy professor. "It would show us as on deck and would help us to take their measure. Who knows but it might be the means of staving off a series of medallion portraits of the board themselves!"

"An idea, yes," reiterated Giles. "But it lays out a terrible lot of work for us. Such a job would be enormous."

"Tackle it," said Abner Joyce. He claimed as a matter of course the right to be present at such conferences. Joyce himself had the strength and the pluck to tackle anything.

"Well, *let's* try it on," assented Giles. "We've got to cut in first, that's sure—if we can. Come, let's put out our feelers."

This was more or less in harmony with Virgilia's parting advice. "Show them to themselves in historical perspective," she had suggested to Dill in bidding him good-night at the front door,—"the last link in one long, glittering chain. Flatter them; associate them with the Romans and Venetians—bring in the Assyrians if need be. Tell them how the Bardi and the Peruzzi ruled the roost in old Florence. Work in Sir Thomas Gresham and the Royal Exchange—ruffs, rapiers, farthingales, Drake, Shakespeare and the whole 'spacious' time of Elizabeth. Make them a part of the poetry of it—make them a part of the picturesqueness of it. That will bring Mr. Gibbons around easily enough, and ought to budge two or three of the others."

Daffingdon took his great scheme to the bank, but it failed to charm. Andrew P. Hill poked at Daffingdon's neatly drawn-up memorandum with a callous finger and blighted it with an indifferent look out of a lack-lustre eye. The *mensarii* of Rome and the trapezites of Athens seemed a long way off. The picturesque beginnings of the Bank of Genoa left him cold. The raid of the Stuart king on the Tower mint appeared to have very little to do with the case. And Jeremiah McNulty, who happened to be about the premises, showed himself but slightly disposed to fan Hill's feeble interest to a flame.

"This is not just what we want," said Hill. "It is not at all what any of us had in mind. It is very little in accord, I must say, with the ideas I gave you last week. I don't think it will do. Still, if you want to get up some drawings to show about how it would come out, and bring them around in a week or so...."

Daffingdon groaned inwardly; after all, they were wedded to their own notion. He explained to them the unfairness of their proposal—detailing the cost of models, the matter of draperies, the time required for study, the labours and difficulties of composition. To do experimentally what they were asking him to do would be to execute half the entire work on a mere chance.

"Well, we won't buy a pig in a poke," said old Jeremiah sturdily. He was now on the familiar chequered pavement of black and white and felt a good deal at home. "We've got to see what we're going to pay for. That's business."

"Never mind," said Andrew. "After all, we want something nearer to our own time and closer to our own town. We want to show ourselves loyal to the place where we've made our money. We want to put on record the humble beginnings of this great metropolis. The early days of our own city are plenty good enough for us."

"That's right," said Jeremiah. He saw himself a lusty young fellow of twenty-five, the proud new head of a contractor's shop, with his own lumber pile, a dozen lengths of sewer pipe, a mortar bed, a wheelbarrow or two and a horse and cart. No need of going farther back than that. Those early days were glorious and fully worthy to be immortalized.

"We want to make our new building talked about," said Hill. "We want every daily paper in town, and throughout the whole country, to be full of it. We want to make it an object of interest to every man, woman and child in our own community. When the little boys and girls come down Saturday morning to deposit their pennies—for we shall open a savings department that will welcome the humblest—we want them to learn from our walls the story of the struggles and the triumphs of their fathers' early days——"

"That's right," said Jeremiah again. "If you had lived here as long as I have, young man, you would understand that there's no need of going outside our own bor-r-ders for anything we may require."

"Yes, a great deal of history has been transacted on this site," said Hill,—"more than enough to meet the requirements of our present purpose. I have here"—he opened a drawer in one side of his desk and drew out a paper—"I have here a list of subjects that I think would do. Mr. McNulty and I drew it up together. Take it and look it over; it might be an— —"

A shadow darkened the door. It was another interruption from the Morrell Twins. This time it was not Richard Morrell, but Robin, his brother. His pocket bulged with what seemed to be papers of importance, and his face signalled to Andrew P. Hill to clear the deck of lesser matters.

"—it might be an advantage to you," Andrew concluded. "This about represents our ideas; see what you can do with it."

Andrew passed the paper over to Jeremiah, and Jeremiah passed it on to Daffingdon with an expression of unalterable firmness and decision. "You *must* do something with this, if you are going to do anything for us at all," his air said. "It's this or nothing. It is our own idea; we're proud of it, and we insist upon it. Go."

XI

The Morrell Twins were among the newer powers. They had rolled up a surprisingly big fortune—if it *was* a fortune—in a surprisingly short time, and were looked up to as very perfect gentle knights by all the ambitious young fry of the "street." They were the head and front of the Pin-and-Needle Combine. They did not deal with the Grindstone only; they had made their business the business of half the banks of the town,—for how could these institutions be expected to stand out when all the investors and speculators of the street were pressing forward eager to add to their collections a few good specimens of the admirably engraved and printed certificates of the Combine, and more than willing to pay any price that anybody might ask? Some of the banks—the more fortunate among them—were attending to this business during business hours; others of them worked on it overtime, and one or two were beginning to work on it all night as well as all day. They worried. The Twins were not worrying nearly so much,—they knew they must be seen through.

The Twins had been grinding pins and needles for a year or two with striking acumen and dexterity. Sometimes Richard would turn the handle and Robin would hold the poor dull pins to the stone; and then again they would change places. Whichever arrangement happened to be in force, people said the work had never been done more neatly, more precisely. And now the Twins had enlarged their field and had begun to grind noses. They were showing themselves past masters in the art. They had all the legislation of nose-grinding at their fingers' ends; the lack of legislation, too, as well as the probabilities of legislation yet to come. They knew just how fast the wheel might be turned in this State, and just how close the nose might be held in that, and just how loud the victim must cry out before the Rescue Band might be moved to issue from some Committee Room to stop the treatment. They knew where nose-grinding was prohibited altogether, and they knew where enactments against it had thus far completely failed.

They knew where the penalty was likely to be enforced, and they knew where it might be evaded. "Learn familiarly the whole body of legislative enactment, state by state, and then keep a little in advance of it,"—such was their simple rule.

No man is to be denied the right to profit by his own discovery, and so, though the glory of the Twins was envied, their right to luxuriate in it was seldom questioned. They were seen in all sorts of prominent and expensive places—at the opera, at the horse-show, on the golf links, and were very much envied and admired,—envied by other young men that were trying to do as they had done, but not succeeding; admired by multitudes of young women who felt pretty sure that to "have things," and to have them with great abundance and promptness and conspicuousness, was all that made life worth living. In this environment Richard Morrell could hardly fail to be fairly well satisfied with himself. To ask and to receive would come to the same thing. And so he spoke to Virgilia one crisp October morning, between the fifth and sixth holes in Smoky Hollow, and awaited in all confidence her reply. But Virgilia quickly made it plain that he would not do—not for her, at least. She was by no means one of the kind to be impressed by tally-ho coaches, however loudly and discordantly the grooms might trumpet, nor to be brought round by country-club dinners, however deafening the chatter or however preponderant the phalanx of long-necked bottles. So his raw, red face turned a shade redder still; and as he sat, later, on the club veranda, hectoring the waiter and scowling into his empty glass, he growled to himself in a thick undertone:

"What's the matter with the girl, anyway? If she doesn't want me, who does she want?"

Virgilia wanted, in a general way, an intimate and equal companionship, a trafficking in the things that interested her—the higher things, she sometimes called them to herself. She wanted a gentleman; she wanted cultivation, refinement—even to its last debilitating excess. What she wanted least of all was a "provider," a steward, an agent, a business machine. "We must *live*," she would say, looking forward toward her matrimonial ideal; "we mustn't let our whole life run out in a mere stupid endeavour to accumulate the means of living, and then find ourselves only beginning when at the finish:"—an idea held substantially by so different a young person as Preciosa McNulty, who was preparing to set aside her mother's careful ambitions and to take a step forward on her own account. Only, Preciosa was looking less for cultivation and gentility than for "temperament." Less the dry specialist, however successful in the accumulation of this world's goods, than the resonant adventurer that would bring her full chance at all the manifold haps and mishaps of life as it runs.

"Nothing more tedious than a set programme," declared Preciosa. "If my whole future were to be arranged for me to-morrow, I should want to die the day after. A whole play"—Preciosa was a most persevering little theatre-goer—"carried through with one stage-setting—how tiresome that would be!"

XII

"Come, now," said Little O'Grady; "help the lame duck over the stile. Be a good Gowan—give the poor fellow the use of your studio. Mordreth's isn't enough better to be worth asking for, and Stalinski is working from the model. Come,—as a personal favour to me. It was I let you in on the bank scheme and gave you a chance to make big money; and now you must just let Ignace have the use of your place for a few hours—he can't paint the girl's picture in that little hole upstairs."

"Much you let me in!" retorted Gowan with a grin. "Tell me who is in, anyway, and how far, and for how much, and I'll give you half I get."

"Haven't I seen them?" returned Little O'Grady. "Didn't I address the whole board? Didn't I go for them with the architect himself to help me? Haven't I got the mantel-piece in the president's parlour? And now if Ignace can only get a chance to paint the fav'rite grandchild of one of the——Yes, sir; I talked to them as a business-man to business-men, and it went. They're square; they're solid; they'll treat us right. Never you fear. In a year from now you'll be wearing diamonds and saying: 'O'Grady, you're the wan that hung them on me.' *Now* will you give Ignace your room?"

"Why, he's no portrait painter, is he?"

"She thinks he is. And it's what the girls think of us that makes us what we are. As for me, I believe he can do anything. Come, give the poor lad a show."

"What could he do in an hour or two?"

"He could get acquainted with her," said Little O'Grady.

Preciosa, thanks to O'Grady's chatterings through the Temple of Art— he blew in and out with great freedom and was as much at home there as in the humbler establishment—had come to some knowledge of Ignace Prochnow. She learned his name—in itself an immense advance, and the location of his studio; and she arranged with the Gibbons girls, who, by reason of their fencing, were developing great self-reliance and a high capacity for initiative, to search him out in his private haunts.

"Set the day," chirped Little O'Grady, "and we'll be ready for you."

Preciosa set the day; Little O'Grady traced Prochnow's name in elaborate letterings and clapped this new placard over Gowan's own; and all waited intent to see just what of interest would develop in the countenance of the daughter of the McNultys, and just what Ignace Prochnow would be able to make of it.

Preciosa wore her green velvet toque, and let her chestnut hair stray and ramble whithersoever it would, and sat in Gowan's best high-backed mahogany chair with the brass rosettes, and tried to view with kindly indulgence his flimsy knick-knacks and shabby hangings (they came nowhere near Dill's) on account of her interest in their supposed proprietor. Nor did she find in her painter any of Dill's soft suavity. Prochnow was direct and downright almost to brusqueness, seeming to see no need of such graduated preliminaries as even O'Grady found place and reason for. He admired her, and admired her extremely, as she perceived at once; but he offered none of the appropriate deferences that she had received on occasion from obscure young men of less than modest fortune. He was intent, he was earnest, he was even a bit peremptory; but she felt perfectly certain that he was not treating her as a subject and a subject merely. His black eyes looked at her with a sort of sharp severity across the leg of the easel, and his rasping crayon promptly scratched down his impressions upon the promising blank of his canvas. Preciosa was slightly puzzled, but on the whole pleased. She knew she was worth looking at, and felt herself fit to stand the keenest scrutiny. She leaned back easily in her chair. Let time attend to the rest.

"Doesn't she *compose*!" said Little O'Grady in a poignant whisper to Elizabeth Gibbons, as he thrust out his arms akimbo and squinted learnedly at Preciosa through his fingers. "And hasn't the lad got *line*!" he presently added in a rapturous undertone, as the black and white tracing began to take shape. Prochnow was drawing with immense freedom, decision, confidence; every stroke told, and told the first time. "He knows how! He knows *how*!" moaned Little O'Grady, locking his hands and forearms in a strange twist and rocking to and fro with emotion. "He's got the wrist!—the *wrist*!" he exclaimed further, liberating his hands and fanning the air with long pendulous fingers. "There, he's caught her already!" he cried, leaning forward,—"inside of five minutes. Not a line more, Ignace; not a line more!"

Prochnow turned on him with a grim tight smile—a smile that slightly dilated the nostrils of his good firm nose and shifted in ever so small a degree the smutch of black beneath that was slowly advancing to the status of a moustache. It was an acknowledgment from one who *could* to one who *knew*. "Ah, si jeunesse...!" ejaculates the poet; but here *jeunesse*, by a doubling of forces, both *pouvait* and *savait*.

Then Prochnow turned the canvas itself round toward Preciosa. "Does Mademoiselle recognise herself?"

"It's you, Preciosa, to the life," said the daughter of Roscoe Orlando Gibbons.

"Oh, Ig!" cried Little O'Grady, much moved, "you're the king-pin sure. People *shall* know you; people *must* know you!" He faced about toward Preciosa. "Ah, my fair young thing, he's got you dead. Why, Daff himself couldn't have reached this in an hour!"

Preciosa was like most of the rest of us—inclined to take good workmanship for granted; where there was nothing to criticise there was nothing to take hold of. But the words and actions of Little O'Grady—he was now hopping about on one leg, holding the other in his hand—made the matter perfectly certain. Her painter had done a notable thing, and done it easily, promptly, without revisions, without fumblings. His own face and attitude expressed his consciousness of this. "Nobody could have done it better," she read in his eyes; "and you, you blooming young creature, have been the inspiration." He had called her "Mademoiselle" too; could anything be more charming? Nothing save his accent itself,—a trick of the tongue, an intonation ever so slightly alien that addressed her ear just as some perfume's rich but smothered pungency might address the nose. Yes, the first stage in her apotheosis was an undoubted success. All that was needed now was her translation from black and white to colour. Well, the chariot was ready to take her up still higher.

"I have found you very easily, Mademoiselle,"—Preciosa felt a sugary little shudder at this repetition of the word,—"I have found you very easily," said Prochnow, casting about for his palette and brushes; "and now I may just as easily lose you."

"Oh no," said Elizabeth Gibbons, with great earnestness.

"Never fear," said Little O'Grady confidently. "Though the likeness generally gets submerged at first, it comes to the surface again in the end."

"Don't risk it," continued Elizabeth Gibbons.

"What has been done once," said Prochnow, motioning with a brush-handle toward the charcoal sketch, "can be done once more."

Prochnow handled his brushes with the same firmness and confidence that he had shown in handling his crayon. The "resemblance" soon sank beneath the waves, as prophesied, but Little O'Grady continued to ride on the topmost crest with unabated enthusiasm. "Whee! hasn't he got the nerve! hasn't he got the stroke! Doesn't he just more than slather it on!" he cried. "Catch the shadows in that green velvet! R-r-rip!—and the high light on that tan jacket!" he proceeded in a smothered shout, as he nudged Elizabeth Gibbons in the side. Elizabeth had never been nudged before, and moved farther down the settle, after giving him a *look*. Little O'Grady, who never knew when he was squelched—he never, as a fact, had been squelched by anybody whomsoever—moved along after her. "Oh, my! Can't he *paint*! Can't he more than lay it *on*! Did you get that last one, now?"

Buoyed up by such support as this, Prochnow forged ahead with quadrupled *brio*, and Preciosa felt the chariot rising heavenward cloud by cloud. Little O'Grady continued to lead the performance, prompting Preciosa to look her prettiest and Prochnow to do his best. "Ah, my sweet child," he declared, "you've fallen into good hands. You're trying to get away, true: you've nearly lost those bright eyes, and I wouldn't want to swear to your ears or your chin, just yet; but your blessed old-gold hair is there all right, and it's put on to stay. The rest of you will be coming back tomorrow, or next day, or the day after. And then you'll be all on deck, jew'l. You'll see; you'll hear; you'll speak, by heaven! Won't she, Lizzie?"

Miss Gibbons gave Little O'Grady another *look*. Preciosa paused in her heavenward ascent, and seemed to be wondering with a questioning little glance just how far along, after all, she had got. When she finally left her high-backed chair—"That's as far as we will go to-day," Prochnow had said—she felt herself very close to earth again: the cherished "resemblance" had vanished altogether. But Prochnow seemed satisfied with the result, and Little O'Grady was rapturously fluent over the brushwork. "Ignace is a wunder-kind," he declared to the doubting girl. "I never saw such swing, such certainty. He'll fish you back, and he'll have you to the life in less than a week. Or I'll eat my hat."

There was a knock at the door. O'Grady rushed to open it. "Go right away," Miss Gibbons thought she heard him say, in a tense undertone.

> The face of Kitty Gowan showed in the doorway, puzzled, protesting. Medora Joyce was behind, her hands full of parcels.

"Go away?" repeated Mrs. Gowan. "What does this mean? Let me in at once."

"Depart!" hissed Little O'Grady. "This is not Mr. Prochnow's day. Come to-morrow."

"Step aside, O'Grady," said Kitty Gowan spunkily. "Let me pass." An afternoon of shopping had tired her and shortened her temper.

"Well, as a visitor, possibly," said O'Grady condescendingly. "Ignace, do you feel disposed to — —" He glanced back and forth between Prochnow and the petitioners.

Prochnow took down the canvas and set its face against the wall.

Kitty Gowan strode in holding her head high. "How do?" she said carelessly, by way of general salute. "Sit there, Medora," she directed Mrs. Joyce, indicating a chair.

"Sit here, Medora," said O'Grady firmly, placing another. "Prochnow, Preciosa dear, allow me to present— —" and so on. "And you sit here," he said to Kitty Gowan, placing a third chair. "You're a visitor, remember," he whispered to her fiercely; "so behave like one. Stay where you're put and don't own the earth. We have loaned the shop for the day. Understand?"

Preciosa passed lightly over Kitty Gowan, whom she found brusque in her manners and plain in her looks; but she fixed her best attention on Medora, with whom she was as much charmed as at the first. Idealist and heroine-worshipper, she was always ready to prostrate herself before a young married woman of Medora's gracious and fashionable cast.

O'Grady lingered over Medora's chair. "We've had a wonderful session," he said, laying his hand affectionately on her shoulder. "You ought to have come a bit sooner, my dear."

Preciosa shivered. It was like the profanation of an idol.

Medora unconcernedly pushed away his hand. Preciosa envied such serenity and self-poise.

"Why, how's this?" asked O'Grady, studying his hand curiously, as some detached thing, some superfluity rejected and returned. "Ain't we friends? Ain't we old pals? You can't mean to stand me off with your London clothes and your London manners? Don't say you're trying to do that, Dodie!"

Preciosa shuddered. Medora laughed carelessly—oh, how could she! Kitty Gowan jumped up and boxed O'Grady's ear with one of Medora's long, flat parcels. "Get away, you saucy child!" she said.

O'Grady grimaced and nursed his ear. "It serves you right!" said Elizabeth Gibbons tartly.

Preciosa was placated; the great retribution had fallen. She banished the wish that she herself might have had the daring to be a third avenging fury, and fell to studying the folds of Medora's bottle-green cloak. She wondered if she herself were not as pretty as Mrs. Joyce—oh, in an entirely different way!—and if she were glad or sorry that Medora and her companion had come a little late for seeing the picture. Would it be a success—this portrait? Was it all that Mr. Prochnow's lively little friend seemed to think?

Prochnow, putting away his palette and brushes, grandly overlooked the late irruption of trivialities. He glanced across to Preciosa, and she felt that he was thanking her for having held herself quite aloof from them.

Preciosa went away not completely reassured, yet on the whole pretty well pleased. She felt that she had been taken hold of by a strong, decided hand. She had made an excursion into a new land where feeble compliments were dispensed with and where meek-eyed ingratiation seemed not to exist. Yes, he was a forcible, clever fellow. That Virgilia Jeffreys should have tried to make her think anything else, and that she should have permitted Virgilia to make the attempt! She should see Virgilia soon, somewhere, and should regain the lost ground; she should not allow herself to be walked over a second time. She should probably say something very cutting, too—if she could but find the right words. Suppose she were younger than Virgilia and less expert? Was that any reason why she should be played with, be cajoled into making fun of a——Yes, Ignace Prochnow was a fine clever fellow; good-looking too, in a way; and masterful, beyond a doubt. Had she been kind enough to him to cancel her cruelty at their first meeting? She was afraid not. Should she have been kinder but for the abundance of company and the absorbing nature of the work? Probably so. Should she be kinder next time? That would depend on him;—yes, if he became a little less professional and a little more personal. Would he become so? She hoped he might. And if he didn't? Then he might be encouraged to. How? Preciosa opened her purse for her fare and postponed an answer.

At that same moment, Prochnow, banished along with the canvas to his own room by the return of Gowan, sat staring at the portrait as it stood propped against his trunk. Little O'Grady, if he had been present, instead of being occupied on the other side of the partition in sweeping up the dried plaster that littered his floor, would have decided that the personal interest was in fair proportion to the professional, and would have rated Prochnow no higher as an artist than as a man.

XIII

Virgilia, after dismissing Daffingdon with the detailed memoranda of her great decorative scheme, went through the vain forms of going upstairs and getting to bed. But sleep was out of the question. Her brain still kept at work, elaborating the ideas already proposed and adding still others to the plan. Why hadn't she laid more stress on the Medici? How had she contrived to overlook John Law and the South Sea Bubble, with all its attendant wigs, hooped petticoats and shoe-buckles? Then the Pine-Tree Shilling jumped to her eyes, and Virginia's use of tobacco as a currency;—possibly the entire scheme might be arranged on a purely American basis, in case sympathy for her wider outlook were to fail.

Virgilia ate her breakfast soberly enough; she checked all tendency toward expansiveness with her own people, who were sadly earth-bound and utilitarian. But immediately after breakfast she put on her things and stepped round the corner to have a confab with her aunt. She found Eudoxia upstairs, clad in a voluminous dressing-gown and struggling with her over-plump arms against the rebelliousness of her all but inaccessible back hair. Virgilia was very vivid and sprightly in her report on the evening's conference, and Eudoxia, studying her with some closeness, was barely able to apply the check when she found herself asking:

"Has he—has he——?"

Virgilia dropped her eyes. No, he hadn't.

But the acceptance of these magnificent proposals might easily make another proposal possible, and again Eudoxia Pence asked herself:

"Do I want it, or don't I? Certainly only the bank's acceptance of Daff's scheme will make possible Virgilia's acceptance of Daff himself."

That evening Dill called again on Virgilia, bringing the Hill-McNulty plan.

"So *this* is the sort of thing they want?" she cried. "They insist on it, after all, do they?" She cast her eye over the paper and hardly knew whether to laugh or to weep. "'The First Fire-Engine House,'" she read. "'Old Fort

Kinzie'; 'The Grape-Vine Ferry'; 'The Early Water-Works'—oh, this is terrible!" she exclaimed.

"Read on," said Dill plaintively.

"'The Wigwam'— —"

"What in heaven's name is that?"

"A place where they used to hold conventions, I believe. 'The Succotash Tavern'— —"

"What does that mean?"

"I've heard it spoken of, I think," said Virgilia faintly. "It was built of cottonwood logs and stood at the fork in the river. 'The Hard-Shell Baptist Church,'— —" she read on.

"Do you know anything about that?"

"I think I've seen it in old photographs. It stood on one side of Court-House Square."

"Did it have a steeple?" asked Dill droopingly.

"I believe it did—quite a tall one."

"Of course it did!" he groaned. "And so it goes. One building hugs the ground and the next cleaves the sky. Yet they've all got to be used for the decorative filling of a lot of spaces precisely alike."

"What does Giles think of this?" asked Virgilia.

"He's crazy."

"And Adams, at the Academy?"

"He's gone out to buy a rope."

"And Little O'Grady?"

"He fell over in a dead faint. He's lying in it yet. But before he lost consciousness he made one suggestion— —"

"What was it?"

Dill paused. "Have you ever heard of a painter named Proch—Prochnow?" he presently asked, with some disrelish. "A newcomer, I believe."

"I don't think I have."

"He has lately taken a studio in the Warren. O'Grady has seen his work and speaks well of it."

"What particular kind of work?"

"Decorative. Portraits too, I understand. He has been doing one of that little Miss McNulty."

Virgilia frowned. "What!" she was thinking to herself, "have I been taken in by that viper, that traitress?—by a child who looked like an innocent flower and is turning out to be the serpent under it? Prochnow!—the hard name that nobody could pronounce! It's easy enough: Prochnow; Prochnow. She could have pronounced it fast enough if she had wanted to! And now she has gone over to the other side and taken O'Grady with her—and her grandfather too!" Then, aloud:

"Well?"

"O'Grady says he's full of—ideas——"

"And what has O'Grady got to do with it?" asked Virgilia tartly. "Has anybody asked his help? Why is he mixing up in the matter, anyway? And if he wants to suggest, let him stop suggesting painters and suggest a few sculptors. I haven't heard of his doing anything like that!"

Dill sighed wearily. "You can't keep O'Grady out if he wants to get in. But I must say I hadn't expected to be loaded down with any more of the Warren people. Gowan is more a drag than a help, and O'Grady is doing all he can to bring us under a cloud. The directors can't understand such freedom, such language, such shabbiness, such Bohemianism. Take it all around, they are making it a heavier load than I can carry through."

"And now they want to add another of their miserable crowd to it. Well, there will be no room for Prochnows and their ideas," declared Virgilia, wounded in her tenderest point. "*We* will attend to the ideas. Let us take Hill's absurd notion, if we must, and rush in and wrench victory from defeat. Let us take his cabins and taverns and towers and steeples and use them in the background——"

"That would be the only way."

"—and then put in people—Hill and McNulty can't be insisting upon mere 'views.' Fill up your foregrounds with traders and hunters and Indians and 'early settlers' and 'prairie-schooners'——"

"Giles has gone out to bring them round to something like that."

"They really won't have the Bank of Genoa? They won't listen to Phidion of Argos?"

"I couldn't bring them within hailing distance of him."

"Where is Roscoe Orlando Gibbons in such an hour as this?"

"I haven't been able to find him."

"*I* shall find him. Aunt Eudoxia is a large stock-holder in that wretched bank, and he's the only man of taste and refinement on the board. If we have lost Jeremiah, that's all the more reason why we should have Roscoe Orlando. I shall get her and go to his office at once. He can't refuse support to our plan; he won't let this barbarous notion of Hill's make any headway."

Dill looked at Virgilia with mounting appreciation. Where was her equal for resource, for elasticity, for devotion, for erudition? She was at home in Grote and Sismondi, and she was just as much at home in the early local annals of the town itself. She knew about the Parthenon and Giotto's Tower, and she knew about the Succotash Tavern and the Hard-Shell Baptist Meeting-House too. With matchless promptitude and resiliency she began the broad sketching out of an entirely new scheme—a thoroughly local one. Was there not Pere Marquette and the Sieur Joliet and La Salle and Governor D'Artaguette? Was there not the Fort Kinzie Massacre and the Last War-Dance of the Pottawatomies? Was there not the prairie mail-coach and the arrival of the first vessel in the harbour? Were there not traders and treaties and Indian commissioners? "There!" she cried, "you and Stephen Giles just sharpen your teeth on such matters as those! We have almost got the Nine Old Ogres on the run, and we mustn't slow up on them for a single minute!"

Dill stared at her with dazzled eyes. Such vim, such spirit, such knowledge, such loyalty!—and all for him, all in his service! He felt confusedly that he was upon the verge of taking her hand and saying in broken trembling tones that she was his guiding star, his ruling spirit, his steadfast hope—what lesser expressions could fitly voice his gratitude, his admiration, his devotion? Then he caught himself: things were still in the air. His fortune was yet to be made, and who could say but that its making might yet be marred? Let him once come to an understanding with those trying old fellows, let him but have a hard-and-fast agreement with them in downright black and white, and then—who could tell what might be said and done?

XIV

Dill and his coadjutors had two or three more conferences, and a second detailed scheme was sent over to the bank. History in general was decisively thrust aside,—the only history worth recording was the history the Nine themselves had helped to make. "We will go to the libraries for 'ana,'" said Gowan; "they will help us with the earlier years of the last century."

"And to the Historical Association for more," said Giles. "Old Oliver Dowd is an ex-secretary of it, and him at least we can capture beyond a doubt."

"Hurray!" cried Little O'Grady, who had insisted on being present. That very afternoon he threw his "First Coinage of Venetian Sequins" back into the clay-box and started in on a relief of "The Earliest Issue of Wild-Cat Currency."

"We've got a good thing this time," said Adams. "It's homogeneous; it's picturesque; it's local. It gives all they want and a great deal more. I think we can tussle with it successfully and not be ashamed of the outcome."

"As business-men they ought to appreciate the completeness of our new scheme," said Giles, "and our promptness in furnishing it."

"They will," said Joyce. "This beats the other idea all hollow. Go in and win."

Each one of them spoke in terms of unwonted confidence. Little O'Grady himself was in such a state of irrepressible buoyancy that he left the earth and fairly sailed among the clouds. All this reacted on Dill. For the first time he felt the great commission fully within his grasp and the net profits as safely to be counted upon. He began to warm to his subjects. To him, who had learned a good deal in regard to shipping and the handling of water from lounging about the ports of Marseilles and Leghorn, had fallen the arrival of the first vessel: he would reconstruct the primitive lighthouse that Mr. Hill had set his heart on, and would eke out the angular emptiness of the subject by a varied group of expectant pioneers big in the foreground. He had also taken the Baptist church, of whose Bible-class Andrew P. Hill had been a member. He would suppress the spire, and would show the pillared front on some Sunday morning in midsummer, with an abundance of wide petticoats and deep bonnets of the period of 1845, or thereabouts, displayed upon its front steps. And finally, as he was fairly strong on figures in action, he had intrepidly undertaken the Pottawatomie war-dance; and as soon as the conference in Giles's studio broke up, he took the express-train out to the Memorial Museum to see what the ethnological department there could do for him in the way of moccasins, tomahawks and war-bonnets.

He made his way through several halls filled with tall glass cases, skirting the Polynesians, bearing away from the Eskimos and finally reaching the North Americans. Their room was empty, save for a slender girl in brown who was making notes on a collection of war-bonnets in a morocco memorandum-book. It was Virgilia.

"Why, what are you doing out here?" he asked.

"Turning the odd moments to account. Collecting data for you on the aborigines,—I am sure we can put them to use. I ran out to hear the lecture on Earthquakes in Japan—you know I have a chance to go there with the Knotts in April—and I thought I might incidentally pick up a few notions for the War-Dance."

So authentic and thoroughgoing a piece of loyalty as this affected Dill tremendously; the hint of an Oriental exodus scarcely less so. Never should she go to Japan with the Knotts; she should go with him. His share in the work at the Grindstone would make this the easiest as well as the most delightful of possibilities. Now was the time; no matter about waiting for the contract. He felt the flood rising within him. Here at last was the moment for taking her hand (she had put the memorandum-book back into her pocket), and for looking earnestly into her eyes with all the ardour perfect good taste would permit, and for saying in a voice tremulous with well-bred passion the words that would make her his loyal coadjutor through life. These different things he now said and did with a flawless technique (Virgilia recalled how sadly the young real-estate dealer had boggled), and a row of gaudy Buddhistic idols that looked in through the wide door leading to the Chinese section stood witnesses to her unaffected surrender. The pair passed back through the Aztecs and the South Sea Islanders in a maze of happy murmurs and whisperings, and when next Eudoxia Pence asked her niece:

"Has he—has he——?"

Virgilia, as she again dropped her eyes, was able to reply, this time:

"He has."

Daffingdon and Virgilia passed out through the great row of Ionic columns and down the wide flight of steps into the bare, brown wind-swept landscapes of the park.

"And about Japan?" asked Dill. "You can wait a year longer for that, can't you? We shall find the earthquakes just the same."

Virgilia laughed happily. "Of course I can. What will such a year count for as a mere delay?—a year so short, so full, so busy, so happy, so successful! By *next* February we shall be famous, we shall be rich, the whole country will be ringing with our pictures——"

Dill found it easy to fall in with her mood. He foresaw the immediate acceptance of a scheme so complete and so well-considered; the early signing of a binding contract; the receipt, without undue delay, of his honorarium—a business-like tribute from a methodical and trustworthy body of business-men; growing fame, increasing prosperity——After all, why dwell on Japan? The world was beautiful everywhere, even in the bare, flat rawness of the suburbs.

XV

A few days later, and his bold step seemed justified. The directors were an elusive body, and even when got together they found it hard to act with anything like unanimity and despatch; but one afternoon Stephen Giles encountered Mr. Holbrook in the office of one of the hotels and was told that the plan was receiving favourable consideration and was not unlikely to be accepted. As Mr. Holbrook was the most passive member of the directorate, drifting quietly along with the general current, it seemed safe to accept him as representing the feeling of that body.

Giles carried the good news to Adams, at the Academy. Adams hurried home with it to his wife and little Frankie.

A few days more, and it laboriously transpired that old Jeremiah McNulty was readjusting himself to the plan as modified and elaborated by Dill and his associates. Old Jeremiah was particularly taken by the idea of the First Ferry—suggesting only that the scene be slightly enlarged, so as to take in the site of his early "yard."

"At last we're gathering them in!" declared Adams to his wife. They began to figure up their share of the spoils and to study how they would lay this immense sum out.

First of all they would bring a smile to the wan face of a patient landlord by paying the back rent in full. As for the rest, Frankie must have a pair of new shoes; and a thousand dollars at least must be placed on deposit in some good savings bank.

"For we have never been able to put anything by, and now at last comes this chance to provide for the rainy day." They looked at each other in mutual content and admiration—this was prudence, this was thrift.

Next, word came to Dill that the attorney for the bank was actually engaged in drawing up the contract. "We may even be able to sign it tomorrow," he said to Virgilia. "We shall have Japan in good season, and much more in between. Tell me; are we not selfish in keeping our happiness to ourselves? Shall you not——"

"I am ready to let the whole world know, dear Daff," she responded. "And oh, to think that I have had my part in bringing your great good fortune about!"

At the very moment when Daffingdon and Virgilia were taking notes on the aborigines and planning for Japan, Preciosa McNulty was strolling with Ignace Prochnow through the galleries of the Art Academy. The portrait was now finished. The submerged "resemblance" had risen once more to the surface, as Little O'Grady had foretold, and the canvas had been borne home in triumph to Preciosa's fond, admiring family.

"Who did it?" asked her grandfather, boundlessly pleased.

"That young man," replied Preciosa.

"What young man?"

"The one who came here that night and threw those big sheets of paper all over the furniture."

"It's you to the life, my child," he said.

"Grandpa," proceeded Preciosa, "I want him to come here again and throw some more sheets over the furniture. He's awfully smart, and he's just bursting with ideas."

Her grandfather scratched his chin. There were so many smart young men bursting with ideas—the wrong sort of ideas. "Let him go to Mr. Hill."

"They're better than those others were."

Still the old man shook his head. "Let him go to Mr. Hill," he repeated.

"With a letter or something from you?"

"Let him go and talk for himself."

"No. You just sit down and write it now." Then, to herself: "There! I think Virgilia Jeffreys will find she can't wind me round her finger quite as easily as she thought she could!"

Preciosa gave Prochnow his letter in front of the Parthenon pediment (where the current of visitors was thinnest), and counselled him to advance on the Grindstone. He was as quick and clever as any of them, she declared, and was entitled to take his share.

Prochnow tossed his head. "I don't know that I care for a 'share,'" he said.

"Do you want to do it all?" asked Preciosa, awe-struck.

"All or none," replied Prochnow loftily. "I am not one to co-operate. I could do the whole as easily as a part."

They strolled on through one spacious hall after another; none seemed too roomy for the manoeuvres of this young genius. The largest studio in the Burrow, Gowan's own, cramped him—most of all on the days when

Mrs. Gowan came down, set forth the tea-pot, lit up her candles and gave her moving little imitation of the handsomer functions that took place through the upper tiers of the Temple of Art. Prochnow had scant patience with the mild hospitalities that accompanied, obbligato-like, art's onward course; he could not accommodate himself, he could not fit in. There were days when the streets and the parks themselves seemed none too spacious, and Preciosa, who was beginning to accompany him abroad, soon got the widest notion of his limitless expansiveness. He saw things with an eye that was new, informed, penetrating, and he spread comments acute, critical, pungent, with the freest possible tongue. He showed her the tawdry, restless vulgarity of the architecture along the most splendid of her favourite thoroughfares, and the ludicrousness of much of the sculpture that cumbered the public parks; and with the mercilessness of youth for mediocrity in his seniors, the *arrives*, he would run through the canvases of current exhibitions, displaying an abrupt arrogance, a bald, raw, cursory cruelty that only the Uebermensch of art would have ventured to employ.

"And what do you think of our front parlour furniture?" asked Preciosa; "and of all that fancy woodwork on our cupola?"

Prochnow placed his hand over his mouth and turned away. It seemed as if these things were too awful for characterization, yet he would spare them for her sake. Let him laugh, though, if he wished; and she would laugh with him.

Thus her world daily became smaller, more insignificant, less to be regarded, while Ignace himself grew bigger, more preponderant. How could she refuse confidence in one who had such boundless confidence in himself?

In the course of these strolls he told her something about his own early life. He had been born, she made out, somewhere between the Danube and the Oder; he spoke familiarly of the frontier of Silesia. He had studied in Munich and Vienna, and some of his things—sumptuous, highly-charged, over-luscious—showed clearly enough the influence of Makart and the lawless vicinity of gipsy Hungary. He had crossed to America with his family five years before; they were still in New Jersey. "They came half-way," he declared; "and I have come all the way—an adventurer in a new land."

Preciosa tried to realize the newness, which she had always taken for granted, and the remoteness, which had never made itself particularly plain to her consciousness; all this that she might reach some appreciation of his venturesomeness,—a gallant, spirited quality not misplaced in one so youthful, so self-confident, so fitted for success and mastery.

"Well, you're ready for one adventure, anyway," declared Preciosa, motioning toward the letter still held in Prochnow's brown, veined hand. She saw herself helping him into the saddle and passing him up his lance.

"So I am," he acquiesced. He brought his eyes back from the large, pale, formidable Amazonian figures before him to the warm-hearted, warm-coloured little creature by his side. Her wealth of chestnut hair was glowing in its most artful disorder; and there was limitless enticement in the turn of her long curling eyelashes, just on a level with his moustache-to-be. Her slim little body was subordinated to her head and to her spreading hat in precisely the degree imposed by modern taste and recognised by the canons of modern art; nothing less grandiose, pallid, remote was to be imagined. Her dress, full of rich, daring colours and latter-day complications of design, completed the spell; those very large white women in crinkled draperies might remain where they were, when such a one as this was here, as close to him as his own self, as contemporaneous as the last stroke of the clock, as rich and brilliant in colouring as any of the canvases of his master's master, as necessary as bread and wine. He must put to its best use the weapon she had placed in his hand, when there was so much—all the world, in fact—to gain.

> "Do your best," said Preciosa, mindful of the portfolios that Little O'Grady had lugged downstairs and had opened in Festus Gowan's studio. "Leave them all behind," she added, feeling as keenly as ever the smart of her feeble complaisance toward Virgilia Jeffreys.

"Can I fail with such encouragement?" asked Prochnow, in an intonation unwontedly tender, as he tried to look under those long curling lashes.

Preciosa flushed—a thing those great, over-admired marble women would have tried in vain to do. Yes, she was no closer to him than she was necessary to him. He began to look forward to the time when he might take her by the hand, restraining such modest impulse as she was now showing to move on to the next room, and reproduce that blush by telling her all she was to him and must be ever. Only the wills, the whims, the prejudices of a few unenlightened old men stood in his way; these he must bend, dissipate, brush aside. He felt himself equal to the task.

XVI

Eudoxia Pence, after receiving the news of Virgilia's engagement, felt more easy in her mind; she knew, now, just what ground she stood on and saw just what she had to do. She realized that she had rather liked Daffingdon Dill all along and had secretly been hoping that he and Virgilia would hit it off. What she must see to was that Daffingdon got the commission from the Grindstone, or his proper share in it: those nine old men must accept his ideas and his sketches if this marriage were to become a fact. Virgilia, who always ran with wealthy people, often gave the impression of possessing greater means than she really commanded; this was doubly serious when it came to her taking up with a man who was altogether dependent on his wits, his skill and his invention, and subject to the passing whims of a fickle public taste. She went down to the library, to discuss the affair with her husband.

"It isn't as if Palmyra had been left with abundant means and only one daughter," she submitted. "It's different when Virgilia is one of four. And her brother is too taken up with his own wife and children to be of— —Are you listening, Palmer?"

"Eh? What's that?" asked her husband, lifting his elderly face from a mass of papers that lay in the bright circle made by the library lamp. He was generally deep in his own concerns, and they were large ones. He seldom gave more than scant attention to such domestic details as developed from relations through marriage.

Eudoxia sighed and forbore to tax him further. And when, next morning, Virgilia came round to report the fate of the second decorative scheme she sighed again.

For the new plan had not been successful, after all; it had failed ignominiously at the eleventh hour. A great deal of effort had been expended in the private office of this director and that, and a futile attempt made to bring four or five of them together at the office of the bank itself, that the matter might be clenched and the contract signed. But the directors were elusive, and cost a great deal of time; and when found, evasive, and cost a great deal of patience. But it was the delay that had worked the ruin. It gave opportunity for tangles and hitches, for the reconsideration of points already settled, for the insinuation of doubts as to this, that and the other.

Andrew P. Hill developed a sulky dislike for all the laboured superfluities that now encumbered the chaste simplicity of his original conception, and Roscoe Orlando Gibbons began to question (though, to tell the truth, he was just about to bring forward a candidate of his own) whether the artists thus far considered were sufficiently skilled to carry out the work. As a matter of fact, the only striking and convincing demonstration of ability witnessed thus far was that reported by his daughter from the studio of Festus Gowan.

No, that overwrought presentation of early local history was not quite what they wanted. The contract remained unsigned, and presently it slid off into the waste-paper basket under Andrew P. Hill's desk.

The whole circle boiled at this outrage. Joyce, who was highly articulate and who possessed a tremendous capacity for indignation, would have made himself a mouth-piece to voice the protests of his infuriate friends; but Little O'Grady wrenched the task from him.

O'Grady could not contain himself—nor did he try to. "This is business-dealing with business-men, is it?" he cried to Dill. "This is what comes of treating with solid citizens of means and method, is it? Where is my hat? I'll go round to that bank and just tell them what I— —"

"O'Grady!" protested Dill. "Behave! or you'll have the fat in the fire for good and all."

"No, Daff," insisted Little O'Grady. "I got you into this, and now— —"

"I don't understand it so," said Dill coldly.

"Oh yes, I did. And now I'll see you through. Where is my hat?"

While Daffingdon was trying to hold O'Grady in check, Virgilia was making moan to her aunt.

She sat down on Eudoxia's bed with a desperate flounce. "They don't want it! What, in heaven's name, do they want?" she asked angrily. "I think it is time for you, aunt, to make yourself felt. You are as much interested in the bank as any of them, and as much entitled to speak. Go down there as a stock-holder and find out what they are trying to do."

"I will if you wish," said her aunt. "In the meantime, why don't you go round and talk to Mr. Gibbons? He's an agreeable enough man, and the only one of the lot that knows anything about such things. Learn from him, if you can, what the trouble is."

Virgilia found Roscoe Orlando Gibbons in the midst of his plats and charts—he was pushing a new subdivision to the northward; but he gallantly dropped his work at the entrance of a lady.

Virgilia asked for his support; she appealed to him both as a man of business who should be willing to carry on things in a business way, and as a cultivated amateur whose influence should not fail in supporting a fine scheme contrived by reputable artists.

"Ah—um, yes," replied Roscoe Orlando vaguely. "The town is developing a number of strong talents—really, we are pushing ahead wonderfully. I—ah, in fact, I may say," he went on, with some little grandiloquence, "that I have just been the means of bringing such a talent to light myself—an absolute discovery, and one of no little importance."

"Indeed?" said Virgilia coldly.

"Yes; a young Pole—a young Bohemian—a young I-don't-know-what." Roscoe Orlando waved his fingers with a vague, easy carelessness. "His name is Prochnow. Very, very gifted. I found him living out on the West Side—incredible distance—impossible neighbourhood—starving in the midst of masterpieces," pursued Roscoe Orlando complacently. "I bought a few."

"Prochnow!" thought Virgilia angrily; "that fellow who painted Preciosa McNulty's portrait!" He had doubtless won over old Jeremiah by that stroke, and now he was running off with Roscoe Orlando Gibbons. It was little less than a landslide; she and her aunt must stop it.

"One of his pictures is in my own drawing-room," said Gibbons. "The other I have presented to our club. Such colour!" he cried, rolling his eyes. "Such composition!" he added, running his fat fingers through his whiskers. "A talent of the first order; more—an out-and-out genius!" he concluded.

Yes, it was Roscoe Orlando who had purchased Prochnow's pictures and thus enabled him to take quarters in the Burrow. They were large unwieldy things, painted in the latter days of his Viennese apprenticeship, and they had cost him cruelly for freight and storage; but he had always clung to the belief that he could sell them sometime, to somebody: at least, they would serve to show what he could do. Or rather, what he had once done and been satisfied to do. He should hardly care to do such things now; he was not ashamed of them—he had merely left them a little behind.

"Oh, Ig, Ig, Ig!" Little O'Grady had cried upon learning of all this, "why won't you be fair and above-board? Why will you be so secretive, so self-sufficient? Why didn't you tell me it was Roscoe Orlando Gibbons who had bought those pictures?"

"Why, what difference does it make?" asked the other, in wonder.

"It makes all the difference in the world—to anybody who knows this town and its people. Has nobody ever told you that Roscoe Orlando Gibbons was one of the directors of the Grindstone?"

"No."

"Well, he is, and you've got him on your side. Did you say he had given one of 'em to some club?"

"Yes. Why?"

"What club?"

"The——. Is there such a club as the Michigan?"

"Yes. And old Oliver Dowd is the president of it. Now you can get *him* too."

"Him?"

"Yes; he's another of the directors. Oh, Ignace, you poor lost lamb, why haven't you told your Terence all these things before?"

As a fact, Roscoe Orlando's gift to the club (it had not cost him any great sum) had been accepted with empressement and given a good place in the general lounge. The younger members welcomed it gladly. It presented an odalisque, very small in the waist and with a wealth of tawny hair black in the shadows; the foreground was a matter of fountain basins and barbaric rugs; infants with prominent foreheads waved palm-branches in the corners; and one or two muscular bronzed slaves loomed up in the dim background. Dill, who had some acquaintance among the members of the club and was now and then asked in to lunch, was promptly brought up to look at it. To him it had a public, official aspect, not amiss in that place— surely the lady offered herself most admirably to the general male gaze. The thing was done knowingly, and with a certain *brio*, he acknowledged; but it seemed rather exotic and already slightly out of date. He saw Roscoe Orlando Gibbons openly gloating over its floridity, and bringing up other members, old and young, to gloat with him; but he thought it more than doubtful whether its dripping lusciousness would prove grateful to the dry mind and sapless person of Oliver Dowd. And he was glad to notice that Abner Joyce, who had lately joined (in the hope that the club's well-known interest in public affairs would offer him some opportunity to work for civic and national betterment), turned away from Gibbons's ill-judged offering with disdain and disgust.

"The fellow has training and facility," said Daffingdon; "but a great monumental scheme conceived in such a spirit as that——No, we have nothing to fear from him."

But there was much to fear from the complacency of Roscoe Orlando Gibbons. Could he, as he asked Virgilia with a maddening, self-satisfied smile, withdraw his support from a talent that he had introduced into his own house and indorsed in the eyes of the commercial and professional public? Virgilia saw that what she had to contend against was vanity, and she went away in very low spirits. If Prochnow had but come to Roscoe Orlando's notice through the ordinary channels! If his patron were not glowing, palpitating, expanding with the conscious joy of discovery! But crude ore brought to light by our own pick and shovel is more precious to us than refined gold that enters into circulation through the assayer and the mint.

"Ugh!" said Virgilia to her aunt; "you should have heard him. He simply—*blatted*. It was disgusting. And now, what are we going to do?"

XVII

"We must get at the girl herself," declared Eudoxia,—"that is, if it isn't too late, if she isn't utterly infatuated with him."

"I don't think I've heard as much as *that* said," replied Virgilia. She knew of but one young woman who might justly go to such a length. "What shall you do first? Shall you ask her to pour tea?"

"No need, yet, of going as far as that. Can't you get together a little party and give her a sort of lunch out at the Whip and Spur? Then one of us, I suppose, might call on her mother—if she's got one."

"Whatever you suggest," said Virgilia, with a suppressed sob. "You may think I'm a perpetual fount of ideas, but I'm not." The Grindstone's rejection of her second scheme had hurt her cruelly. She put her handkerchief to her eyes—as if she had become, instead, a fount of tears.

And as such she next appeared to Dill. "I felt so sure, dear Daff, that we could put it through," she mourned. "And now—and now——"

Daffingdon drew her discouraged head down against his shoulder, in his most noble and manful mode. "Let the lions take us, if they will," he seemed to say, casting his eyes around the arena.

Little O'Grady came over, bearing a martyr's palm. The universal sadness was reflected in his face. Little Frankie Adams was to go along wearing his old shoes, and Kitty Gowan, who had been figuring on a belated winter suit, had tearfully thrown a handful of samples in the fire and put the fond notion aside.

Little O'Grady wiped a sympathetic eye. "Oh, Daff, I'm so sorry for you; just at the time, too, when——" He dared not proceed, awed by Dill's protesting pathos. "Come, now," he ventured presently, "why shouldn't we let Ignace in on this? He's so inventive; he's so full of ideas——"

Daffingdon recalled the sensuous Oriental masterpiece at the club and saw no reason why the possessor of such a particular talent could be expected to succeed in a bank. He shook his head; no member of another sect—no heretical Viennese—should share his martyrdom with him. This left Prochnow free to rush upon the lions on his own account. Little O'Grady, returning to the Rabbit-Hutch, found his neighbour's loins fully girded for the task—the fine frenzy of inspiration had already turned the place upside down.

"That's right, Ignace!" he called from the threshold; "sail in. What is the plan this time?" he asked, tiptoeing along over the scattered sheets that littered the floor.

Prochnow ran his nervous fingers through his wild black forelock, and cast on Little O'Grady a piercing, inspirational glance from a pair of glittering eyes.

"The two great modern forces," he pronounced, "are Science and Democracy. I shall show how each has contributed to the progress of society. Science shall have the six lunettes on the right and Democracy the six on the left."

"H'm," said Little O'Grady; "an allegory?"

"Precisely. No better basis for a grand monumental work."

"Well, Ignace," declared Little O'Grady, "you'll put it through if anybody can!"

He hurried back to his own room, shrugged himself into his plaster-flecked blouse of robin's-egg blue, threw "The First Issue of Wild-Cat Currency" (a group of frontier financiers in chokers and high beaver hats) back into the clay-box, and began at once on a bold relief of "Science and Democracy Opening the Way for the Car of Progress."

"Science," he explained to Prochnow, next day, "will be clearing the air of the bats of ignorance, and Democracy will be clearing the ground of the imps of aristocracy—or maybe they'll be demons. And between the two, right in the middle, of course, the Car of Progress will advance in very low relief. I haven't quite got it all where it will pull together yet, and I can see the foreshortening of the horses will be something terrible; but I'm pretty sure I shall find some way out within a week or so. Let me tell you one thing, though, about your own job, Ignace. Your allegory will go down easier if— —Say, you wouldn't take Hill's hints, would you?"

"No," said Prochnow, with the loftiest contempt.

"It will go down easier, I say, if you'll just work in some portraits of our Nine Worthies. Ghirlandajo did that racket, for instance; so did Holbein. So did plenty of others. Wouldn't Andrew P. Hill's chin-beard come in great on Fortitude? And if you've got any gratitude in your composition, Roscoe Orlando ought to go in as Prosperity. Give him two cornucopias, instead of one, to balance those side-whiskers— —"

"Hush!" called Prochnow reprovingly. He never jested about his patrons and he never made facetious observations about art.

"Well, don't get mad," said Little O'Grady, slightly abashed. "I'm doing just that thing with Simon Rosenberg; he's going to be my archdemon of aristocracy."

Prochnow remained smilelessly severe; and Little O'Grady, after one or two more feeble efforts to save his "face," slunk away—vastly impressed, as he never failed to be when he met the rare person that could put him down.

"What makes Ignace so grouchy to-day, I wonder?" he muttered, as he returned to the Car of Progress.

Prochnow soon forgot this interruption and jumped back into his work with redoubled vigour. He took a serious view of himself, of his art, of things in general; above all, he took a serious view of his immediate future and of the place that Preciosa McNulty might come to have in it. Little O'Grady, an easygoing bachelor, everybody's friend, and too much the champion of the whole gentler sex to set any one of its members apart from all the rest, might indulge in such jestings about his own life and his own work as he saw fit. But for himself, a man of the warmest and highest ambitions, yet with the most restricted means for realizing them, play by the roadside was quite out of the question.

XVIII

While Ignace Prochnow was busy in adjusting science, democracy and progress to the requirements of finance, Preciosa, in whose behalf this great work had been undertaken, was lunching with Virgilia Jeffreys at the Whip and Spur. A mild, snowless season and dry firm roads had induced the managers of this club to try the experiment of reopening for the remainder of the winter: surely enough devotees of out-of-door activity, desirous of filling in the weeks that intervened between now and spring, must exist to make the step worth while.

At first Preciosa had had her doubts. But Virgilia had known how to execute a cordial grasp with her cold slim hand and how to put a warm friendly look into those cool narrow eyes. After all, Preciosa was not one to hold a grudge; besides, she could think of none of those cutting things she had once wished to say.

Virgilia had asked Elizabeth Gibbons, from whom she had heard the particulars about the portrait, and whom she hoped to bring round even if she had not succeeded with the girl's father. She had asked Dill too, and his sister Judith, both of whom were to show themselves very gracious and winning with the granddaughter of Jeremiah McNulty and the supporter of a rival painter. And she had added two or three other young men, who might be expected to appreciate this chance of making a fresh, youthful addition to their own limited and tiresome circle. There was a crackling fire in the big dining-room chimney-place; and three or four other little parties, scattered about, helped to remove some of the empty chill from the great, bare, shining place so full of disused chairs and tables.

Preciosa, who somehow found it impossible to take the thing simply, was decked out to considerable effect; most of the other young women struck her as rather underdressed, and she wondered that they could seem so very much at home. She felt they viewed her, as they passed, first with a slight curiosity (giving questioning glances that referred the matter to their sweet, whimsical Virgilia), and then with a slighting indifference. Clearly, in their eyes, she was here for just this once; she would not occur again, and they need not bother Virgilia by asking reasons. Preciosa began to feel very cold and lonely.

But Virgilia had no idea of permitting any such effect as this. She had been very gracious all the way out, and now she stared her inquiring friends into the background and worked with redoubled vigour to restore Preciosa's circulation. The fire helped; so did the good cheer—including some excellent bouillon; and so did the rattling remarks of the two or three young men, who were not at all overcome by Preciosa and who treated her with an ingenuously condescending informality that she took for the friendliest goodwill.

But most of all was the dear child affected by the confidential hints and whisperings of Virgilia, as they came to her in the wardrobe, or before the great fireplace, or across the corner of the table itself, or up in the bay-window, overlooking the gray lake, where they cosily took their coffee. This delightful function, Virgilia as much as intimated, might be but the beginning of many; this, if little Preciosa rightly understood, was only the withdrawal of the first of the filmy, silvery curtains that intervened between her and the full splendour of society. Virgilia murmured of the present opening of the golf season—it would come early this year; and she did not stop with proposing Preciosa for the Knockabout (which was good enough for a certain sort of people), but even suggested the possibility of her little friend's reception within her own club, the Fairview itself. She had charming acquaintances too, it delicately transpired, who had taken an opera-box for the season, but who were kept away from it by a sudden death in the family; and she, Virgilia, had the use of the tickets as freely as another. Certain dear friends of hers, she added, were expecting to give a cotillon next month—and why should they call her friend if she were not at liberty to ask cards for a friend or two of her own? And it was an easy probability, she intimated further, that Mamma McNulty might receive the honour of a call from one lady or another of the Pence connection and even be invited to assist at her aunt's charity bazar for the benefit of the Well-Connected Poor....

Yes, the veils lifted one by one, and the shining heavenly host of society drew nearer and nearer. And finally, as in the Lohengrin Vorspiel, the surcharged moment came when the violins, though pushed to their utmost, could go no further, and the clashing cymbals took up the bursting tale. The last clouds rolled away, the Ultimate Effulgence was revealed, and Preciosa McNulty was vouchsafed a vision of herself as the central figure in a blinding apocalypse: she was pouring tea at one of Mrs. Palmer Pence's authentic Thursday afternoons, with the curtains drawn, the candles glimmering, the right girls lending their aid, the street outside blocked with shimmering carriages, and the great ones of the earth saying to an alien, inexperienced little nonentity, "No lemon, thank you," or, "Another lump of sugar, please,"—a palpitating child who felt that now it but rested with her to readjust her halo and clap her wings and soar onward and upward with the departing host toward the realm of glory.

Preciosa was in a glow. She forgot the nippy ride out through the bare, bleak suburbs, and the weltering waste of the raw gray lake just below, and the cold glare from the dozens of disused table-tops, and the cool stares of people who wondered why she was here. Let them but wait a little, and they might soon meet her elsewhere.

Then Virgilia took Preciosa up into the bay-window on the landing and set her to sipping her coffee and delicately indicated to her the price she was to pay. She spoke of Mr. Dill's recognised primacy among the city's painters, and of the exertions by which he had won his place. She reminded Preciosa that he, as a fact, had been the first to take up and study the great problem proposed by the Grindstone, and that both professional courtesy and plain, everyday honesty forbade his summary supplanting by another. Preciosa listened with lowered eyes,—eyes that once or twice slid down the stairs and rested upon the prepossessing young gentleman for whom this plea was made. She felt that she was trapped; Virgilia Jeffreys had set a snare for her once more. She was conscious of the sidelong glance out of Virgilia's narrow green eyes, and of Virgilia's sharp nose and vibrating nostrils and fine intent eyebrows; they were all at work upon her to subdue her to Virgilia's will. She felt very feeble, very defenceless, greatly embarrassed, thoroughly uncomfortable. She thought suddenly of Medora Joyce, with her long bottle-green cloak and her friendly face. Why were not more of the "nice" people powers in the social world? Why must the gates be kept by the selfish, the insincere, the calculating? Medora, she felt sure, would have lent a hand without asking one to give up, in return, one's own thumb and forefinger....

There was a sudden stir outside—the sound of crunching wheels and grinding machinery and escaping steam. The two girls looked down from the bay. A bulky figure got out of an automobile, gave a command or two in a peremptory tone, entered the house and made his wants known to the steward.

"H'm," said Virgilia; "one of the Morrells."

The newcomer picked up all the men available and invited them to assist in his libations. Robin Morrell, the second of the Twins, had passed an active forenoon in the popularization of those unequalled certificates, and now he was more than willing to spend money freely in the eyes of the right people. Everybody he had approached earlier had met his views as to the value of those documents (they were at two-hundred-and-thirty, or some such incredible figure)—including a bank president or so, who had accepted them as collateral on this basis; and all whom he invited, or summoned, now (refusal seemed impossible), must needs show a like unanimity in sharing his pleasures. He was big and red, and took up a great deal of room. By contrast, Daffingdon Dill looked more of a gentleman than ever.

"He's like his brother—just!" said Virgilia to herself. "Imagine!" she added elliptically.

While Morrell collected the men and impressed his very urgent and particular demands upon the intimidated steward, Virgilia, leaving Preciosa, bestowed a few moments' exertions upon Elizabeth Gibbons. Virgilia gently but decidedly held the girl's father up to reprobation. Elizabeth professed herself utterly shocked by this disclosure of her parent's divagations and conveyed the impression that he should be brought back into the right path and should turn from Prochnow and all his works.

"What sort of a thing did he make of it?" asked Virgilia, thinking of the portrait.

"Why, really, do you know, it came out very well."

"What kind of a person is he?"

"Clever enough, I should say; but not by any means what you would call a gentleman."

"Um," murmured Virgilia darkly. How could anybody be interested in a painter that was not a gentleman? This was more than she could understand. "Don't let it go any further, dear," she counselled gently.

"Certainly not," said Elizabeth promptly, and put the matter out of her mind for once and for all.

After Morrell had imposed himself upon the men he turned his attention to the women. Virgilia had always impressed him as a trifle meagre and acidulous, and Elizabeth Gibbons had never impressed him at all; but he instantly caught at the flamboyant and high-charged beauty of little Preciosa McNulty. However, she was too chill and lonely once more to be greatly affected by the blusterous gallantries of this prosperous swain. She was very subdued in her acceptance of his heavy attentions;—"more so than I should—well, than I should have expected," as he himself observed. Really, she was too young for so much poise, too "temperamental," by every indication of her physiognomy, for such complete self-control.

"I say, she has a very good tone, do you know," he took occasion to remark to Dill. And he spoke as a man whose authority in such delicate matters was beyond dispute. There is only one way to impress the pusher, and that way Preciosa had unconsciously taken. The more she repulsed him the more worthy he thought her. "I must see her again, somewhere," he decided.

"Millions," whispered Virgilia to Preciosa, behind Robin Morrell's broad back. "Quite one of *us*. And you can see for yourself how immensely he is taken with you."

Yes, here was something more glorious even than the Thursday tea.

On the way home Preciosa was quiet and thoughtful. Her mother, devoured by a hungry curiosity and a sharp solicitude, plied her with questions. Whom had she met? What had they said and done? How had they dressed and acted? For the love of heaven, names, descriptions, particulars!

Preciosa looked back at her mother and held an unbroken silence.

XIX

Prochnow spent the whole day working for Preciosa, oblivious of Virgilia's snares or of the debut of Robin Morrell. He heaved history, tradition, legend, mythology into the furnace, worked the bellows with indefatigable hand, blew his brains to a white heat and kept them there, and dropped down at dusk with his project complete. He had outlined two or three of his cartoons as well, and had even dashed out, on a small scale, the colour-scheme of the one that made the most immediate appeal.

Little O'Grady, who had had all the trouble he anticipated with the chariot of Progress—and a good deal more—came in for a cup of Prochnow's potent, bewitching coffee.

"Ignace!" he cried, wiping his clay-encrusted hands on the blue blouse, "you beat us all! You'll run away ahead of any one of us! Only, you'll kill yourself doing it!"

"My first great chance," replied Prochnow. "I mustn't let it slip by."

Within a few days this third scheme was brought into intelligible shape and sent off in pursuit of the scattered sons of finance. "It's a dead go!" cried Little O'Grady; "this time we get 'em sure!" His confidence was the light from the blazing furnace, just as Prochnow's intensity was its heat. When each believed so fully in himself and in the other how could the thought of failure intrude?

"Ignace," said Little O'Grady, "this time they'll treat us right. You must take a better room than you have here. You must move downstairs, where people can find you, and where you will be able to let them in when they do. Ladies, now—how could you possibly receive them in such quarters as these?"

Prochnow easily allowed himself to be persuaded. He was already beginning to see about how the cat jumped and to understand how much depended upon the gentle patronage of the luminaries of society. There was one little star, surely, whose light he should be glad to focus on himself once more—nor be indebted to another's kindness for the privilege. He had indeed ventured to call on Preciosa once or twice at her own home—in particular there was the evening on which, defying niggardly Fortune, he had invited her to the theatre, her passion; but Euphrosyne McNulty had not seemed fully able to understand him. She appeared to view him as a sort of unclassifiable young artisan and to find slight justification for his presence. She had other ideas for her daughter.

"Come, make a stagger," said Little O'Grady encouragingly. "Take that other big room down there next to Gowan's. I'll cough up a few for you, and I'll let you have all the traps of mine you need. Take the Aztec jars and both the priceless Navajos that I have clung to through all my days of misery and privation."

Prochnow made the move. Preciosa was among his first callers. His studio came to little compared with Dill's, and to little more compared with Gowan's; but the jars and the blankets did their part, the mandolin and the coffee-pot theirs; the portfolios were broken open to decorate the walls, and,— —

"You'll do," said Little O'Grady.

Preciosa's back missed the tall mahogany chair with the brass rosettes. "We've loaned it to Gowan," explained Little O'Grady; "we're helping him out on a portrait."

Preciosa's feet missed the thick-piled Persian rug. "It was getting full of moths and dust," said Little O'Grady. "We've given it to some poor chaps upstairs for a coverlet."

"Are they very destitute?" asked Preciosa tenderly.

"Turrible," replied Little O'Grady. "There's one sufferer up there who's just about cleaned out—nothing left but his bed and one chair. He's eating his mattress. It'll last a week longer."

Preciosa leaned back luxuriously on the wood-box, which was covered by one of the blankets, and tapped her delicate little foot on the other, spread over the floor. How fortunate that Ignace was spared all these privations!

Prochnow himself could not feel that he was poor. *She* was here; his drawings were with the bank; his Odalisque was at the club; and his Fall of Madame Lucifer, in a bright new frame, adorned the chaste walls of Roscoe Orlando Gibbons. The future was bright with promise. He dared to speak now. He would. He did.

As soon as Little O'Grady had the grace to make a move toward departure, Prochnow hastened it on. O'Grady went upstairs to banish one or two more obstacles from the way of the Car of Progress, and Prochnow took Preciosa over to the Academy to see the Winter Exhibition.

Preciosa, as has already been said, was not a girl of many ideas; yet a single one, detached, isolated, and presented to her with some ardour and directness, was easily within her grasp. The idea was now presented, and Preciosa forgot all about the pictures. For surely he who offered it was a most complete and admirable mechanism; the pulse of his heart, the beat of his brain, the flash of his eye, the tremor of his masterful hands—all these now worked in fullest harmony and told her here was a man. Preciosa, never inclined to make too much of worldly considerations, now set them aside altogether. Any idea of mere lucre slipped from her mind, and if she thought at all of a mother's strained social ambitions for a favourite child, it was but to feel with a wilful joy that she was extricating herself from the selfish grasp of Virgilia Jeffreys. Her own humble and obscure origin stirred within her,—her, the granddaughter of peasants who had trotted their bogs,—and she gave no heed to her lover's gentility or lack of it, in her unconscious tendency, even her active willingness, to "revert."

Prochnow felt the utmost confidence in his own powers, in his future, in the great scheme now under the scrutiny of the Grindstone. He glanced round the walls of the gallery, and here and there a canvas due to one hand or another that had co-operated in the rival scheme came to his view. He made silent, acidulous comments on certain manifestations of mediocrity placed there by men so much better quartered, better known, better circumstanced than himself. "Never mind," he said; "next year *I* shall be here, and then the difference will be seen by everybody." Well might the director welcome work from one who had distanced all others in a fair race and who unaided had brought to a triumphal issue the greatest piece of monumental decoration the town had ever known. And this little thing close by his side, panting, palpitating, flushing divinely, had helped him to conquer his success.

"It will be your triumph, too!" he told her.

"Mine?" she asked, in self-depreciation. "Why, I have not made you a single suggestion." Too truly she was no Virgilia Jeffreys.

"You have had a hand in every drawing," he insisted warmly. "You have moved the crayon over every sheet. The whole work is full of you—it is You yourself."

Preciosa accepted this full, round declaration with easy passivity; she was not clever, only happy. If he thought thus, and felt thus—why, that was enough. He was a strong young man—let him have his way. It all fell in with his "handling" of the whole situation. Little enough had he depended upon soft seduction, upon gallantry, upon flattery; still less had he tried to wheedle, to propitiate. He had grasped her with an intent, smileless severity, and he was not to be opposed. His words, like his works, were full of sweep and decision, and empty of all light humours, and they lifted her up and carried her away.

"Yes," she said, "it will be my triumph too." And she seemed to have said the words he wished to hear.

XX

A week or two went by. The paladins of finance found it as hard as ever to get together. Nothing moved ahead save the new building itself. Even the Car of Progress stood stock-still in the roadway, while Little O'Grady gnawed his nails. Only the contractors and their men had any advance to show. They had put on the roof and had begun to plaster the interior. The vagaries and uncertainties of a few struggling, befogged old gentlemen had no terrors for them—*their* contracts had been signed hard and fast months before, and their receipts of money had kept close and exact step with the progress of the work itself. "I wish I was a bricklayer—or even a hod-carrier!" said Little O'Grady, throwing a despairing eye upon the Car, stuck fast in the mire.

Prochnow was still confident. He saw a bride, a home, a year of satisfying and profitable activity; he even saw more than one new ring on Preciosa's dear, overloaded little fingers. Yes, he had fully justified his summary snatching of this child of luxury from that front parlour full of contorted chairs with gilded arms and with backs of pink brocade. He even heard Euphrosyne McNulty say to him in a voice tremulous with generous feeling: "Dear Ignace, you are all I hoped to find you—and more. You have made little Preciosa's mother completely content."

At last the Grindstone made a revolution. Andrew P. Hill, weary of waiting for the help of his associates, none of whom save Roscoe Orlando Gibbons could be brought to the scratch, took hold of the handle and struck out a few sparks.

Together Hill and Gibbons considered "Science and Democracy." Prochnow had devised a scheme that was properly severe and monumental; though the intellectual cherubs and the muscular blacks were present in modified form, all odalisques and such had been suppressed. Still, the general tone was too luscious for Andrew, who, even in his young days, had been a pattern of sapless rectitude; and on the other hand, it was not luscious enough for Roscoe Orlando, who, in *his* young days, had been quite the reverse. Andrew had no affinity for fluttering garments and sensuously waving palm-fronds—little did they consort with the angular severity of "business." Roscoe Orlando, on the other hand, had an intense affinity for such things as the Fall of Madame Lucifer, and was hoping for something more of the same sort. Madame was falling in red tights and Parisian slippers, with black bat-wings inserted between her straight, slim legs and her outstretched arms, while Lucifer himself, a much smaller figure, fell some distance behind her; and her staring eyes and open mouth and streaming hair were a sight to see—even upside down. As Roscoe Orlando turned over Prochnow's sketches with a discontented hand he asked querulously where was the *chic*, the snap that he had hoped to see. No, no; the boy had done his best work already; he was on the down grade—that was plain.

"And then, all this allegory," objected Andrew. "It's too blind; it's too complicated. People can't stop to figure it out. Besides, I'm not so sure that every bit of it is perfectly proper."

So the Grindstone made another revolution and took off the tip of poor Prochnow's nose. He came into Little O'Grady's dirty and disorderly place, and O'Grady, even before he could scramble forward through his ruck of dusty casts and beplastered scantlings, saw that the blow had fallen.

He gave one look at Prochnow's face, drawn, haggard, black with disappointment and anger, and began to work himself out of his blouse. "Where is my hat?" he muttered wildly.

"Where are you going?" asked Prochnow. His voice was hoarse. O'Grady looked at him a second time, to make sure who was speaking.

"I got you into this, Ignace; and now I——"

"You did not," said Prochnow. His pride of intellect, still unhumbled, forbade his acknowledgment of any such claim.

"Oh, yes, I did, Ignace; and now I must get you out of it."

"Are you going to see those men?"

"I am."

"Don't. There is still some hope left," said Prochnow thickly, "and you would only make matters worse. A great deal of unsuspected talent has been developed, it appears, by these experiments, as I have heard them called," he went on chokingly, with blazing eyes, in a gallant attempt at cold irony; "and much more may be waiting still. Enough, in fact, to justify a *concours*—how do you say?—a competition." He clenched his fists against his rigid thighs and turned his face away.

"A competition? They say that now?" Little O'Grady threw off his blouse and jumped on it with both feet. "Where *is* my hat?" he cried, running his fingers through his long, fluffy hair and toppling over a disregarded cast or two.

Prochnow caught him by the arm. "You must not go," he said.

But Little O'Grady was obsessed by a vision of the Grindstone directors—the whole Nine—assembled round the council-board in that shabby, out-of-date parlour. It had been hard to get them together for Dill and Giles and Prochnow and Adams, but there they sat now, waiting for him. A new figure entered the vision, the little Terence O'Grady they were expecting: the spokesman for honour, for fair play; the champion of the poor girls whose tenderest hopes had been blighted; the whip of scorpions that was to lash the ignorance, the ineptitude and the careless cruelty that had brought so many hearts and talents to fury and despair.

"Get out of my way!" cried Little O'Grady. He pushed Prochnow aside, clapped on his hat and rushed from the room.

He tumbled down five flights of stairs. At the bottom he met Gowan.

"A competition!" cried O'Grady, with raging scorn.

"I know," returned Gowan. "But there's something later. They have formed a committee, under the lead of an 'expert'—somebody that *I* never heard, of—to pass the Winter Exhibition in review. They want to see which of us do the best work and to determine whether any of us at all can do good enough for their wants."

"Ow!" shrieked O'Grady.

"Furthermore, old Rosenberg has proposed to cut down the appropriation for decorations from twenty-five thousand to four. If they're bad, after all, so much less will the loss be."

"Ow!" shrieked O'Grady again, as he tried to bolt past.

"Where are you going?" asked Gowan.

"To the Bank! To the Bank!" It was as if Revolutionary Paris were yelling, "*A la lanterne! a la lanterne!*"

Again O'Grady saw the Nine in conference. Again he heard their voices. "There's nobody here," said Holbrook, making, to do him justice, his first and only suggestion; "send East." "There's nobody here," said Gibbons,—oh, how Little O'Grady hated him now!—"send abroad." "No," came the voice of Hill, "we need not go outside of our own city. Surely we can find within the corporate limits somebody or other to do our bidding;" and Jeremiah McNulty agreed with him. "Why spend four thousand dollars?" asked Simon Rosenberg; "why spend one? Calcimine and have done, and save the money;" and Oliver Dowd took the same view. All these enormities rang clearly in Little O'Grady's ears and put wings to his heels.

"Get out of my way, Gowan!" he cried, and ran full speed down the street.

XXI

"Yes, they're all in there," said the watchman who stood, decorated with a police star, in front of the partition of black walnut and frosted glass. "But you can't see them now; they're busy."

"I can't, eh?" said Little O'Grady. "We'll find out if I can't!" He dodged the watchman, wrenched open the flimsy door and threw himself upon the board.

Yes, they were all there, including the two or three that Little O'Grady had not seen the time before—that first time of all. And the Morrell Twins were there too, one of them remorseful and the other defiant. And Andrew P. Hill, who presided, was in a blue funk—O'Grady could see his chin-beard waggle and could almost hear his teeth chatter; for it was Andrew who had amassed all that Pin-and-Needle collateral, accepting it at the street's own mad valuation. Pin-and-Needle, pushed too far, blown too big, was now shaky at the knees, and Andrew and all the Nine were trembling sympathetically from top to toe. The Grindstone might survive in a single serviceable mass, or it might fly to pieces, dispersed in a thousand useless fragments.

Little O'Grady looked round upon the other faces; they were all like Andrew's. Remorse, shame, contrition sat upon them. Ah, these men knew they had not given fair treatment to him and to Ignace and to Dill and to Preciosa and all the rest. "Just see how they're looking at me!" he said to himself. "Never mind; I won't let up on them. I'll rub it in; I'll drive it home."

What drawn faces! What anxious eyes! What sharp noses!—who had been grinding them? Answer: the Morrell Twins. Not for nothing their long practice in sharpening pins and needles! It had come into play here. Richard had turned the crank and Robin had held down each official proboscis, and the board had winced. Then Richard and Robin had changed places, and the board had groaned. Now Richard and Robin were changing back, and soon the board might scream. "I'll take a hand too," said O'Grady.

He began at once; he gave the discomfited directors no chance to forestall him. He taxed them roundly with their delays, their double-dealings, their invertebrate wabblings. They had blown hot and cold. They had played fast and loose. He and his friends had worked, had thought, had studied, had invented, had torn their very brains from their heads; and what had they to show for it? Nothing; nothing at all. On the contrary— —

"Get out of here," said Andrew P. Hill sternly. "This is a business meeting."

"Business meeting!" cried Little O'Grady scornfully. "What do any of you know about business, I'd like to ask? Nobody who wanted to do business by business methods would come here to do it, I'm thinking! No, sir; he'd go to *our* shop, where we do as we say we will, and do it up sharp and ship-shape, no matter how unreasonable the demands of the shilly-shallying old grannies we have to deal with. Business! You don't bluff me!"

"Take care, young man," said Hill, "or— —"

"Or nothing!" cried Little O'Grady undaunted. "And now, for a finisher, you offer us a competition. You wind us, and then ask us to run against a fresh batch that haven't even left the stable! After we've pulled our brains out of our heads strand by strand, you'd have us stuff them back and pull them out all over again, would you? Nobody but a man with cotton-batting *for* brains could ask a thing like that!"

"Brains!" said Dowd contemptuously. He had always looked upon himself as a lofty intellectual force. In his view there was no great play for intellect outside of finance and law.

Little O'Grady pounced upon this insolence at once. "There's not one of you here, I'll venture, that has had an idea in the last twenty years. You just sit beside your little old machine and turn the crank—why, the crank almost turns itself. We, on the other hand, live on our ideas. We keep alive on our own brains and hearts and blood and emotions— —"

"Emotions!" said Dowd, carelessly crumpling up a paper and throwing it into the waste-basket. He himself had not had an emotion—foolish, superfluous things—in his life. Little O'Grady looked at his nose. It was the sharpest of the lot.

"Get out of here, young man," said Simon Rosenberg. "This is no place for you."

O'Grady passed over Rosenberg's nose in contempt.

"We turn in scheme after scheme," he pursued;—"schemes to be welcomed and appreciated anywhere—but here. And what is your own? All you can think of is a mongrel heap of cabins and spires and chimneys and shacks that would set a tombstone to grinning. What chance is there for art in such a hotch-potch as that? What could a self-respecting— —"

Up rose Andrew P. Hill. He expressed all his nervous dread, his vexation, his irritability by one tremendous whack of his fist on the table.

"To hell with art!" he said. "What I wanted to do was to advertise my business."

Dead silence. Nobody had ever heard Andrew P. Hill swear before; nobody had supposed that he could. But the unlooked-for, the impossible had happened.

To Little O'Grady this profanity was no more than the profanity of anybody else. It did not stop him.

"To advertise your business?" he mocked. "Then why didn't you say so before? It ain't too late to do so yet, is it? I'll do it for you myself. I'll advertise you and your business and your building fit to make you dizzy. I'll make you celebrated. I'll make you talked about. You won't have to pay twenty-five thousand dollars for it, either. Nor four. Nor one. Just give me a week's time and a scaffolding—I worked on a panorama once—and I'll see that you're advertised. I'll do it with my eyes bandaged and with one hand—either one—tied behind me. I'll see to it that you get the Merry Laugh. I'll see that you get the Broad Grin. I'll see that you get the Unrestrained Cachinnation. I'll get you into the guide-books and the art journals—nit! Why, you poor creatures"—Little O'Grady's liberal glance took in the entire assembly—"who do you think bestow the sort of celebrity you have presumed to hope for? *Your* kind? Not on your life. The cheap twaddlers of cheap daily stuff for cheap people? Never imagine it. Who, then? The few, wherever they may be, who *know*. Good work by good men; and then a single word from the right source, however distant, starts the ball rolling and the stream running. The city feels proud of your taste and liberality, travelling strangers turn aside to see the fruit of it, and you get praise and celebrity indeed. But nothing of that kind will ever happen to you, whether you think yourselves art patrons or not;"—here O'Grady dealt a deadly look at Roscoe Orlando Gibbons. "Do what you like; people will snicker and guffaw and hold their sides and pant for somebody to fan them and bring them to. As for me, I utterly scorn and loathe the whole pack of you. I curse you; I rue the day when first I——"

Little O'Grady thrust out his angry hands to rend his garment, but found that he had left it behind. Balked here, he was about to let them loose on his hair, when the Morrell Twins, at a sign from Andrew P. Hill, now speechless with anger, sprang up and seized Little O'Grady by both shoulders and hustled him out of the room. Robin Morrell gave him a cuff on the ear to boot—a cuff that was to cost him dearer than any other action of his life. Little O'Grady paused on the other side of the partition to curse the board again, but the watchman hustled him out into the street. He paused on the curbstone to curse the bank, but a policeman told him to move along. On his way back to the Warren, Little O'Grady went a block out of his road to curse the new building, now almost ready for occupancy. He lifted up his arm against it and anathematized it, and a passing patrol-wagon almost paused, as if wondering whether he were not best picked up.

"Don't bother about me," said Little O'Grady to the patrol-wagon. "I'm all right." He looked again at the long row of columns: they were still standing. "There yet?" he said. "Well, you'll be down before long, if I'm any guesser."

XXII

The columns were still standing a week later; and the Pin-and-Needle Combine, too, still managed to hang together. But every moment was precious, and Roscoe Orlando Gibbons lost no time in giving a dinner for Preciosa McNulty.

Robin Morrell's first impression of Preciosa had lost nothing of its intensity—on the contrary. He had taken every possible occasion for seeing more of her. He had invaded a stage-box at the theatre where she happened to be sitting; he had made an invitation to call upon her at home impossible to withhold, and he had called. Elizabeth Gibbons, who was hand and glove with Preciosa (except that, like everybody else, she knew nothing of her engagement), speculated aloud on the probable outcome of all this, and her father himself, overhearing, had laid these considerations before old Jeremiah. Briefly, Preciosa must marry Robin, and Roscoe Orlando himself would help to the extent of bringing them together once more by means of a dinner.

Jeremiah blinked solemnly at Roscoe Orlando's florid side-whiskers and wide sensuous mouth. Both the affairs of the heart and the functions of society life were far removed from the range of Jeremiah's interests and sympathies.

"Save Morrell, and you save the bank," urged Roscoe Orlando.

Jeremiah blinked again. He was fully able to do this, if he chose. He was immensely well off. He drew rentals from every quarter of the city. Those gilded Louis Quinze chairs and sofas in his front parlour were, as everybody knew, stuffed with bonds and mortgages, and coupons and interest-notes were always bursting out and having to be crammed back in place again. Yes, Jeremiah was the richest member of the board; but he was also one of the smallest among the stock-holders. He shook his head. Why risk so much to save so little?

"Then save your grandchild," pursued Roscoe Orlando.

Jeremiah stopped blinking and opened his eyes to a wide stare. "Aha! this fetches him!" thought Roscoe Orlando.

"Will you have her marry a business-man of means and ability," he went on, "or will you have her tie up to a poor devil of a painter, with no friends, no position, no influence, no future?" Roscoe Orlando's brief period of easy patronage was over; no longer was he the caressing amateur, but the imperilled stockholder (rather a large one, too), and Ignace Prochnow need look for no further support from his quarter. Roscoe told Jeremiah bluntly that his granddaughter was as good as engaged (this was his own daughter's guess) to that obscure young man from nowhere, and asked him if he wanted the thing to end in matrimony.

Jeremiah scratched his chin. Roscoe Orlando saw with disappointment that neither explosion nor panic was to ensue. Yes, Jeremiah remembered Prochnow; he recalled the bold, brainy young fellow, so full of vigour and vitality. He himself had reached an age when such things made their impression, and when he wistfully envied so signally full a repository of youthful hope, energy, persistence.

Gibbons eyed him narrowly; clearly his argument was failing. "However," he went on hurriedly, therefore, "this is no affair for us. Speak to the child's mother; she will know how to handle it. Meanwhile, my daughters will arrange for the dinner."

Euphrosyne McNulty jumped at the dinner. As for Preciosa's infatuation for Prochnow (upon which Jeremiah had touched very lightly), she refused to consider any such possibility. At most it was but a passing fancy, due to the painting of that portrait; it would quickly dissipate: least said, soonest mended. A girl like Preciosa, brought up so carefully, a girl who had always had everything and who would always need to have everything, would know how to choose between two such men. As for Robin Morrell, Euphrosyne had been greatly taken with him. He blew into her arid parlour the long-awaited whiff from the golden fields of "society." He was big, loud, self-confident, tremendously and immediately at home (in a condescending way, though this she hardly grasped),—a man to open up his own path and trample through the world, Preciosa by his side, and Preciosa's mother not far behind. So, up to the very hour of the Gibbons dinner, she sang his praises in Preciosa's ear.

Preciosa was preparing to revert; she sought the soil, but she was determined it should be the soil of her own choosing. She found Morrell coarse, dry, hard, sandy, gritty. What she sought was some dank, rich loam, dark, moist, productive. To be sure, great towering things grew in the sand—pine-trees, for example, with vast trunks and with broad heads that spread out far above the humbler growths below; but on the whole she preferred some lustrous-leaved shrub full of buds that would soon open into beautiful red flowers. She told her mother that she had no interest in the Gibbons dinner and did not mean to go.

"But I mean that you shall!" retorted Euphrosyne. "After all that's been done to get you into society you turn round now, do you, and cut off your own parents from it? You'll go, make sure of that; and your father and I will go with you."

XXIII

Daffingdon and Virgilia were bidden to the Gibbons dinner, along with the rest.

"It's a sop," declared Virgilia; "it's to propitiate us. It's to make amends—he knows he hasn't treated us fairly. Shall we go?"

"He has treated us no worse than he has treated everybody else," said Dill, bent upon the preservation of his *amour propre*. "Look at that young Prochnow—picked up one day and dropped the next."

"They say he's really clever," replied Virgilia. "If we failed, we failed in good company. Just how good, we might see by going. Mr. Gibbons has something of his at the house, you remember."

"We haven't failed yet," persisted Daffingdon. "The field is clear—just as it was to start with. We may be able to bring them round yet. Anyway, we'll keep up the pretence of good terms. Let's go."

Virgilia and Daffingdon had given over all mention of Japan, and had left off the shy, desultory house-hunting that had occupied the spare hours of their engagement. This great question with the bank must be settled first. Nor was Virgilia sure that Daff was proving to be all she had fancied him. He had shown less head than he might have shown in planning the scheme, and less spunk than he should have shown in pushing it. As she thought things over she felt that all the ideas and all the efforts had been her own. And now the question of money. Money; it did not come in, and yet it was the prime need. These considerations filled her mind as they bowled along in the cab together, and she was not sure but that their engagement was a mistake. At Roscoe Orlando's carriage-block their cab was close behind the livery brougham of the Joyces—Abner and his wife were going everywhere, now; and she looked after Medora half in envy, as upon a woman whose future, whether small or great, was at least assured. Nothing consoled her but Daffingdon's seeming determination not to give up. Yes, there was room for more ideas, for further efforts. But whose? His or hers?

Elizabeth Gibbons welcomed her father's guests, and Madame Lucifer backed her up bravely. Dill gave this canvas the closest scrutiny. "It *is* strong," he said; "it has *chic* without end." But it had no earthly bearing on the great problem. Another point in his own favour: he was here and Prochnow wasn't.

Yes, he was here, and he tried to take advantage of the fact. Before long he met Gibbons himself in front of the picture—a juncture he had privately hoped to bring about—and was speaking of its merits and of its author and of their common participation in the great scheme and of the prospects and possibilities of the early future. Roscoe Orlando tried to seem smiling and cordial and encouraging, but clearly his thoughts were somewhere else. And his eyes. And his ears. They were wherever Preciosa McNulty and Robin Morrell happened to be sitting or standing together. It was no longer a question of decorations, nor of the walls that were to give them place, nor of the colonnade through which the public would pass to view them. It was a question of the very vaults themselves; of the capital, the deposits, the surplus, the undivided profits, of his own five hundred shares; of safety, of credit, of honour—oh, might this painter but eat his dinner in quiet and let the matter of art go hang!

Eudoxia Pence looked at the new picture too, comparing its spirit and quality with a number she had recently added to her own gallery. She also attempted a word with her host about the thwarted pageantry at the Grindstone, but Roscoe Orlando put off her just as he had put off Dill.

"Very well, sir," said Eudoxia firmly, within herself; "if I can't speak here, then I will speak elsewhere. If not to you, then to others. Have eyes and ears if you will for that poor little vulgarian alone; all the same, I shall know how to make my point."

Preciosa was in full feather and in high colour; she seemed like a sumptuous pocket-edition of some work bound more richly, perhaps, than it deserved to be. She was in yellow tulle, and her mother had clapped an immense bunch of red roses upon the child's corsage and had crowded innumerable rings upon her plump little fingers. Her chestnut hair fell in careless affluence round her neck and blew breezily about her temples, and a bright spot in each cheek gave her even more than her wonted colour. Robin Morrell, who was, of course, to take her out to dinner, seized upon her at the very start. It was as if he had wrenched a peach from the tree and had hastily set his greedy teeth in it—one almost saw the juices running down his chin. Yet his satisfaction was not without its drawbacks; the peach seemed a clingstone, after all; and there was a bitter tang to its skin. Preciosa's eyes blazed as well as her cheeks, but not, as some thought, from exhilaration or from gratified vanity; rather from protestant indignation and a full determination not to be moved. Virgilia, from her place, saw how Euphrosyne McNulty constantly watched the child on one side and how Roscoe Orlando Gibbons as constantly watched her on the other; and when Dill asked her, "What does it mean?" she replied: "Leave it to me; this is nothing that a mere man can hope to master. I shall know all about it before I quit this house."

Roscoe Orlando put the men through their liqueurs and cigars in short order—more important concerns were at hand; Joyce, who was now beginning to feel himself an authority in such matters, almost found in his host's unceremonious haste good cause for resentment. James W. McNulty, who saw nothing but the surface, supposed himself here by virtue of his growing importance in the business world, and was fain to acknowledge the attention by the recital of a number of appropriate "stories." During the slight delay thus occasioned, the ladies made shift, as usual, to entertain one another. Preciosa, relieved temporarily of the pressing attentions of Morrell, sat with Medora Joyce on the drawing-room sofa, proud and flattered to have the undivided regards of the most charming "young matron" present. At the same time, Virgilia, in a shaded corner of the library, was sounding Elizabeth for a clew. Elizabeth had little, consciously, to tell; but, like many persons in that position, she told more than she realized. It was not enough for the purpose, but it dovetailed in with other information that came from other sources the day following. When Morrell led Preciosa into the conservatory, at the earliest possible moment, Virgilia was as keen over their exit as Euphrosyne McNulty or as Roscoe Orlando himself. She knew what was impending and she almost knew why.

And when Robin Morrell issued from the conservatory she knew just what had happened. Nobody could be so dashed, so dumfounded for nothing. Yes, that incredible child had refused him. Richard had not been good enough for the one, but surely Robin was good enough for the other.

Preciosa's no had been without qualification or addition. Morrell knew as little as her own mother that she considered herself fully pledged to Ignace Prochnow.

Roscoe Orlando came up to Eudoxia. His lips were white.

"A little plan I had set my heart upon," he said, trying to smile lightly, "has received a slight check. May I not rely on you to help it through?"

"A little plan I had set *my* heart upon," she returned significantly, "has received a slight check. May I not rely on *you*? In other words, I have my problem, just as you have yours. I must insist that justice be done to Mr. Dill."

Roscoe Orlando bowed—only too glad to acquiesce in anything. "One straggler brought back to camp," said Eudoxia. "To-morrow I shall try to bring back one or two others."

XXIV

Eudoxia Pence immediately got herself into motion. During the watches of the night she evolved plans for such a function as she thought the present situation required. Her picture gallery, re-enforced by those six or eight new masterpieces from Paris, she should throw open to the general public. She would call the thing an afternoon reception, and there would be tea. People were to be invited with some regard to form, but the opportunity would be made rather general—almost anybody might come who was willing to pay a dollar. This crush would supplement her bazar, and would be announced as for the benefit of—oh, well, of any one of the half-dozen charities that looked to her for support. She would throw open the whole house and tea should flow like water. These doings must take place within three days, at the outside. Time was precious and none of her friends would take seriously anything of hers given at so short a notice. No matter, then, who paid; no matter who poured; no matter about anything, if only her net took in all the different people she wanted to catch.

Next morning she rose for a busy day. She had brought back Gibbons, and now she must bring back Hill. Young Prochnow was off the board, but that did not put Daffingdon Dill back upon it; nor would he be there till she should have placed him there. "We *must* have that commission," said Virgilia. "You shall, if I've got any influence," replied her aunt.

> She had long foreseen that, one day or another, she must seize her Grindstone stock in her talons, beat her wings about the head of Andrew P. Hill, raise a threatening beak against his obdurate front, and ask him what he meant by behaving so.

She drove to the bank. The old office stood empty; a last load of ancient ledgers and of shabby furniture was just driving away. She ordered her coupe to go to the new building. Here she found Andrew adjusting himself to his grandiose environment, and delivered her assault.

What had he and the directors meant by such a game of fast-and-loose? Why had they treated an artist of Mr. Dill's standing with such inconsiderateness and injustice? Why had they tried to handle so important a question by themselves? Why had they not consulted the stock-holders? Why had they not consulted *her*—a stock-holder since the foundation of the bank and an amateur of approved standing? And many more interrogatories no less hard to answer.

Hill listened to her cowed, intimidated; it was one more trouble in a time of trouble. He presently found his voice—or a part of it—and explained in low, trembling tones that concerns of much greater importance had come to the front; that this entire matter of decoration must be set aside for the present, perhaps for all time; that some other— —

Eudoxia threw an indignant frown upon him and drove off to see his wife.

Almira Hill was at home—in these latter days she was seldom anywhere else. Socially speaking, she had evaporated years ago; but there was no reason why she should not precipitate herself and appear once more in concrete form. Eudoxia had an intuitive sense that Almira would welcome the chance.

"Receive with us," Eudoxia urged her. What easier way for Almira to see some of her old friends? She considered. She consented.

Then Eudoxia opened against the bank. "Give me your help for my— nephew," she said to end with.

"Mr. Hill has spoken of this to me," replied the old lady slowly; "but he is so worried, so anxious, about something these days, that I hardly— —"

"*We* are worried; we are anxious, too, my dear Mrs. Hill. Figure the situation. Imagine the strain upon two young people— —"

Almira had not lost all her sentiment, nor all her interest in the concerns of youth. She promised to give what help she could.

Eudoxia sped on to see Euphrosyne McNulty. She found the household in a state of suppressed tumult. The servant who opened the door was all at sea; obscure sounds of sobbing came from somewhere above; and when Euphrosyne finally washed in she was like the ocean half-subsided after a storm. She had just learned that Preciosa had refused Robin Morrell.

"Such a caller at such a time!" she had articulated over Eudoxia's card. It took away half the sweetness of the triumph. She rushed to her toilet-table, hoping, meanwhile, that Norah had not boggled with the tray and that her father-in-law had not left his pipe on top of the piano.

Eudoxia was brief. She made no vain passes of regret that Euphrosyne had not taken her place earlier on her invitation-list. She invited her, now, with all emphasis, to attend her "art reception," and hoped that she would allow her dear daughter to help pour tea. A sunburst exploded before Euphrosyne's unready eyes. She recovered herself and accepted for both.

Eudoxia drove to the office of the Pin-and-Needle Combine. Like every other moneyed person in town, she had a finger in that pie. Why shouldn't she drop in on the cooks?

Robin Morrell was not there; she was received by Richard. Richard had heard from Gibbons what was in the wind, but knew nothing as yet, of course, about his brother's rejection.

Eudoxia understood that Richard was hand and glove with Hill. She asked his influence as a matter of justice to Daffingdon Dill. Richard had been impatient and resentful to begin with; now he became dogged and surly. She had come at the wrong time and about the wrong business. Virgilia had dismissed him with no gentle hand—people had smiled over his discomfiture for a week. The memory of this still rankled. Why in the world should he exert himself for Daffingdon Dill?

Let him exert himself for his brother then. But he became more dogged and surly still. Why should his brother succeed when he himself had failed? Why should his brother need help anyway? Why must this woman come poking into a man's most private affairs? Eudoxia surmised, through the medium of his sullen mood, a house divided against itself. She left Morrell in anger and drove to her husband's office.

Every man had rebuffed her. Only the women had been complaisant—and even these she had had to pay. As she sat by her husband's desk, waiting for his attention, her wrath rose against the Grindstone and Hill, against the Morrells and their Combine.

"I'll take my Grindstone stock," she declared, "and hawk it up and down the street at eighty—half what it's worth. Let us see where Andrew Hill will be *then*!"

Pence turned on her slowly. "I doubt whether you could get eighteen for it to-day. The street is talking—talking low, but it's talking."

"Why, is anything wrong with the Grindstone?"

"Well, rather. Hill, I judge, has come as close to the edge as a man can without falling over. I'm glad your holdings are no heavier."

"Ah!" said Eudoxia; "that's why he has choked off Dill! Well," she resumed with unimpaired energy, "I'll take my Pin-and-Needle and sell it for next to nothing. I'll give it away. I'll stick it under the cracks of doors. I'll present it with every pound, or rather every cup of tea. Let us see, then, how Richard Morrell——"

"Do that," said her husband, "and half the banks in town will fail. You're not ready for such a crash as that, are you?"

"Why, what's the matter with Pin-and-Needle?" asked Eudoxia.

"It's at death's door. It's gasping. Unless something is injected, unless somebody galvanizes it——"

"Ah!" cried Eudoxia; "so that's why Orlando Gibbons gave the McNulty dinner! Oh, things must hold off a few days longer! Make them, Palmer! That girl must marry him, so that I can save my Grindstone stock and my Pin-and-Needle investments, and so that Daff can get those pictures to paint, and so that Virgilia can get him!" Oh, heavens! She had once aspired to guide the chariot of finance, yet all she had to offer against this threatening squadron of calamities was an "art reception" with tea!

XXV

"Go? Of course we'll go!" said Little O'Grady spiritedly. "Anybody may go who's able to pay a dollar and who's got a friend to name him. I hope you and I can cough up as much as that, Ignace; and then if we have to live the rest of the week on sawdust, why, we will. Go? I guess yes. If I'm ever to make the Queen's acquaintance and get her profile, this is no chance to throw away."

Prochnow was in a deplorable state and needed all the support Little O'Grady could give him. He had not seen Preciosa for several days. He had called at the house once or twice—that vast florid pile, which had always looked lackadaisical rather than cruel; but it had refused to admit him. Euphrosyne had repulsed him with the utmost contumely; even old Jeremiah (who may not have meant to be harsh, but who seemed to be acting under superior orders) told him he must not appear there again. Nothing came to console him except three or four tear-stained little scrawls from Preciosa herself. In these she vowed in simple and slightly varying phrases to be faithful; nobody should come between them, nobody should make her untrue, nobody should prevent her from keeping her promise, nobody should take her away from him, and the like.

"What does it mean, Terence?" asked Prochnow, vastly perturbed by these blind reiterations.

Little O'Grady pondered. "Her folks are against us, that's all," he replied. "They're trying to marry her to somebody else," he told himself. "Who can it be?" Then, aloud and cheerfully: "If you can't see her at one house, why, just see her at another. Come along with you."

They found the town moving on Eudoxia Pence *en masse*, with several policemen in front to keep order. On the front steps they grazed elbows with the Joyces and the Gowans; and with these and other members of the general public they swept on, joining the vast throng of those who were so eager to press the great lady's Smyrna rugs with their own feet and fumble her silk hangings with their own fingers and rap her Japanese jars with their own knuckles and smell her new paintings with their own noses and see Mrs. Palmer Pence herself with their own eyes. "Gee! ain't it swell!" whispered Little O'Grady, who could make swans out of geese or geese out of swans with equal facility.

Prochnow ignored the swells, the jars, the pictures and all the rest; he sought only Preciosa. Little O'Grady was not in a new field for nothing, and he looked at everybody. First of all, there was the great Eudoxia herself, and her profile was as lovely as ever. When, when, when should he reach the point of modelling it? She stood there with a vain pretence of receiving,— she was too conventional to dispense with the recognised forms even on the occasion of a mere popular outpouring. Little O'Grady went up to her boldly and shook hands; he was outside the general understanding that made her, in so promiscuous a function, something to be looked at rather than touched—save by a few intimates. Only let him bring her within range of his aura, he thought, and her subjugation would inevitably follow. Then he stepped back and watched her. There was still a determined cordiality in her smile, but a furtive anxiety marked the glance she sent now and then into the second or third room beyond, where a pressing crowd and a subdued glare of candle-light seemed to indicate a focus of interest hardly second to the picture gallery itself. Little O'Grady caught this anxious look. "Is she afraid for her bric-a-brac or her spoons?" he wondered. "No, it's something more than that."

Beside Eudoxia stood Almira Hill,—"a mother in Israel, if ever there was one," O'Grady commented. "And what's the matter with *her*? Shy? Awkward? No, she's too old and experienced for that. There, she's looking in the same direction. Something's up. What is it?"

It was this: Almira's husband had told her that morning how it all depended upon Preciosa McNulty.

Roscoe Orlando Gibbons came through the crowd, with a great effect of smiling joviality. But he too glanced over the press of heads toward the glare of candle-light with a strained intensity not to be concealed.

Roscoe Orlando suddenly turned aside toward an old fellow who sat on a pink brocade sofa. "See, there's her grandfather," whispered Prochnow. Old Jeremiah had instinctively taken refuge on the one piece of furniture that reminded him of home. Here he sat, awkwardly twisting his hands and blinking every now and then at the great light that shone afar off. "I could never in the world have got him to anything resembling a dinner," declared Eudoxia. "He acts like a stray cat," said Little O'Grady. "But he needn't,—there seem to be plenty of the same sort here, after all." Yes, at a second glance old Jeremiah appeared to be less the victim of society than of circumstances; and when Roscoe Orlando Gibbons bowed over him and whispered and they both looked toward the illumination while Eudoxia Pence looked at them, Little O'Grady was surer than ever that something was in the air.

He felt Prochnow suddenly slipping behind him. "Her mother!" the young fellow explained. Yes, it was Euphrosyne in full fig and in very active circulation. She rustled, she swooped, she darted, she was as if on springs. "Well, she feels her oats," commented Little O'Grady. He looked at her again. No, what moved her was not vainglory, not a restless sense of triumph. She was keyed up to the most racking pitch of anxious expectation. She looked whither Eudoxia and Roscoe Orlando and all the others had looked, but with an intensified expression, and Little O'Grady almost felt as if challenged to solve some obscure yet widely ramified enigma.

He turned round as if in search of help. In a doorway near-by he saw another familiar face. "Why, there's Daff!" he cried. "It's Dill, our hated rival," he explained to Prochnow. "And that girl with him is Miss Jeffreys, the one he's going to marry."

Prochnow looked at the tall handsome figure in the long frock-coat with the bunch of violets, and felt abashed by his own short jacket and indifferent shoes. He noted too the assumption of ease and suavity with which the other was entertaining a little knot of ladies. It was this person, then, an out-and-out man of the world, against whom he, uncouth and unpractised boy, had presumed to pit himself!

Little O'Grady was not able immediately to detach Dill's attention from his associates. Meanwhile he studied both Dill and Virgilia. The general effect was brilliant enough, yet——Yes, surely they were too loquacious, too demonstrative; they were talking against time, they were working under cover, they were kicking up a dust. And, yes—both Daff and Virgilia, in the midst of this gay chatter, shot certain furtive, sidelong glances whither so many had been sent before.

> The group in the doorway showed signs of breaking up. "Daff," said Little O'Grady, "for the Lord's sake, what's on?"

"Ah, O'Grady," said Dill, in a cool, formal manner; "are you here?" Since that calamitous episode at the bank, he had cared less than ever for O'Grady: they had been quite right in throwing him out. He had found it hard to tolerate his forwardness at the beginning of the negotiations, and to carry the burden of his Bohemian eccentricity through them; and harder still to pardon the slap-dash sally that had thrown the common fat into the fire. Now up popped the fellow, knowing him as intimately and familiarly as ever.

"Oh, Daff," said Little O'Grady earnestly, and all unmindful of any possible rebuff, "what's out in that room?"

Daffingdon smiled at Virgilia. "Why don't you go and see?" he asked.

"But don't break off the match!" said Virgilia, with a nervous titter. What state of overtension could have prompted her to a piece of bravado so rash, so superfluous?

Little O'Grady gave her one look and sped away.

After pushing through two or three roomfuls of tall people, he finally reached the desired threshold. He felt a hand upon his arm and found Prochnow beside him. They both saw the same sight together.

It was a table like Dill's—only larger, with candles on it—five times as many, and flowers—ten times as handsome, and silver and glass and china—only a hundred times more brilliant, and girls seated about it—a thousand times more fetching than poor sister Judith. Among them was Preciosa, with a big feathered hat toppling on her head and the desperate look of some hunted creature on her face. Yes, they had hung her with chains and tied her to the stake. "If she is to pour here, after all," Eudoxia had said grimly, "let her pay for the privilege." And close to the girl's elbow sat the chief inquisitor, Robin Morrell, big, bold, unabashed, persevering, bringing all possible pressure to force her to recant. People about them—his unconscious familiars—sipped and chattered, and fluttered up and away, but he remained fixed throughout. He must have her, he was determined to dominate her; in the end she could not but yield. There was no other way out for her, and none for him. And that sole way must be taken at once.

Little O'Grady recognised the red face, the broad shoulders, the thick neck, the heavy hand; he still felt those fingers in his collar, that palm against his ear. "A-a-ah!" he emitted in a long sibilant cry of repressed rage.

"Stay where you are a minute," he said to Prochnow, and slipped away. Ignace stared now at his rival in love just as before he had stared at his rival in art,—yet held in check both by the intimidating splendour of the ceremonial and by his own uncertainty as to the precise significance of the situation.

O'Grady hurried back to Dill. "Daff, Daff!" he cried with wide eyes and with a tremulous finger that pointed back toward the tea-table, "is that the man?"

"What man?"

"The big brute sitting beside her."

"Robin Morrell to a 't,'" said Virgilia. "Or Richard, either."

"Are they trying to make her marry him?" demanded Little O'Grady, his gray-green eyes staring their widest.

"That is the plan, I believe," returned Dill.

"It won't come off!" cried Little O'Grady, and dashed away.

He pushed and trampled his course back to Prochnow. In the library he brushed against Medora Joyce.

"Oh, Dodie," he panted, "they're sacrificin' our little Preciosa to that big brute of a Morrell!"

"I was afraid so," said Medora, with concern. "Stop it."

"I'm going to!" said O'Grady.

As he regained Prochnow's side Preciosa was just rising from the table, and Elizabeth Gibbons was slipping into her place. Preciosa left the room by another door, and Morrell walked close beside her.

He looked about the crowded place with an air that was both determined and desperate. People here, there, everywhere; the rabble swarmed in the library, the morning-room, the den, chattering, staring, gaping, wondering. It was disgusting, it was barbarous, it made matters impossible. Every corner bespoken, every angle occupied. Nothing left save a nook under the great stairway—a nook shaded by dwarf palms, however, and not too open to the general eye. He half led, half crowded Preciosa toward it. He should speak now, a second time, and trust to bear her down.

He spoke a second time, and a second time Preciosa refused. She had but one idea,—an idea a bit obscured by Prochnow's absence,—yet she held it fast.

"You will not marry me, then?"

"No."

"You have a reason?"

"The best."

"What is it?"

"I am engaged to marry some one else."

"Who is he?"

Prochnow appeared in the hall, with Little O'Grady close behind him. Little O'Grady's mobile face was taxed to the utmost to express all that was within him, but Preciosa saw sympathy and the promise of instant help as clearly as Morrell saw detestation and mocking mischievousness. O'Grady pushed aside a palm-frond and pointed toward Prochnow. "We've come for you, darlin'," he said.

Preciosa rose; the one idea to which she had clung throughout came uppermost and crystallized before her eyes. "Who is he?" Morrell had asked. She raised her arm, pointed to Ignace like a true little heroine of the drama, and said:

"There he stands!"

She went out to meet them, and the three instinctively began to push toward the front door. She had her hat—never mind her jacket. Dill saw them moving away and bit his lip. Roscoe Orlando Gibbons grasped a door-jamb for support. A smothered scream was heard behind the palms; it was Euphrosyne McNulty, fainting away, as Preciosa, Prochnow and Little O'Grady went out through the vestibule and down the front steps together.

XXVI

The Pin-and-Needle Combine fell apart the next day. The Grindstone National Bank followed it the day after. Richard and Robin had turned the handle a little too briskly and the Grindstone had flown to pieces. Three or four other banks followed.

Little O'Grady danced with joy. His curse had told. And the great hulking bully that had dared to cuff him was flat on his back with the rest. When O'Grady fully realized what he—*he*—had done his breast heaved proudly. He ran over to see the fatal placard fastened on one of the Grindstone's great polished columns, and then tramped on down the avenue of ruin with the step and mien of a conqueror. All this devastation was due to him—whatever the foolish newspapers, groping in the dark, might say. He alone was the Thunderer; he alone wielded the lightning.

There was but one drawback; never should he get Eudoxia Pence's profile—now.

Eudoxia felt that the McNultys had disgraced her,—"as people of that sort always will if you give them a chance." Virgilia lingered in the limbo of engagement; impossible to say, now, when matrimony might ensue. The question of money was the question still. Dill was no Prochnow, to carry her off by main force, nor was she a Preciosa to permit it. She could not conceive of existence beyond the pale of society; the impulsive action of a pair of social outcasts could scarcely serve as a precedent. "I must wait," said Virgilia. Unconsciously she compared Daffingdon with Ignace Prochnow and realized how easy it would be for her to wait quite a while without discomfort, regret or protest.

Prochnow and Preciosa were married in the midst of the crash. Little O'Grady and Medora Joyce took the other two seats in their carriage and saw them through the ceremony. Preciosa knew that her mother would never forgive her, but she thought it not improbable that her grandfather might acquiesce. In any event, she would marry the man of her choice.

Little O'Grady patted Preciosa's hand patronizingly as the carriage rolled along. He, none other, was the good angel of the whole affair. "What do we care, darlin'," he said, "for the Morrell Combine?—hasn't it kept us on pins and needles long enough? What do we care for the Grindstone, either?—hasn't it ground our noses as long and hard as it could? Down wid 'em both—and let 'em stay down, too! And let anybody think twice, my children, before he tries to prick the skin or grind the nose of little Terence O'Grady!"

DR. GOWDY AND THE SQUASH

I

When Dr. Gowdy finally yielded to the urgings of Print, Push, and Co.—a new firm whose youthful persistency made refusal impossible—and agreed to steal from his sermon-writing the number of half-hours needed for putting together the book they would and must and did have, he certainly looked for a reward far beyond any recognisable in the liberal check that had started up his pen. For *Onward and Upward* was to do some good in the world: the years might come and go for an indefinite period, yet throughout their long procession young men—it was for them he was writing—would rise up here, there, and everywhere and call him blessed. To scrimp his sermons in such a cause was surely justifiable; more, it was commendable. "Where it has been dozens it will now be thousands," said the good Doctor. "I will guide their feet into the right path, and the thanks of many earnest strugglers shall be my real recompense."

Onward and Upward was full of the customary things—things that get said and believed (said from mere habit and believed from mere inertia),—things that must be said and believed (said by the few and believed by a fair proportion of the many) if the world is to keep on hanging together and moving along in the exercise of its usual functions. In fact, the book had but one novel feature—a chapter on art.

Dr. Gowdy was very strong on art. Raphael and Phidias were always getting into his pulpit. Truth was beauty, and beauty was truth. He never wearied of maintaining the uplifting quality resident in the Sunday afternoon contemplation of works of painting and sculpture, and nothing, to his mind, was more calculated to ennoble and refine human nature than the practice of art itself. The Doctor was one of the trustees of the Art Academy; he went to every exhibition, and dragged as many of his friends with him as could be induced to listen to his orotund commentaries; and he had almost reached the point where it was a tacit assumption with him that the regeneration and salvation of the human race came to little more than a mere matter of putting paint upon canvas.

These were the notions that coloured the art chapter of *Onward and Upward*. I hardly know where the good Doctor got them; surely not from the ordinary run of things in the Paris studios, nor from any familiarity with the private lives of the painters of the Italian Renaissance, which show, if anything does, that one may possess a fine and rigorous conscience as an artist, yet lapse into any irregularity or descend to any depravity as a man. But Dr. Gowdy ignored all this. Art—the contemplation of it, the practice of it—worked toward the building up of character, and promoted all that was noblest in human life.

These views of his were spread far and wide. They competed with the novel of adventure on the news-stands, and were tossed into your lap on all the through trains. One copy penetrated to Hayesville, Illinois, and fell into the hands of Jared Stiles.

II

Jared was an ignorant and rather bumptious young fellow of twenty-four, who was hoping to make something of himself, and was feeling about for the means. He had a firm jaw, a canny eye, and vague but determined ambitions. These sufficed.

Jared lived on a farm. He liked the farm life, but not the farm work—a fine distinction that caused his fellow-labourers to look upon him as something of a shirk. He would rove the fields while the rest were working in them. He thought his own thoughts, such as they were, and when a book came his way, as now and then happened, he read it.

Onward and Upward was lent to him by the daughter of the county attorney. She thought it would tone him up and bring his nebulousness toward solidity—she too being anxious that Jared should make something of himself, and unwilling to wait indefinitely. Jared took the book and looked at it. He passed quite lightly over the good Doctor's platitudes on honesty, perseverance, and the like, having already encountered them elsewhere; but the platitudes on art arrested his attention. "I shouldn't wonder but what all this might be so," said Jared to himself; "I don't know but what I should like to try it"—meaning not that he had any desire to refine and ennoble himself, but only a strong hankering to "get his hand in," as the phrase goes.

It was about this time that the Western Art Circuit began to evangelize Hayesville. The Western Art Circuit had been started up by a handful of painters and literary men in "the city"; among them, Abner Joyce, notable verist; Adrian Bond, aesthete, yet not without praiseworthy leanings toward the naturalistic; Stephen Giles, decorator of the mansions of the great, but still not wholly forgetful of his own rustic origins; and one or two of the professors at the Art Academy. All these too believed that it was the mission of art to redeem the rural regions. It was their cardinal tenet that a report on an aspect of nature was a work of art, and they clung tenaciously to the notion that it would be of inestimable benefit to the farmers of Illinois to see coloured representations of the corn-fields of Indiana done by the Indianians themselves. So presently some thirty or forty canvases that had been pushed along the line through Bainesville and Miller and Crawford Junction arrived at Hayesville, and competed in their gilt frames with the canned peaches and the drawn-work of the county fair.

"There, Jared," said the county attorney's daughter, who was corresponding secretary of the woman's club that had brought about this artistic visitation, "you see now what can be done."

Jared saw. He walked the farm, and drew beads on the barn-yard, and indulged in long "sights" over the featureless prairie landscape. The wish to do, to be at it, was settling in his finger-tips, where the stores of electric energy seemed to be growing greater every day.

"I believe I could do something of the kind myself," said Jared. "I like the country, and I'm handy at light jobs; and if somebody would give me an idea of how to start in...."

The Hayesville Seminary had just celebrated the opening of its fifth fall term by adding an "art department"; a dozen young women were busy painting a variety of objects under the guidance, good as far as it went, of an eager lady graduate of Dr. Gowdy's Academy.

"Why don't you get Miss Webb to show you?" asked the county attorney's daughter.

"I can't study with a lot of girls," muttered Jared loutishly.

"Of course not," quickly replied the other. "Make it a private, individual matter. Get some ideas from her, and then go ahead alone."

Jared picked up a few elementary facts about colours, canvas, and composition in the art atmosphere of the Seminary, and then set to work by himself. "Something sizable and simple, to start with," he said. Autumn was over the land; nothing seemed more sizable, more simple, more accessible, than the winter squash. "Some of 'em do grapes and peaches," he observed, in reminiscence of the display of the Circuit at the fair, "but round here it's mostly corn and squashes. I guess I'll stick to the facts—that is, to the verities," he amended, in accord with the art jargon whose virus had begun to inoculate the town.

He elected the squash. And he never went far beyond it. But the squash sufficed. It led him on to fame (fame of a certain curious kind) and to fortune (at least a fortune far beyond any ever reached by his associates on the farm).

III

Yes, Jared kept to the squash, and made it famous; and in due course the squash made him famous. He came to be known all over Ringgold County, and even beyond, as the "squash man." He painted this rotund and noble product of the truck-farm in varying aspects and with varying accessories. Sometimes he posed it, gallantly cleft asunder, on the corner of the branbin, with its umber and chrome standing out boldly against a background of murky bitumen; and sometimes he placed it on the threshold of the barn door, with a rake or a pitchfork alongside, and other squashes (none too certain in their perspective) looming up from the dusky interior.

Jared mastered the squash with all the ease of true genius. He painted industriously throughout the early winter. He had saved two or three of his best models from the fall crop, and they served him for several months. Squashes keep. Their expression alters but slowly. This one fact alone makes them easier to paint than many other things—the human countenance, for example. By the end of January Jared was emboldened to exhibit one of his squashes at a church sociable.

"Well, Jared," said the minister's wife, "you *be* a genius. I don't know that I ever see anything more natural." Other ladies were equally generous in their praise. Jared felt that at last he had found his life-work. Henceforward it was to be onward and upward indeed.

The men were more reserved; they did not know what to make of him. But none of them openly called him a fool—a sort of negative praise not without its value. Nor was this forbearance misplaced—as was seen when, along in March, Jared's father ended his fifty unprofitable years of farm routine by dying suddenly and leaving things more or less at loose ends. Farming was not his forte—perhaps it is nobody's. He had never been able to make it pay, and he had gone in seeming willingness to shuffle off the general unsatisfactoriness of it all on to other shoulders.

In the settlement that followed, nobody got the better of Jared. There were itching fingers among the neighbours, and sharp wits too in the family itself, but Jared shrewdly held his own. He climbed into the saddle and stuck there. He cajoled when he could, and browbeat when he must. "No, he ain't no fool," said Cousin Jehiel, who had come up from Bainesville, with his eye on a certain harvester and binder. "He may make the farm pay, even if the old man didn't."

About this time Jared, partly for solace, subscribed to an art journal. It came once a month, and its revelations astounded him. He took a day off and went into "the city," and spent eleven dollars to satisfy himself that such things could really be.

"I declare, Melissa," he reported to the daughter of the county attorney on his return to Hayesville, "but it was an eye-opener. The way the people poured into that place!—and just to look at creeks and corn-fields and sacks of potatoes!"

"Of course," replied the girl. "Why not? Doesn't your paper tell you that the hope of American art is in the West, and that the best thing we can do is to paint the familiar things of daily life? That's all the cry just now, and you want to take advantage of it."

"And there was a sort of book," pursued Jared, "hung up by the door near the desk where that girl sat and kept track of things. I see people looking at it, so I looked too. You won't believe me! 'No. 137, two hundred and fifty dollars. No. 294, six hundred and seventy-five dollars.' I looked for No. 137, and what do you suppose it was when I found it? It wasn't more'n two foot by eighteen inches—just a river and a haystack and a cow or two. No. 294 was some bigger, but there wasn't nothin' in it except a corn-field—just a plain corn-field, with some hills 'way off and mebbe a few clouds. And there was a ticket on it, and it said 'Sold.' What do you think of that?"

"That's all right," said Melissa. "If you want to get money, you've got to get it out of the people that have got it. And you've got to go where they are *to* get it."

"And there was another picture that the book said was 'still life'—apples and ears of corn and a bunch of celery or such and a summer squash. Not my kind, but a squash all the same. About a foot square—one hundred and twenty dollars. What do you think of that?"

"I think the squash has its chance, the same as anything else."

"I asked the girl who it was painted all these things. 'This is the second annual ex'bition of the Society of Western Artists,' says she."

"There!" cried Melissa. "'Western artists'!"

"'Are they all for sale?' says I.

"'Cert'nly,' says she.

"'Are folks interested?' says I.

"'Look around you,' says she.

"I did look around. People was walking along close to the wall, one after another, a-smellin' every picture in turn. In the other rooms there was women standin' on clouds, and there was children with wings on and nothin' else; but everybody give them things the complete go-by. Yes, sir, let me tell you, Melissa Crabb, all those folks was once just country folks like you and me. Those there city people had all come from the country some time or other, and they was all a-longin' for country sights and country smells. They're Western people, too, and they want Western scenes painted for them by Western artists. There's fame a-waitin' for the man who can do that—and money too. I guess I'm beginning to see a way to make the old farm pay, after all.''

IV

Jared during his visit to the city had not confined his attention to the display of the Western artists. He had talked with several dealers, and had visited one or two makers of picture-frames, and had taken note of the prominence given to "art" in the offices and corridors of the great hotels.

"I tell *you*," he declared roundly, "paintin' 's got the call everywhere. You go into one of them bang-up hotels, and what is the first thing you notice? A painting—scenery; ten or twelve feet long, too—some of 'em. Well, that's all right; I can paint as big as they want 'em, and frame 'em too, I guess."

He had formed some ideas of his own about framing. The prices mentioned by the frame-makers astonished him as much as those entered in the sale catalogue by the fond artists themselves. "No gilt for me. That's clear." He thought of a wide flat frame he had seen at the exhibition. "It was just a piece of plain boarding daubed over with some sort of gilt paint. It had a fish-net kind o' strung round it, I recollect."

"What was that for?" asked Melissa.

"It was a sea view, with boats and things. Seemed a pretty good notion to me."

"Why, yes."

"But there was one old codger come along who didn't seem to like it. Specs and white whiskers standing out. Lot of women with him. 'Well, I declare,' says he, 'what are we coming to? I can't understand how Mr. English could have let in such a thing as that!' He was going for the frame. I stepped over to the girl at the desk——"

"Seems to me you talked a good deal to that girl."

"Well, I did. She was from Ringgold County too, it turned out; hadn't been in town but six months. She was up to all sorts of dodges, though—knew the whole show like a book."

"Oh, she did, did she?"

"Well, she wasn't so very young, nor so very good-looking, if that's what you're after."

"Oh, she wasn't, wasn't she?" said Melissa, somewhat mollified.

"'Who is that funny old feller?' says I to her. He was poking out his arms every which way and talking like all possessed.

"'Why,' says she, sort o' scared like, 'that's Doctor Gowdy.' You might have thought I had let drive at the President himself. I see I had put my foot in it, so I pulled out as fast as I could."

"Gowdy," reflected Melissa; "haven't I heard that name before?"

"It didn't seem altogether new, somehow," acknowledged Jared.

But neither of them immediately associated this name with the authorship of *Onward and Upward*. They laid no more stress on the title-page of a book than you, dear reader, lay on the identity of the restaurant cook that gets up your dinner.

"It seemed all right enough," said Jared, reverting to the frame.

"Why, yes," assented Melissa. "I don't see what could have been more appropriate."

"Well, you watch me," said Jared, "and I'll get up something equally as good." For this choice collocation of words he was indebted to a political editorial in the county weekly.

Next morning he was strolling along the roadway, carefully scrutinizing a stretch of dilapidated fence.

"What you up to, Jared?" inquired Uncle Nathan Hoskins, who happened to be driving past. The fresh morning air had a tonic effect upon Uncle Nathan; he showed himself disposed to be sprightly and facetious.

"Lookin' after my fences," said Jared shortly.

"'Bout time, ain't it?—he, he!" continued Uncle Nathan.

"Just about," assented Jared.

"Might 'a' begun a little sooner, mebbe," proceeded Uncle Nathan, running his eye over several rods of flat, four-inch stuff, weather-worn and lichen-stained, that sagged and wobbled along the road-side. "So far gone ye hardly know where to begin, eh?"

"Where would *you* begin?"

"Well, that len'th right in front of you has got a little more moss on it than 'most any of the others."

"All right; I'll begin here," returned Jared. He struggled up through the tangled growth of smartweed and bittersweet, tore a length of lichened boarding from the swaying posts, and walked down the road with it.

Here at last was a suitable setting for the Squash.

V

Yes, *the* Squash, before which all other squashes were to pale. It was to be his best and biggest work, and worthy of the post he designed it to take at the next Exhibition of Western Artists. He enlarged its scope so as to take in a good part of the barn's interior; he boldly added a shovel—an implement that he had never attempted before; and he put in not only bins, but barrels—chancing a faulty perspective in the hoops. All these things formed a repellent background of chill gray-blue, but they brought out the Squash. It shone. Yes, it shone like a beacon-light calling the weary and sophisticate town-dwellers back to the peace and simplicity of country life. And it was inclosed by four neatly mortised lengths of fencing, lichened and silvered by a half-century, it may be, of weather taken as it was sent. Furthermore, the abundance of simulated seeds developed by his bold halving of his model was re-enforced by a few real seeds pasted upon the lower part of the frame.

"If all that don't fetch 'em," said Jared, "what will?"

But the exhibition jury frowned upon this ingenuous offering. Stephen Giles pitied it; Daffingdon Dill, an influential member, and a painter not especially affiliated with the Circuit, derided it cruelly; Abner Joyce himself, when appealed to as a man and a brother by the disappointed farmer-artist, bleakly turned away. Not even the proprietors of the sales-galleries seemed willing to extend a welcome. Jared was puzzled and indignant. Then he bethought himself of the hotels, with their canons and jungles and views along the Canadian Pacific.

"Yes, the hotels—there's where I'll try. That's where you get your public, anyway."

But the hotels were cold. One after another they refused him. Just one was left, and this was so magnificent that he had never even thought of carrying his proposal into it.

He did so now—nothing else was left to do. The clerk was even more magnificent and intimidating than the house, but Jared faced him, and asked for space in which to show his work.

Jared had one of his minor works under his arm—style of painting and style of framing being fully representative of his biggest and best. "It's this kind, only larger," submitted Jared.

The clerk condescended to look, and was interested. He even became affable. His imposing facade was merely for use in the business, and for cloaking the dire fact that, but two short years back, he himself had been a raw country boy from a raw country town. He looked at the picture, and at Jared—his knuckles, his neck-tie, the scalloped hair on his forehead. "Could *I* have been anything like that?" he thought. He refused consideration to such a calamitous possibility, and became a little more grandly formal as he went on listening to Jared's business.

"Oh, George!" he presently called across his slab of Mexican onyx; "come here."

George came. He was a "drummer": nobody could have supposed for an instant that he was anything else.

"What do you think of this?" The clerk took the picture out of Jared's hands and twirled it round on one corner of its clumsy frame.

George looked at it studiously. "Why, it ain't so worse," he said. "That squash is great—big as life and twice as natural."

"What do you think of the frame?" asked the clerk, venturing with no little fondness to run a ringer over the lichens.

"Made out of fencing, ain't it? Why, I like it first-rate. Maybe I haven't kicked my bare heels on just such a fence many a time!"

So had the clerk, but refrained from confession.

"Buying it?" asked George.

"No; house-room," responded the clerk, with a motion toward Jared.

"Yours?" asked the drummer.

"Yes, sir; I painted it."

"Frame your idea, too?"

"Yes."

"From the country, I suppose?"

"Yes."

"Well, so are most of the rest of us, I expect. Why, yes, give it room—why not?" the drummer counselled his friend, and turned on his heel and walked off.

The clerk clanged his bell. "Just have Tim come here," he directed. "How much you expecting to get for it?" he asked Jared.

"Well, for *this* one about a hundred and fifty, I should think."

"Right," commented the clerk. "Put a good price on a thing if you expect people to look at it. Never mind about Tim," he called, reminded by Jared's emphasis that the "house-room" was not for this painting, but for another. "Well, you get your picture round here to-morrow, and I'll have it put in the writing-room or somewhere." And he turned toward a new arrival bent over the register.

VI

After the squash had triumphed in the rotunda of the Great Western, the surrender of the other hotels was but a matter of time. They reconsidered; Jared was able to place a specimen of his handiwork, varying in size if not in character, with almost every large house of public entertainment. He walked daily from caravansary to caravansary, observing the growth of interest, straining his ear for comments, and proffering commentaries of his own wherever there seemed a possibility of acceptance. He dwelt upon his aims and ambitions too, and gave to the ear that promised sympathy the rustic details of his biography. At first there was some tendency to quiz him, especially among the commercial travellers, who seemed to be, of all the patrons of the hotels, the most numerous and authoritative. But they soon came to a better understanding of him. Beneath all his talk about being a poor farmer boy and a lover of nature whose greatest desire was to make others share the joy that nature gave him, they saw that his eye was as firmly set on "business" as theirs, and a sort of natural freemasonry kept them from making game of him. He had chosen a singular means, true, but the end in view was in substantial accord with their own.

About this time a great synod, or conference, or something of the kind, flooded the hotels with ministers from town and country alike. One forenoon the chief clerk of the Pandemonium—these functionaries were all on familiar terms with Jared by this time, and had begun to class him with the exhibitors of reclining-chairs and with the inventors of self-laying railways—called our artist's attention (temporarily diverted) back to his own work, before which a group of black-clad men were standing. A stalwart figure in the midst of them, with shining spectacles and bushy white whiskers, was waving his arms and growing red in the face as he poured forth a flood of words that, at a moderate remove, might have passed either for exposition or for expostulation.

"*There's* a big gun," said the clerk.

Jared followed the other's quick nod.

"Why," said Jared, "it's Doctor—Doctor— —"

"Dr. Gowdy," supplied the clerk. "The Rev. William S. Gowdy, D. D.," he continued, amplifying. "He's the king-pin."

"The Rev. William S. Gow——" repeated Jared. The title-page of *Onward and Upward* flashed suddenly before his eyes. The man to whom he owed his earliest quickening impulse, the man whose book had shone before his vision like a first light in a great darkness, stood there almost within reach of his grateful hand. He stepped forward to introduce himself and to voice his obligations.

But Dr. Gowdy, with what, to a disinterested spectator, would have seemed a final gesture of utter rejection and condemnation, turned on his heel and stalked down a long corridor, with his country members (who were prepared to like the Squash, but now no longer dared) pattering and shuffling behind.

"Of all the false and mistaken things! Of all the odious daubs!" purled Dr. Gowdy to his cowed and abashed following. For Dr. Gowdy, town-bred and town-born, had no sympathy for ill-considered rusticity, and was too rigorous a purist to give any quarter to such a discordant mingling of the simulated and the real.

"I've never seen anything worse," he continued, as he swept his party on; "unless it's that." He pointed to another painting past which they were moving—a den of lions behind real bars. "That's the final depth," he said.

The country parsons, left to themselves, would have admired the ingenuity of this zoological presentation, but Dr. Gowdy's intimidating strictures froze their appreciation. They pattered and shuffled along all the faster.

Meanwhile Jared, proud to have awakened the interest of the "Rev. Gowdy" (as the reading of the Ringgold County *Gazette* had taught him to express it), was busy whirling the leaves of the hotel's directory to learn the good man's address.

VII

Before Jared could catch up with the Doctor a new tidal wave broke upon the town and slopped through the corridors of the hotels. The provincials (both clerical and lay) were enticed to the metropolis by a "Trade Carnival." The Squash met them everywhere. Here, in the midst of the city's strange and shifting life, was something simple, tangible, familiar, appealing. Jared had had the happy thought to mount one or two of his best pieces on easels fitted out with a receptacle for holding a real squash. "Which is which?" cried the dear people, delightedly. The country merchants expressed their appreciation to the commercial travellers, and these factors in modern life, whose business it was to know what the "public wanted" and to act accordingly, passed on the word (casually, perhaps) to the heads of the great mercantile houses. In this way the eminent firm of Meyer, Van Horn, and Co. became conscious of the Squash.

Now, individually considered, the members of this firm made no great figure. Nobody knew Meyer from Adam. Nobody knew Van Horn from a hole in the wall. Who the "Co." might be there was nobody outside of certain trade circles that had the slightest notion. But collectively these people were a power. Except the street-railway companies, they were the greatest influence of the town. They paved the thoroughfares around their premises to suit themselves; they threw out show-windows and bridged alleys in complete disregard of the city ordinances; they advertised so extensively that they dictated the make-up of the newspapers, and almost their policy. Above all, they were the arbiters of taste, the directors of popular education. That they sold shoes, hardware, soda-water, and sofa-pillows to myriads was nothing; that they pulled your teeth, took your photograph, kept your bank account, was little more. For they supplied the public with ideas and ideals. They determined the public's reading by booming this book and barring that; their pianos clanged all day with the kind of music people ought to like and to buy; and the display in their fifteen great windows (during the Christmas season people came from the remotest suburbs expressly to see them) solidified and confirmed the popular notions on art.

Well, Meyer, Van Horn, and Co. had set their minds on having a "ten-thousand-dollar painting." It would be a good advertisement.

They sent for Jared.

"Ten thousand dollars!" gasped the young fellow. He saw the heavens opening. "Why, I could get up a *great* thing for that!"

"I guess you could!" retorted old Meyer brusquely. "You could do it for five hundred. That's what you *will* do it for, if you do it at all." He treated Jared with no more consideration than he would have given a peddler vending shoe-strings and suspenders from the curb.

"Why," said Jared, abashed, indignant, "you said ten thou——"

"Let me explain," put in Van Horn, a little less inconsiderately. "We want a ten-thousand-dollar painting, and we're willing to pay five hundred dollars for it."

"Who'd come to see a painting billed at five hundred dollars, do you think?" snarled Meyer. "Nobody. You can see that kind of thing anywhere, can't you?"

"I s'pose you can," assented Jared, mindful of his first exhibition.

"But ten thousand will fetch 'em."

"Five hundred dollars, then," said Van Horn; "that's what we'll give you. And it wants to be bigger than anything you've got on show anywhere, and the frame wants to be twice as wide. I suppose you've got plenty more of that fence left?"

"Yes," assented Jared.

"Well," said Meyer, "you'll never have a chance to realize any more on it than you've got right here. And don't economize with your seeds—stick 'em on good and plenty."

"We'll give you a whole window, or a place at the foot of the main stairs close to the fountain," proceeded Van Horn. "We put it out as a ten-thousand-dollar production and bill you big as the artist. Everybody in town will see it, and the advertising you'll get—why, ten thousand won't begin to express it."

"And we want you to put in a lot of farm stuff," said Meyer junior, whose taste in window-dressing had often roused the admiration of the entire town. "Vines and grasses, and a lot of squashes—real ones. I suppose you've got enough faith in your work to face the comparison?"

"I s'pose I have," said Jared. "I guess I've faced it before this."

"I want some real squashes on the frame too," said the elder Meyer, from whom the son's fine taste was directly derived. "Ever tried that?"

"In a small way," said Jared.

"Try it now in a large way. Half a squash, like a big rosette, on each corner of the frame—the half with the handle on it, y'understand." Meyer saw the squash as a kind of minor pumpkin.

"If I put it in the window," said the son thoughtfully, "I shall want some saw-horses and bushel baskets and——"

"Take 'em right out of stock," said his fond father.

—"something to make a real country scene, in fact. And possibly a farmer sitting alongside in jeans. Just the place for the artist himself. It might be better, though, to put the whole show by the fountain. In that case I'd have a band, and it would play, 'On the Banks of the Kankakee.'"

"Have you got that song on hand?" asked his father.

"It ain't written yet, but it will be inside of a week; and in a week more the whole town will be going wild over it, or my name——"

Van Horn cut short the youthful visionary. "Well," he said to Jared, "you hustle off and get the show together. Check for five hundred on delivery. And mum's the word," he added, with good-natured vulgarity, "on both sides."

"Ain't nobody ever said I talked too much," mumbled Jared, reaching for his hat.

VIII

Soon the Squash dawned on the town—the Last, the Ultimate. Jared had soothed his ruffled feelings and gone back to his old barn and worked for a fortnight. The result was in all men's eyes: a "Golden Hubbard"—an agricultural novelty—backed up by all the pomp and circumstance a pillaged farm could yield.

"There it stands, Melissa," he said to the girl, who had come out with an admiring little company to bid Jared's masterpiece godspeed. "And here *I* stand—a ten-thousand-dollar artist, and the only one in the country."

"I'm proud of you, Jared," panted Melissa, with little effort to conceal the affectionate admiration that filled her.

"And I'm grateful to you. You believed in me—you encouraged me——"

"Yes, I did, Jared," said Melissa shyly. They were alone, behind the shelter of the barn door.

"And next to Dr. Gowdy—"

"You've seen him? You've thanked him?"

"Not yet. But I'm going to as soon as I get this picture in place. This here ain't the end, Melissa; it ain't hardly the beginning. There ain't a picture of mine all over town that won't be worth double next week what it is this—and people anxious to pay the money, too. Just wait a little, Melissa; there's a good deal more to follow yet"—an ambiguous utterance to which the girl gave the meaning that her most vital hope required.

A few days later the city press was teeming with matter pertinent to young Mr. Meyer's newest display—the paper that refused to teem would have had to tell him why. Jared stood in the calcium-light of absolute unshaded publicity. "An American Boy's Triumph." "A New Idea in American Art." "The Western Angelus"—this last from a serf that submitted, indeed, yet grimaced in submitting. Under head-lines such as these were detailed his crude ideas and the scanty incidents of his life. And there were editorials, too, that contrasted the sturdy and wholesome truthfulness of his genius with the vain imaginings of so-called idealists. These accounts rolled back to Ringgold County. "Ten thousand dollars! ten thousand dollars!" rang through township after township. "Ten thousand dollars! ten thousand dollars!" murmured the crowds that blocked the street before the big entrance to Meyer, Van Horn, and Co.'s. All this homage helped Jared to gloss over the paltriness of their actual check. By reason of this double hosanna he was a ten-thousand-dollar man in very truth.

"And *now*," said Jared, "I will go and see Dr. Gowdy."

IX

"Dr. Gowdy is not at home this afternoon," they told Jared in response to his ring; "he is addressing a public meeting down town."

This would have applied to half the days of every calendar month throughout the year. When Dr. Gowdy let a day pass without making some public utterance, he counted that day as good as lost. He spoke at every opportunity, and was as much at home on the platform as in the pulpit. Perhaps even more so; there were those who said that he carried the style of the rostrum and the hustings into the house of prayer. Certainly his "way" was immensely "popular"—vigorous, nervous, downright, jocular, familiar. Whether he talked on Armenia, or Indian famines, or street-railway franchises, or primary-election reform, or the evils of department stores (he was very strong on this last topic), the reports—he was invariably reported—were sure to be sprinkled freely with "laughter" and "applause." To-day Dr. Gowdy was talking on art.

"It's going to be a hot one!" said the students among themselves. And they packed the assembly-hall of the Academy half an hour before the Doctor's arrival.

The lecturer who was delivering the Wednesday afternoon course on Modern French Sculpture had failed to come to time, and Dr. Gowdy, almost on the spur of the moment, had volunteered to fill the breach. He telephoned down that he would talk on Recent Developments in Art. This meant the display of Meyer, Van Horn, and Co.

Dr. Gowdy had seen the abominable exhibition—who, during the past week, had not?—and had been stirred to wrath. He fumed, he boiled, he bubbled. But it was not merely this that had roused his blood to fever-heat. No; Jared Stiles, emboldened by his success in the shopping district, had applied to Mr. English, the director of the Academy, for a room in which to make a collective exhibit of the masterpieces at present scattered through various places of public resort and entertainment. Mr. English had of course refused, and Dr. Gowdy, of course, had warmly backed him up. But Mr. Hill, the vice-president, and Mr. Dale, the chairman of the finance committee, had taken the other side. They had both been country boys—one from Ogle County, the other from the ague belt of Indiana—and their hearts warmed to Jared's display over on Broad Street. Their eyes filled, their breasts heaved, their gullets gulped, their rustic boyhood was with them poignantly once more. They murmured that English was a hidebound New-Englander who was incapable of appreciating the expansive ideals of Western life, and that Gowdy, city-born and city-bred, was wholly out of sympathy with the sturdy aims and wholesome ambitions of the farm and prairie. For once Art might well take a back seat and give honest human feeling a fair show. They hinted, too, that the approaching annual election might bring a general shake-up; English might find himself supplanted by some other man more in touch with the local life and with that of the tributary territory; and Gowdy—well, Gowdy might be asked to resign, for there were plenty of citizens who would make quite as good a trustee as he had been.

Some inkling of these sentiments had come to Dr. Gowdy's ears. He scented the battle afar off. He said "Ha! ha!" to the trumpets. He pranced, he reared, he caracoled, he went through the whole *manege*. He outdid himself. The students, his to the last man, simply went mad.

For the past year there had been a feud between Dr. Gowdy and Andrew P. Hill. Hill, relying on his own taste and judgment, had presented the city with a symbolical group of statuary, which had been set up in the open space before the Academy. This group, done by a jobber and accepted by a crass lot of city officials, was of an awful, an incredible badness, and the better sentiment of the community had finally crystallized and insisted upon its removal. Dr. Gowdy and Professor English stood on the steps of the Academy and watched the departure of the truck that was carrying away the last section of this ambitious but mistaken monument.

"Well," said English, with a quizzical affectation of plaintive patience, "we learn by doing."

"And sometimes by undoing," retorted Dr. Gowdy tartly.

Hill heard of this observation, and came to the scratch with animadversions on Dr. Gowdy's maladroit management of the finances of the Famine Fund (a matter that cannot be gone into here). This was blow for blow, and ever since then Dr. Gowdy had panted to open the second round.

Jared Stiles, standing on his own merits or demerits, might have got off more lightly, but Jared Stiles, as a possible protege of Andrew P. Hill, was marked for slaughter. This new heresy and all its supporters must be stamped out—especially the supporters.

X

Dr. Gowdy stamped it out—and the crowd stamped with him. The fiery denunciations of the Doctor kindled an answering flame in the breasts of his youthful auditory. In five minutes hands, lungs, and feet were all at work. The youths before him awakened the hot, headlong youth still within him, and he launched forth upon a tirade of invective that was wild and reckless even for him.

"This folly, this falsity, this bumptious vulgarity—shall we not put an end to it?" cried the Doctor.

"Yes, yes," responded the house.

"No; go on," said a single voice.

The Doctor laughed with the rest, and a wave of delighted applause swept over the place.

"Shall we not purify the temple of art? Shall we not drive out the money-changers?"

"Yes, yes," called the audience. For Jared had never drawn from the antique—he was trying to climb in like a thief and a robber.

"Shall we not?" repeated the Doctor, searching the house for that single voice.

"Sure," said the voice, and another wave of applause rolled from the foyer to the rostrum.

"Ten thousand dollars!" shouted the Doctor. "The man who says he paid ten thousand dollars for that agglomeration of barn-yard truck is one of two things: if he did pay it, he's a fool; and if he didn't, he's a liar! Which is he?"

"He's a fool!" cried half the men.

"He's a liar!" cried the other half.

"Oh—h!" shrilled the young women.

The Doctor wiped his streaming brow.

"What kind of a community is this, anyhow?" he resumed, stuffing back his handkerchief into his pocket. "Here we have this magnificent school [applause] that for the past fifteen years has been offering the highest possible grade of art instruction. A corps of thirty earnest and competent teachers [loud applause and a few cat-calls] are ministering to the needs of three thousand promising and talented young people, the flower of our great Northwest— —" [Tremendous and long-continued applause, during which the continuity of the speaker's remarks was lost.] The Doctor filled in the minutes of tumult by taking several sips of water.

"Why, you, we, this Academy, should be the leaven, the yeast, to work upon our great metropolis; not merely the flower, but the self-raising flour"—a pause for appreciation of the pun—"the self-raising flour [loud laughter, easily yielded and unnecessarily prolonged] that is to lift yourselves, and the city with you, from the abyss of no-art, and from the still deeper abyss of false art. That's where we're groping; that's where we're floundering. I declare, when I was elbowing my way through that struggling, gaping crowd [cries of "Oh, Doctor!" and laughter], I could only ask myself the question that I have just asked you here: what kind of a community is this, anyhow?"

Up popped a shock of black hair from northern Michigan.

"It's rotten!" Shouts. Cat-calls.

"I should think it was!" vociferated the Doctor.

He went ahead for half an hour longer, crowding on more steam, acquiring a more perilous momentum, throwing out an ever-widening torrent of reckless personalities, not forgetting the ill-fated monument of Andrew P. Hill. ("Applause" and "laughter" were very frequent just here.) He ended his improvisation without the clearest idea in the world of just what he had said, and went home well pleased.

XI

When Dr. Gowdy took up the *Daily Task* next morning—there were sixteen pages of it—the first thing that met his eye was a picture of himself—the familiar two-column cut that had not had an airing for more than three months. "Gowdy Gives Us Up," said the head-line.

"What now?" wondered the good Doctor. "Or rather, which?" For he knew that every public utterance reported in the daily press of the town was given one of two twists, the local or the personal. This was apparently the local. The personal was to follow—and it did.

Yes, the *Daily Task* had been represented at the Academy, and its young man, by a marvel of mutilation and misrepresentation, had put together a column to convey the impression that Dr. Gowdy was a carping Jeremiah, intent upon inflicting a deadly wound on local pride. "Oh, shucks!" said the worthy man, and went on with his toast and coffee.

But the other papers, though unrepresented at the Academy, had quickly detected the possibilities resident in Dr. Gowdy's abounding personalities, and the evening sheets were full of interviews. What did Jared Stiles think of the attack on him as a representative Western artist? What did Meyer, Van Horn, and Co. think of Dr. Gowdy's characterization of their enterprise and the pointed alternative it presented? What did Andrew P. Hill, as the representative of local wealth and culture, think of Dr Gowdy's strictures on the self-made man's endeavour to adorn the city that had given him success and fortune? What did the distinguished members of the Western Art Circuit think of such treatment toward their most promising and conspicuous protege? All these people had thoughts, and none of them was slow in expressing them.

"I can't understand it, nohow; I swan, I'm completely knocked off my feet," said Jared to the young man of the *Evening Rounder*, in the rustic dialect of the vaudeville. "Why, that there man—I've allus looked on him as my best friend. It was that book of his'n that give me my start, and now he turns agen me. But he's wrong, and I've got the hull town to prove it. And if he's wrong, by gum, he'll have to pay for it. He can't trip up the heels of an honest country boy and not get tripped up hisself. I don't know yet just what I'll do, but——"

With the *Evening Pattern* Jared was more academic. "I acknowledge that this attack comes as a great surprise. I had always regarded the reverend gentleman as the chief of my friends. His own book for young men [name not mentioned—Print, Push, and Co. did not advertise in the *Pattern*] was my earliest inspiration. Such conduct seems as inconsistent as inconsiderate. The public, I think, will be certain to support me. And if the words of the address are correctly reported, I shall be found, I believe, to have good grounds for an action at law. An intelligent jury, I make no doubt— —"

The two Meyers were delighted. This was advertising indeed! Van Horn, a shade less thick-skinned, stuck at the animadversions made so spiritedly by the Doctor and so vociferously supported by his audience. They wore upon him; they seemed almost actionable. He sent for the son of their credit man, a youth enrolled at the Academy, where he was learning to design carpets and curtains, and tried to get from him just what the Doctor had really said. This solicitude reacted upon the Meyers, and Meyer junior, who gave the interview, intimated that such language was actionable beyond a doubt. "Our Mr. Levy will attend to this. We have the endorsement of the general public, and that makes us still less willing to have anybody challenge our business acumen"—all this was but an elegant paraphrase of Sidney Meyer's actual remarks, for he had left school at sixteen and had never looked into a book since—"or our business integrity."

Abner Joyce, on behalf of the Circuit, gave out a grave interview in a few guarded words. Though Joyce by no means looked upon Jared as a protege of his organization, yet his essential sympathy with the country still held full sway, and he felt it possible to regard young Stiles not as a mere freak, but as a human creature like ourselves, and struggling upward, like the rest of us and to the best of his powers, toward the light. But the town did not want restraint and reason just then, and Joyce's well-considered words went—much to his mortification—for next to nothing. Bond, who better apprehended the spirit of the hour, let himself loose in a vein of pure fantasy,—he ventured on the whimsical, the sprightly, the paradoxical. The poor fellow sent to interview him might as well have tried to grasp a bundle of sunbeams or a handful of quicksilver. His report turned out a frightful bungle; the wretched Bond, made clumsy, fatuous, pointless, sodden, when he had meant to show himself as witty and brilliant as possible, was completely crushed. With Joyce going for next to nothing and Bond for worse than nothing, the Art Circuit could hardly be said to shine. It paled, it sickened, it drooped away, and presently it died.

As for Andrew P. Hill, he did not wait for the interviewer; he wrote to his favourite journal over his own signature. If he himself, straying outside of his legitimate field (banking and investments), had failed with "Our

City Enlightening the Universe," Dr. Gowdy, astray in the field of finance, had failed no less egregiously. Yes, his handling of the Famine Fund had been maladroit and eccentric to the point that permitted doubts as to his own personal integrity: why, then, should he be casting doubts upon the veracity, the business honour, of others.

This was a word for Meyer, Van Horn, and Co., who were tenants of Hill's. Landlord and tenant were just now in the midst of some delicate negotiations, and Hill hoped that a word of the right kind from him might help to make adjustment easier. Meyer, Van Horn, and Co. were intending to arrange a summer garden on their roof. Query: was the roof theirs—was it included in the lease? Hill felt sure of carrying his point,—decidedly the roof was an entirely distinct matter from the ten floors beneath it; but the situation might well stand a little lubrication if good feeling were to endure. Therefore Meyer, Van Horn, and Co. had the satisfaction of reading that William S. Gowdy was altogether too impulsive, erratic and unreliable— happily Hill did not employ the word "untrustworthy"—for holding a quasi-public position of some importance. Age was impairing his judgment and setting a term to his usefulness.

Dr. Gowdy flew into a passion. Threatened with legal proceedings!—he, the blameless citizen. Accused of dishonesty!—he, the pattern of integrity. Taunted with failing powers!—he, the inexhaustible reservoir of vigour, of energy! What, after all this, were the pin-pricks daily, hourly inflicted by the press, the post, the tongues of indignant associates, all intent on vindicating the honour of a community he had so wantonly attacked? What were squibs, caricatures, saucy verses, anonymous letters, cold looks from former friends, hot taunts from casual acquaintances? For art had been attacked in the very home and haunt of art! The town had been knifed under the ribs by one of her own sons!—made ridiculous in the eyes of the ribald East, and dubious in the regard of the trusting, tributary West!

Well, what would they have? demanded the Doctor. Should we gain anything whatever by always throwing bouquets at ourselves? Could we go along forever living on the flubdub of self-praise?

But a truce to all this!—for Dr. Gowdy was coming to see, to feel, to consider but one thing—the Squash. Here was the fountain-head of all his woes. "Perdition take that fellow!" he exclaimed, with his thoughts fiercely focused on the unseen Jared Stiles.

XII

Yes, the Squash had begun to run, and nothing, apparently, had the power to stop it. It was putting out leaves here, blossoms there, and tendrils everywhere. Particularly in the press. Interviews continued. Generals, judges, merchants, capitalists—the whole trying tribe of "prominent citizens"—were asked what they thought of such an attack on the fair fame of the city by one of its own sons. Less prominent citizens sent in their views unasked. Professors of crayon portraiture wrote to tell the Doctor he knew nothing of art. Lecturers to classes in civics advised him that he little realized the citizen's duty to his native town. The *Noonday Worm*, which had more than once praised the Doctor's public spirit, now turned on him and called him a renegade. The *Early Morning Fly*, among other buzzings, buzzed this: "If you don't like our city, Doctor, there is Another—higher up. Good-bye; we'll see you later!" The Doctor, who had always felt that he had done as much as any for the town's well-being within, and more than many for its repute abroad, saw now that he had been taking much too favourable a view of himself.

Only the staid old *Hourglass* had a word in his behalf—a sober editorial on the art conditions actually prevalent. The *Hourglass* was in some degree Dr. Gowdy's mouthpiece. It had a yearly contract with him for the publication of his sermons—they came out every Monday morning—and Dr. Gowdy handed over the proceeds to the Board of Foreign Missions. This contract was about to expire, and it was a question whether it should be renewed. Meyer, Van Horn, and Co. said no. Dr. Gowdy had a column or two in the *Hourglass* on one day in the week, but Meyer, Van Horn, and Co. had a whole page every week-day and a double one on Sunday. And they paid for it! They disliked the editorial. They disapproved the sermon. The contract was not renewed, and Dr. Gowdy raged.

On the heels of this came a bill from Meyer, Van Horn, and Co. for tin-ware. It had been purchased but a week before, yet the bill bore these words, stamped in red ink and set askew with a haste that seemed to denote a sudden gust of spite: "Please remit."

"Henrietta!" called the Doctor to his wife; "how's this? You know I never trade at any of those abominable department stores! You know what I think of them: they demoralize trade; they take the bread out of the mouth of the small dealer; they pay sinfully low wages to the poor girls that they enslave— —"

It was the new cook, it appeared, who had purchased a few pie-pans on her own initiative.

"Discharge her!" roared the Doctor.

Two or three days later the Squash put forth a new tendril. It had invaded his home, and now it invaded his pulpit, so to speak. Exacerbated by persecution, Dr. Gowdy had thrown off all restraint. His one real weakness, his inability to keep from talking when talking was going on, grew plainer every hour in exact proportion as his invective, his vituperation, grew stronger. He rushed into print, like some of the others, and his expressions were made matter for consideration at the monthly meeting of the ministers of his own denomination. Briefly, his brethren themselves (brutishly insensible to the abundant provocation) censured him for language that was violent and unchristian.

"I'll resign!" said Dr. Gowdy.

"You'll do nothing of the sort," said his wife.

"Of course I sha'n't," he returned.

Then the Squash invaded the Academy. The shake-up came; Professor English was removed; and Dr. Gowdy was requested to withdraw from the board of trustees.

"I'll resign this time, anyway!" said he.

"I wish you would," said his wife.

Next day came a letter from "our" Mr. Levy. It as good as asked Dr. Gowdy's attendance at the store. Dr. Gowdy tore the letter into very small scraps, thrust them into an envelope, slapped on a stamp with a furious hand, and sent them back.

Then "our" Mr. Levy called at the house, accompanied by a Mr. Kahn, whose particular function was left in some vagueness.

Mr. Kahn felt around the edge of the thing. "It can be settled, I am inclined to think," he said, smoothly.

"So it can," said the Doctor—"by your both going out that door inside of ten seconds."

But Mr. Kahn remained. "Your libellous utterances— —" he began.

"Mine? Those students', you mean. Sue *them*—in a body!"

"We may prefer to sue you."

"Sue away, then! I'll put my standing against that of any department store in existence! This is a mere impudent speculation, impossible to carry out in the face of the public opinion of a Christian community——"

"Is it?" asked Mr. Kahn blandly.

This equivoke checked Dr. Gowdy for an instant. "It used to be," he said, with a fierce smile. The smile vanished and the fierceness remained. "Go," he said. "I'm stronger than both of you together. There's the door. Use it!" He towered over them with red face, threatening arm, bristling white whiskers.

"Drop it," said Mr. Kahn to Mr. Levy, as they went down the Doctor's front steps; "he's a fighter."

XIII

An hour later the Doctor, looking out of his study window, saw a buggy drive up and stop at his carriage-block. It contained a rustic-looking young man, dressed in new and showy garments that had the cachet of the department store, and a young woman brave in such finery as young women wear when approaching the most important hour of their lives. Instinctively the Doctor reached for his prayer-book, an inspired volume that had a way of opening almost automatically at the marriage service.

But only the young man alighted. He came up the front walk with an expression of fell determination about his firm-set mouth. The young woman, holding the reins, frowned at Dr. Gowdy's house-front—in marked repugnance and indignation.

Jared had come to tell Dr. Gowdy what he thought of him—their first and only meeting. Dr. Gowdy at a distance had impressed him as an abstract moral force, but Dr. Gowdy close at hand was a mere man like himself. Jared pushed aside all deference and spoke his mind.

"You set me up an inch," said Jared hardily, "and then you went to work to take me down an ell. You've tried to harm me all you could; you've tried to ruin me. But it couldn't be done. Let me tell you this: I've sold seventeen hundred dollars' worth of my work here, and the first of the month I'm going East with a lot more of it. A man with money in his pocket can get his rights," said Jared truculently.

Dr. Gowdy, to whom Jared too had been an abstraction—an abstraction compact of bumptious heresy as regarded art and of crass ignorance as regarded life in general—finally realized him now as a human being, faulty and ill-regulated, indeed, but not altogether unlikeable, and by no means lacking in a sort of rude capacity. He experienced, not for the first time, the alleviating quality resident sometimes in personal presence, even the presence of an antagonist.

But Jared had no sense of this. "You've made fun of me," he went on; "you've made me ridiculous in my own home. They're all laughin' at me down there. All but her"—with an awkward gesture toward Melissa, visible through the front window. "She's stuck to me right along. She believed in me from the beginning. It was her gave me that book of yours——"

"That book, that book!" groaned Dr. Gowdy. Alas for the refining and ennobling influences of art! Threatened and hectored in his own house by a loutish, daubing plough-boy!

"You've interfered with my success; you've taken money out of my pocket. Do you want to know what I'm goin' to do? I'm goin' to sue you, that's what! Her father is our county attorney, and he'll help me see that I get my rights!"

"Sue me? Do, you poor ignorant young cub!" cried the Doctor. "I've just had one lawsuit to-day, and what I want more than anything else is another!"

Jared glowered at him heavily—a look that was not without its effect on the Doctor. Jared knew nothing of the complexities and delays and expenses and uncertainties of the law, but he had already taught Dr. Gowdy that the overbearing power of sheer ignorance was not to be despised.

"I may be a poor ignorant young cub," he returned, "but, for all that, I know how to take care of myself. And of another too—that right will be mine within half an hour." A second slight gesture toward the window. Dr. Gowdy's accustomed ear recognised the confident tone of the bridegroom.

"Now, see here," said he, with a sudden lurch into what seemed an unceremonious frankness. "Let me make amends." For there was a positive note in Jared that responded to the positive strain within himself. Jared was more likeable than Mr. Kahn, and better worthy of cautious heed as an antagonist. Why, indeed, should he be further antagonized at all?

"Yes, let me make amends," said the Doctor. "Let me"—here the prayer-book opened almost of its own accord—"let me—marry you."

Jared's eyes blazed. "Do you think that Melissa Crabb would——"

"Yes, I do," said the Doctor.

"We're going to Mr. Shears, two blocks down the street." said Jared imperviously.

"You're going to stop here," said the Doctor.

The force of personal relation prevailed—as it almost always does when given a chance. Jared yielded; Melissa acquiesced. She detached her frown from the Doctor's house-front, climbed down out of the buggy, accompanied Jared and the Doctor indoors, and he made them one forthwith.

The Doctor's performance of the marriage ceremony was famous—the town was full of people who would never let anybody but Dr. Gowdy marry them. To those who knew, Mr. Shears was nowhere. The Doctor's method was a wonderful blend of gravity and of intimacy; he made you feel that you were the one man and woman in the world—the world summed up, indeed, in a single pair—and that you were going through a ceremony just a shade more solemn than any other man or woman had ever gone through before. His voice would be shot through with little tremors that showed his sincerity and his individual interest—briefly, Jared and Melissa had no cause to regret Mr. Shears.

The Doctor kissed the bride in hearty, fatherly fashion—Henrietta kissed her too—and refused the fee Jared offered him.

"No," he said; "I've cost you too much already."

Jared wrung the Doctor's hand, and wondered that any mere man could fill his heart with such a tremor and such a glow.

"I'm going to see you again before you leave for the East?" asked the Doctor.

"Well, I have two weeks, at three hundred a week, with the Gayety Theayter," said Jared. "I put the finishing-touches to a picture every night in full view of the audience, and frame it with my own hands."

"Good-bye here, then," said the Doctor.

XIV

This was the turning of the tide for Dr. Gowdy. From this time on, things began to run his way once more. The ministerial body, at its next meeting, reconsidered its resolution of censure; surely their brother had been sorely tried. The threatened suit of Meyer, Van Horn, and Co. was quashed by the Doctor's own dauntless bearing. The *Hourglass* agreed to open its columns to him, though but for a short synopsis and without remuneration—so that he had to go into his own pocket for the Foreign Missions. And finally, the students at the Academy refused to hear of his withdrawal as trustee. They met; they protested; they resolved; they clamoured. "We want our Gowdy back! we want our Gowdy back!"—such was their cry. Their cry was heard; they got their Gowdy back. When next he addressed them (it was only on Ephesian Antiquities—a safe subject) their cry was heard again—heard, possibly, in the interior of the next State. It was the proudest moment of the Doctor's public life.

Jared Stiles's "Golden Autumn," handled and framed in his usual manner, and "valued at" ten thousand dollars—none of Jared's larger pieces now falls below that figure—will soon go trailing, exhibitionwise, through the halls of the Eastern seaboard. But it is an error to assert that the name of the painting was suggested by the Rev. William S. Gowdy. No; he still stubbornly ranges all this work, and indeed all similar work in any other field of art, under the generic name of the Squash.